THE
CREW

DON DICKINSON

*Don Dickinson
Lillooet, B.C.
Oct 29, 1993.*

COTEAU BOOKS

This is a work of fiction. The places and events are made up; any resemblance to persons living or dead is pure luck.

Edited by Andreas Schroeder.

Cover painting, "The Crew," oil on canvas by Antoinette Hérivel.

Painting photographed by Available Light Photographics & Design.

Author photograph by Paul Béland.

Cover design by Kate Kokotailo.

Book design by Val Jakubowski.

Typeset by Lines and Letters.

Printed and bound in Canada.

The author expresses his gratitude to the Canada Council and to the B.C. Cultural Services Branch for their financial assistance in the completion of this book. Thanks also to my editor, Andreas Schroeder, and most especially to my wife and children for their patience and understanding.

The epigraph is excerpted from "Digging" by Seamus Heaney © 1966 *Death of a Naturalist* by Seamus Heaney (Oxford University Press). All rights reserved. Reprinted with permission.

The publisher gratefully acknowledges the financial assistance of the Saskatchewan Arts Board, the Canada Council and Communications Canada.

Canadian Cataloguing in Publication Data

Dickinson, Donald Percy, 1947-

   The crew

   ISBN 1-55050-052-X

I. Title

PS8557.I324C7 1993   C813'.54   C93-098153-7
PR9199.3.D532C7 1993

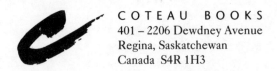

COTEAU BOOKS
401 – 2206 Dewdney Avenue
Regina, Saskatchewan
Canada S4R 1H3

By God, the old man could handle a spade.
Just like his old man.

. . . . Nicking and slicing neatly
. . . . the curt cuts of an edge
Through living roots awaken in my head.
But I've no spade to follow men like them.

Between my finger and my thumb
The squat pen rests.
I'll dig with it.

— from "Digging" by Seamus Heaney

PART ONE

ON THE MORNING THE STRIKE BEGAN KOZICKI ARRIVED AT THE compound early and stood outside the locked gates massaging his privates and wondering at the precise definition of the word *scab*. With one hand laced through the fence links while the other kneaded his groin he considered the frailties of organized labour: union dues, strike votes, and now a burning sensation just south of his belt buckle. In years past it had been bargaining teams and an ulcer. Lockouts and a broken nose. Work-to-rule and frostbite. Pay cuts. A bruised tailbone.

Solidarity, he reflected, was tearing him apart.

Reluctantly he pulled his hand out of his pants. This massage had become a habit. Lately people regarded him askance, suspecting him of obscenity. The other day Dominico had called, 'Hey Mike, whatsa matter, you don' get enough patoong?'

Patoong? Kozicki winced. If peeing was anguish, sex was out of the question. Sometimes, it was true, he awoke in the middle of the night, the demands of his bladder fooling him into an erection while at the same time reaming out his urethra with a Roman candle. But wherever the heat came from, it had nothing to do with sex. Before she'd left with her suitcases and most of the dishes, Charlene had said the same thing. (Kozicki had been dismayed by her observations about sex; dismayed, too, that Charlene took all the crockery. Hadn't they picked it out together?)

'Get it seen to,' Charlene had said about his groin. 'If you're still considering early retirement, get yourself fixed up. You don't want to be one of those people who retires and then does something stupid.'

'Like drop dead, you mean?'

'Sure, let's get morbid. All I'm saying is I can't take it any more.'

'You mean the impotence.'

'I'm not talking about the impotence. It didn't happen that often and anyway it's the symptom, not the disease. There are other things, Mike. You're not the same man.'

'I've still got two arms and two legs.'

'For one thing you don't ask me to marry you any more.'

'I asked you for three years. You always said no.'

'A woman still likes to be asked, Mike.' She'd lugged boxes of books out to her car, shaking off his offer to help. Her grey head had dipped inside the car's trunk and she became a blue-skirted backside on a pair of sturdy legs. When she straightened, she was as tall as he was. 'There are other things,' she said again.

'You got a *list*?'

'The spider's web in your guitar. The sander left out in the rain. Churchill chained up under the porch, day in, day out.'

'Churchill's not chained up. He can walk any time he wants. He's just—reluctant.'

'The letters to Gillian. Those pictures of Emily. You're not the only one who ever lost a spouse, Mike.'

'I know that.' He opened his arms to her, but she backed off.

'No,' she said. 'All I'm saying is get it seen to. Before it drives you crazy.'

'Crazy?' Kozicki had pulled his dictionary from his back pocket. 'Crazy, crazy . . . that's one of those adjectives, isn't it? Hang on . . . here it is: *Crazy: insane, overly enthusiastic.* I thought you said I *wasn't* overly enthusiastic.'

'You know what I mean.'

'Charlene, I'm *kidding*.'

'Well I'm not.' She moved to the driver's side of the car. Her hand—well formed, liver spotted—rested on the door. 'Get it seen to. I phoned Dr. Brandell.'

'Where are you going?'

'I'm staying at my son's place. Jeanette needs help with the kids, and they need to see their grandmother more anyway. You can phone if you like. But don't come over.'

'What if I throw the spider out and play my guitar under your window?'

'My son's a policeman. He owns handcuffs.' She kissed his cheek. 'I'm sorry, Mike. We need a break, that's all.' She slipped behind the steering wheel and smoothed her skirt around her knees. Then she drove away, leaving him standing in the middle of the street under the trees. The sun was setting; at the corner her signal light winked in the dusk before her car disappeared in a sound like tearing paper.

She'd lived with him for nearly four years. They'd met on the university campus where he worked—she a mature student, he a gardener. He'd been lowering rose bushes into holes when his hat fell off and he felt someone gazing at his bald spot. When he looked up she excused herself and asked him if all the stories about roses and horse manure were true. 'Roses love horseshit,' he admitted. 'Excuse my French. Dung is like a day at the beach for 'em. They like to paddle their feet in the stuff.' It turned out her daughter-in-law was having trouble with her roses; turned out, too, that Kozicki had leftover dung in a bag, which he carried to the trunk of her car; turned out that Charlene was a widow and he a widower; turned out that she had green eyes flecked with motes of light.

Once, she'd taken him to a lecture at the university—the only one he'd heard, even though he'd worked on the campus for nineteen years. A rotund professor with a speech impediment talked about the ancient cultures of Peru. 'The Hincas have a wegend,' the professor said, 'that if the head and body of their ancestwal king is weserwected, the Hincas will wise again.' The professor showed slides. Kozicki sat squeezed into a desk next to Charlene, his hat in his hands. The Hincas sure impressed him; their buildings, their canals, the mysterious gigantic figures that lay across their land. The Hincas were optimists. They probably believed that even widows and widowers could wise again.

If this private job he had lined up worked out okay, maybe he could take Charlene to Peru. Maybe they'd learn to speak Peruvic or Incaian or whatever it was. She was nuts about the ancient cities of the Incas.

'How come?'

'They accomplished so much, and then it was taken from them. But even today they haven't lost hope.'

Hope interested Charlene. She was fifty-five years old, her hair was grey and curly and her body as wiry as a shortstop's. When she made love the chest of drawers fell over. She had brains and whaddayoucallit—*joy de veeve*. *Joy de veeve* ran through her like electricity. 'Think of it, Mike. The Spaniards beheaded the Inca king hundreds of years ago, and buried his head in one place and his body in another. If the head regenerates a body, their people will rise again.'

'And you'd like to be in on that?'

'You bet.'

Oh she was tough, Kozicki knew that. Even if he got enough money to secure early retirement, who was to say a trip to Peru would bring her back? The day before she left she told him he was winding up like the Incas—his head was getting away from his body. There was a flaw in him, she said.

Those Incas. On the sly Kozicki had ordered her a book on that big city of theirs, that Machu Picchu. But though he checked the mail every day, it still hadn't arrived. Now it was too late. What was the big deal about heads and bodies, when book companies couldn't even get their act together?

In the middle of the street he'd pulled his dictionary from his hip pocket, thumbed through it, and read: 'Gone. adjective. In verbal senses; lost; hopeless; dead.' He stopped. He must've read the words out loud, for they drifted on the evening air, and blue-haired Mrs. Burkmar, who was weeding her begonias three doors down, looked skyward from her hands and knees as if she'd heard the call of an exotic bird.

Under the porch, Churchill thumped his tail, rolled on his side and farted.

Now, outside the compound, Kozicki waited. The others wouldn't be here for half an hour and Cargill, the picket captain, wouldn't show up until ten minutes after that. *Exactly* ten minutes after that. Cargill was a stickler for punctuality.

Stickler. There was a word. Sounded like a fish. And *scab*—well, everybody knew what a *scab* was. Then again, *scab* could be a dead stickler. Or something you'd *do* to a stickler. *I scabbed a stickler last night.* And *punctuality* was the clunk a time clock made when you punched your card in. Whoever named *punctuality* knew what he was doing. There were lots of words like that. If a guy knew them all, understood them all, he could pretty well get by on his own. He wouldn't need a doctor to tell him what a *carcinoma* was. He could understand his well educated daughter when she wrote that she'd been praised for her critical *perspic, perspicac,*—whaddayoucallit. He might even be able to talk to a woman like Charlene without sounding as if he'd been dropped on his head. The language, the language. A guy could be surrounded by language all his life, and take it for granted. Like it was air. Like it was free.

He was pacing.

Kozicki was a tall, stoop-shouldered man with gangly arms and hands the size of fan rakes. Weathered, his face put others in mind of squinted horizons and fiddle players named Al. He walked in long strides, bent forward at the waist as if at any moment he would scoop up a shovel and start digging. His hair was thin on top, but wildly tangled everywhere else. Sometimes he snagged his chest hair in his shirt buttons and on certain formal occasions such as weddings and funerals these rebellious strands had stirred some people—relatives—to embarrassment. Even his own daughter Gillian, whom he'd sent off to the Ontario Ladies' College and from thence to the University of Toronto where she'd eventually earned a Ph.D. and a life Kozicki knew absolutely nothing about, thought he looked like a farmer. At Christmas she sent him turtleneck sweaters and tweed or corduroy trousers. He preferred khaki.

Kozicki's hands had the gnarled appearance of fruit tree branches, and over the years they'd handled everything from flowers to stones. Until recently they'd strummed a small-bodied, skinny-necked guitar that his first wife Emily had picked up in a pawn shop in 1959; ten bucks, nice tone. Back then he'd tried to play Woody Guthrie, but who listened to those songs any more? Oh, in the sixties the long-haired university kids played acoustic stuff, but then everything went electric. A dozen years later those same kids who'd laboured on his crew had haircuts and houses in the suburbs. They had become business administrators, accountants, teachers. If they saw him again—accidentally in a mall or on a street—they recognized him reluctantly, shielding their spreading middle age with baby strollers and grocery carts, as if the vehicles of their burgeoning affluence could protect them from this calloused, shambling reminder of their firmer, freer youth. 'Kozicki,' they'd say, 'still working up at the university?' and allow their tender hands to be swallowed up in his hoary one. He half expected them to wipe their palms on their trousers, they looked so uncomfortable. At such times he wanted to put a fatherly arm around their shoulders and say, 'It's okay, I just wanted to say hi, that's all. I'm not moving *in* with you.'

He pulled the paperback *Concise Oxford Dictionary* from his back pocket.

Scab, he read. *1. (n) dry rough incrustation formed over a sore in healing. 2. (archaic) mean low fellow. 3. person who refuses to join a strike or trade union or who breaks the rules of his trade union or group.*

He read the entry again, lip-synching the words on the page. There it was, in black and white. *Person who breaks the rules of his trade union or group.* What would all those kids who'd worked on his crew say to that?—those kids who'd scorned the union but still used it to get decent wages and a dental plan and medical coverage, those kids who'd rode his tractor-trailer for four or five summers so they could get their degrees and make real money, while every season he broke in new landscapers and told the same jokes and made two bits more an hour than the greenest one of them? What would they say, if they knew what he had planned?

Kozicki, they'd say. Kozicki, you scab.

Sliding his hand down the front of his pants, he considered the day.

He liked summer mornings—high, clear, breathless, when the white gravel lay dry under recumbent willows and dew glistened on upturned tractor seats behind the compound's fence. Parked in rows the machinery—tractors, tree-spades, gang-mowers, trucks, front-end loaders—waited in massive silence. Above the trees the heat shimmered expectantly. Sucker for work, dressed in green khaki and a khaki hat, Kozicki sniffed the air and got ready to sweat. Somewhere a meadowlark sang as clear as a farm boy's whistle; its song pierced the murmur of traffic and Kozicki's guilt. Never mind, the meadowlark told him. Summer mornings were meant for work.

And Kozicki was a stickler for work.

Stickler: n. person who insists on or pertinaciously supports or advocates.

Pertinaciously? Holy Hannah. How had all these words slipped by him over the years? There was no end to them. One word opened up into another, like those catacombs Dominico said lay under the city of Rome. You could walk down there for miles, Dominico said. Pertinaciously . . . pertinaciously. Jeez. A guy could wander down the tunnels of the English language his whole life and never see the same thing twice.

Nose in his dictionary, Kozicki at first paid no attention to the dogs. They started up most mornings at this time. On the far side of the compound, beyond the line of waxy-leafed willows, the inmates of the Burdock Animal Experimental Station yelped in their kennels.

Yelped. Kozicki lifted his head. Lannie Dougal was slinking over there under the trees, near the kennels. The kid was at it again. What did he do over there every morning? Nice-looking, gentle kid, but some days he walked around with a grin on his face like a crack in a pisspot and his eyes as glazed as doughnuts. Talk about language— you couldn't get two words out of him. What was the poor kid up to, anyway?

Crouched among last year's leaves, Lannie peered along the kennels and in his imagination paced alongside the dogs in their fenced runs. Some mornings he wagged his own tail in anticipation, sniffed musty mole trails in the grass, lifted his snout to the rising sun and raked his claws over the kennel floor. Some mornings he howled, 'Yarrrooow!' and lapped destiny from a dirty green dish.

Today he would teach them silence.

Squatting, he duck-walked from kennel to kennel, pushing the milk bones through the wire. One dog licked his fingers; the collie snuffled his curly hair. All of them grew quiet as he fed them. He crooned in a voice he'd learned from Nurse Pritchard. 'Ar rar rar rar rar,' he sang. His voice stroked the dogs because his hands were too big to fit between the fence links. 'Woof. Woof.'

Like Nurse Pritchard, the dogs liked poetry.

When he reached the last kennel he saw that the Doberman was gone. Kennel One held an Australian blue heeler. He went to where she shivered in a corner. Scrawny and stumpy-legged, she was gun metal dusted with silver. Hackles rose like quills along her backbone, but her heart wasn't in it. The milkbone lay where he'd dropped it.

She said her name was Bluey.

A car horn blared. Through the screen of trees Lannie watched Dominico's big Buick wheel up to the greenhouse compound. Kozicki was still at the gate scratching himself. Little Dominico stepped importantly from his car, hitched up his trousers, adjusted his straw hat, ready for business. Anna rolled up on her bicycle; Trischuk followed on his. Ironeagle stood by himself, trying to quit smoking.

Corny Fergus, in his yellow hard hat and Hawaiian shirt, was saying something to young Paterson.

Lannie watched his fellow workers. For a moment he felt the old uneasiness, as if the Man With the Great Big Gun were near. Lannie didn't often see the Man With the Great Big Gun these days; even so, the Doberman was gone, and likely the Doberman hadn't seen the Man With the Great Big Gun either, until it was too late. Through the trees Lannie studied Kozicki's calm figure, the centre of the crew. The image comforted him. Kozicki spent too much time digging at his nuts, but he wasn't one to shy away from men with rifles. Lannie trusted Kozicki, an achievement which for Lannie was on a par with meeting God in a shopping mall. The only other person he'd trusted in the last few years had been Nurse Pritchard. She used to sponge the mist from the glass in the dayroom and pad his clothes with it. He'd been safe with her.

He stood, reassuring himself that he was still outside, under the trees. The blue heeler's hackles had subsided.

He'd have to go out there, but that was okay. Kozicki was there. And Anna, and the others.

All the way across the bridge Anna had decided to ignore him. Now that the strike was finally on, she'd let Trischuk drift from her consciousness like mist from a river. Perhaps she'd be assigned picket duty with someone else—with Dominico, or Kozicki.

Poor Kozicki. He'd been so embarrassed when she'd caught him massaging himself. Why didn't he go to a doctor? How old was he—fifty-five, sixty? The strike was a perfect chance for him to check into a hospital and get whatever-it-was treated. But if he went into hospital she'd miss him. He was sanity; only Kozicki looked her in the eye. And Trischuk, of course. But Trischuk's eyes scorched her. Passion, humour, strength—it was criminal what Trischuk carried around in his eyes. He was married with two kids, and had no need of a mistress. After Alex, Anna had no need of a man. Yet alone together, she and Trischuk leapt at each other like monkeys.

'We've got to stop this,' she'd said once, doing things with her tongue.

Still, she'd found a new route to ride her bicycle to work, crossed one of the other bridges so she wouldn't feel Trischuk feverish behind her, on *his* bicycle. He brooded over her backside. He'd said so. In some ways he was like all the others. Oh Anna, they'd said—all of them, she couldn't remember one who hadn't— oh Anna your bum is magnificent.

She knew her bum was magnificent. But it was, after all, only a bum, albeit the one vanity she would carry to her grave because she had little choice in the matter. Most people were born with bums, and barring extravagant accidents died with them. At one time she'd been flattered that hers excited so much attention. Men approached her behind as they would a mountain; they wanted to scale it from all angles. And when she was younger, she'd let them, hopeful that sometime during their ascent they'd push on to a more rarefied atmosphere and discover—good God!—that her bum was connected to a mind. Hadn't a mountaineer said he'd climbed Everest because it was there? Anna wanted to make a similar claim for her bum. Its existence had nothing to do with the men who wanted it. It would remain where it was whether they wanted it or not. It was there.

What had Kozicki advised when she'd confided in him? 'If I was you, I'd keep it. It'll hold your pants up and give you something to sit on. If it's good-looking, well, too bad. I know a couple of people who carry their ass on their shoulders—they got a face like a pig's patooey and a rear end like a pie-plate. You oughta feel lucky.'

'Anna?' Trischuk whispered as she leaned her bicycle against the fence. 'I've been thinking. You're right. We have to make it purely physical.'

'I said *if* we could make it purely physical.'

'Right, *if*. So how about this: we won't talk. Every time we're alone together, we'll just do it. We'll shoot the moon.'

'But we haven't shot the moon.'

'That's because we talk. If we shot the moon, we wouldn't talk.'

'If we shot the moon, we'd talk when we were finished. We're always talking. We're talking right now.'

'Should we stop talking and shoot the moon?'

'Don't be ridiculous.'

'You want ridiculous? Here's ridiculous: I'm thinking about telling my wife.'

'Don't do that. Oh please don't do that.'

'Why not? My wife and I talk.'

'Your wife and you shoot the moon, too.'

'Maybe if I told my wife you and I shoot the moon, you and I *would actually shoot the moon.*'

'Stop it.'

'I don't have to stop it. It hasn't started yet.'

'Stop *this.*'

They whispered fiercely. That's how it was with them: all this fierceness. Glaring, they faced one another. Trischuk fisted his hands in his workman's trousers and hunched his weightlifter's shoulders. Years ago he'd been a bodybuilder, and still admitted to pumping iron now and then. From his lips the very words *pumping iron* were fraught with erotic possibility; she saw the two of them coupled athletically among sumptuously padded gym equipment—benches, exercise mats. Trischuk had long lashes and grey eyes and peppered his speech with gym clichés: when the going gets tough, the tough get going; you gotta wanna. God help her; when he rolled his shoulders something massive happened in his back that made her want to wrestle him to the ground and hang on for dear life. Not that she was intimidated, but *his* bum was magnificent, too.

He was staring at her. 'Stop that,' she said.

But he kept looking. 'No pain, no gain.'

She turned and walked away; dignity stiffened her back and kept her looking ahead. Her bum was still back there, though, shifting the way it did. As if it didn't care what she thought. As if it had a mind of its own.

Then Dominico was calling them. She drew herself inward, aimed herself at his words.

'Hey, youa guys, come on, Dio canne. Kozicki, he'sa gonna talk for us. Come on, he's already wait five minutes. What'sa matter you guys, you don' got ears? Come on.'

From under his straw hat Dominico watched them gather around Kozicki. Mio Dio whadda buncha guys! So slow, you think they don' got legs. Holy cow, alla this good luck they don' know they got!

Dominico could tell good fortune from bad. Before he emigrated to Canada he had worked in a Swiss mine where the pit boss had slapped the backs of the miners' legs with a shovel handle if they walked too slow. 'Move your ass, da Vinci.' The pit boss had called all Italians *da Vinci*. 'You're in the trucks today, da Vinci. And you, da

Vinci, you're on number two face.' Da Vinci, da Vinci; the name of the great Maestro played a hymn in Dominico's ears.

As a boy in the village school he and his classmates had been shown copies of some of da Vinci's drawings. Padre Disanto kept them in a large portfolio—delicate sketches of flowers and olive trees, faces, nudes, strange engines, mechanical marvels. The pit boss's thick tongue had tried to profane the name of a great man, but Dio canne, how could he? In his drawings Leonardo showed them what was possible, he showed them *dreams*. Even in Padre Disanto's nicotined fingers those drawings glowed with a peculiar light— maybe even the light of God. Why not the light of God? Stranger things had happened. The Madonna's face, for instance, had appeared to the blacksmith's crippled daughter in the glowing embers of her father's forge. True, she was cross-eyed—the black-smith's daughter, that is—but how could anyone speak against her? For a whole week, she saw what she saw.

The same was true of Dominico. In those copies of da Vinci's drawings, he saw what he saw. Leonardo could talk! With a piece of charcoal he could talk to anyone, even a blockhead Swiss.

'Kozicki, he'sa gonna talk.' Sometimes he envied Kozicki's talk. Those words Kozicki used, the meanings. Holy cow, sometimes in his talk Kozicki was almost a little Leonardo.

Dominico wanted to be like that. A little Leonardo. A little da Vinci.

'Before Cargill gets here with the picket signs I got to let you guys in on something,' Kozicki said. 'We're up shit creek.'

The crew huddled around him. 'Who's we?' Corny Fergus wanted to know.

'We, us. The crew.' Kozicki savoured the word. Later he would look it up—not now, but later. *Crew, noun. body of persons manning a ship, boat aircraft, etc.; such persons other than officers; an associated body, company of persons, set, gang, mob.*

'I been up shit creek before,' said Corny Fergus, a tall, sad man who resembled a stork with the blues. 'Have I got a friggin paddle this time?'

'Not that I can see, Corny.'

'Why not?'

'The word is that our negotiating team and management have left the table. They're not talking, not holding hands, they don't even want to dance. Unless they get a mediator, we could be pounding picket lines until Christmas.' Kozicki paused. 'I've been there before. Brass monkey weather and money tighter than a nun's knees. Then as seasonals we'll get laid off. No wages, and we won't qualify for pogey.'

'That which doesn't kill me makes me stronger,' Trischuk pointed out.

'Yeah, well, you're a better man than I am then. That which doesn't kill me makes me skinny.' A little fuse sizzled somewhere in Kozicki's shorts, sputtered, then swelled into a grape that rolled down a ramp and settled on the floor of his bowels. He tightened his stomach but resisted the temptation to massage. Who knew what he'd find down there? 'Barney Macklin and the executive really don't know how long we could be out. But you got to remember we're seasonals. Even Barney Macklin isn't going grey over us. So last night I went around and had a chat with Mr. Dreedle.'

The crew paused. 'Mr. Dreedle,' someone muttered. As grounds manager and head of the greenhouse, Mr. Dreedle was the only one among them with an office. He wore suits to work, and had a personal assistant, Mr. Bistritz. Rumour claimed that Mr. Dreedle had the ear of the university's president, and had once received a personal phone call from one-time Prime Minister Lester B. Pearson. The crew respected and envied Mr. Dreedle, not merely because he hobnobbed with the powerful, but because—so it was said—he'd begun with a shovel in his hand, like them. Ambition had pushed Mr. Dreedle to study horticulture at night school; hard work had propelled him up the promotional ladder; influence kept him there. If anyone deserved his open-toed sandals and BMW it was Mr. Dreedle. Most of the crew wouldn't have wanted to *be* Mr. Dreedle— he was a cream puff who wore latex gloves when he touched anything dirty—but they were impressed that Mr. Dreedle was Mr. Dreedle. Apparently he'd once been plain Martin. That kind of change didn't happen everyday.

'What does Mr. Dreedle say?' Corny pushed a soiled tensor bandage over a bony elbow. He'd once told Kozicki that his motto was Keep Things Together. Right now he had a Band-Aid pasted across his narrow chin, and a corn plaster on the back of his neck. As lank and loose as a stick insect, Corny had experienced most of the injuries listed in *Prevention of Industrial Accidents: A Worker's Guide.* Tools hated him. Rakes leapt up and smacked his face, rototillers jarred his shoulders, lawn mowers skinned his knuckles or went after his toes. Where machinery purred for others, it snarled at Corny Fergus. Misfortune rode his back like a rabid jockey, and he wore his yellow hard hat even on the car-ride home, not out of habit, Kozicki knew, but out of the deep-seated belief that some day something—a train, say, or a grand piano—would fall from the sky and brain him.

'Mr. Dreedle suggested a private job,' Kozicki said.

The crew fell silent. If sound were any indication, they were holding their breaths. Kozicki expected them to turn blue and fall down.

'Private?' Trischuk stuck out his chin. 'What do you mean, private?'

'I'm glad you asked that, because last night I looked it up. *Private, adjective; kept or removed from public knowledge.*'

'You mean scabbing.'

'I mean private.'

The crew crowded in close. Not only could he hear their breath, he could feel it. Warm, moist, redolent of their various breakfasts. *A company of persons* sort of breath. 'We'd still pull our picket duty,' he said. 'But when we aren't on the pickets, we'll be working.'

'At what?' Anna asked.

'Landscaping. What we're supposed to be doing now.'

Corny tilted his hard hat and scratched his head. 'What the frig would we use for tools?'

'We'll get all the tools and equipment we need from the greenhouse. Plants too. Seed—everything. We can load up the stuff we need while we're picketing.'

'Jesus Christ,' Trischuk said.

Anna laid her hand on Trischuk's arm. 'What would the union say if they found out?' she asked Kozicki.

Trischuk snorted. 'We respect your spirit, because our spirits are one.'

'Rob, *please.*' Anna gripped his arm. 'What would they say?'

Kozicki thought. 'They'd say goodbye—and after that they'd have our butts for bookends. Trischuk's right: technically speaking, we'd be scabs.'

Moses Ironeagle shifted in his unlaced workboots and cleared his throat. The others listened; they always listened to Ironeagle because they could never predict if he was really going to talk. Some days he chattered like a magpie; on others he brooded sullenly. His face gave even Kozicki pause; it was boneless. Ten years in a professional boxing ring had pummelled the cartilage in Ironeagle's face into custard. His nose was a wall hanging, his cheeks a pair of curtains. Scar tissue around his eyes had so tightened his eyelids that he looked smoothly inscrutable or just plain mean. He walked with a springy, pigeon-toed boxer's gait that set his shoulders rolling and fists swinging, as if he was ready at any moment to break into a soft-toed shuffle, pump a couple of lefts to your Adam's apple and finish off with a right hook that came straight from the knees. His voice was a soft monotone, full of whiskey and dark alleys. 'Hey Kozicki,' he said. '*Astum*. You say if we work we'll be scabs. What we gonna be if we don't work?'

'Poor,' Kozicki said.

Ironeagle nodded. 'I been poor a couple of times, eh. I didn't like it.'

Dominico tugged his belt upwards, until his trousers nearly rode his armpits. He twirled his straw hat on his hand and hopped from one foot to another. 'Poor? No, no, you don' wan' poor, poorsa no good for nobody.' He fidgeted directly in front of Kozicki, his sharp face and eager eyes less than a foot away. 'Whadda you think, Mike, how much money we gonna make for thisa private job?'

'Don't stand so close,' Kozicki said.

'How much?'

'I don't have the exact numbers, but I figure after we deduct expenses, we could each make close to four months' wages in eight weeks.'

Dominico whistled triumphantly and clapped his hat on his head. 'Mio Dio! Four months ina just eight weeks. Makea the long time short! Whadda you think, Mike, we can do that? Tell me true.'

'I tell you true, we can do that. Back up a little.'

A green half-ton truck swerved into the road, spraying gravel, scattering the crew. Scrunched behind the wheel was Cargill from Maintenance. Shop steward, picket captain, Cargill was a stubby, apoplectic screamer whose complexion Kozicki used as a living barometer for union-management relations. Catch Cargill flushed pink, Kozicki knew, and there was sunshine on both sides of the contract; add a tint of beetroot and you had a grievance rumbling on the horizon; dip to the colour of plum jam and you were into hurricane negotiations, lockouts, and holes in the Labour Code you could blow a tornado through. Today the man's cheeks hovered somewhere between raspberry wine and spilled blood; Kozicki guessed a stormy return to union principles; closed ranks, closed fists, declarations of war.

Cargill stopped the truck, jumped from the cab and vaulted—athletically for a tubby fellow—into the truck box and flung out picket signs as if they were rifles. 'Arm yourselves, brothers and sisters, arm yourselves!' Part of Cargill's success as a union man was his ability to holler 'brothers and sisters' without a trace of embarrassment. To Kozicki, whose only brother had died of whooping cough in 1932, calling complete strangers family required military daring and maybe even religious fervour. He'd tried 'brothers and sisters' once at a union meeting, but the phrase snagged in the back of his throat, and he'd croaked out 'fellow union members' instead. If he called them brothers and sisters, he'd thought, suddenly panicky, would he have to invite them all over for Thanksgiving? Would they all show up for Christmas? Would some of them phone him at three in the morning and ask him for a loan because poor old Mum needed a gallstone operation? Kozicki wasn't a selfish man, but he wasn't ready for the burden of five hundred and seventy-three siblings, either. He would've settled for a single brother—cough or no cough.

'The brothers and sisters at Maintenance faced two delivery trucks this morning.' Cargill announced. 'But they held 'em back, they turned 'em away. That's the kind of inspiration we need here, brothers and sisters, that's the kind of commitment we've got to have. And have we got it? You bet we've got it! The Faculty Association and the Students' Union are behind us one hundred per cent. Ditto CUPE Local 516. Ditto the farm labourers.' He paused and counted heads. 'Hey. I don't remember the schedule saying *everybody* had to be here.'

'Solidarity meeting,' Kozicki said. 'Keep up the morale.'

'Hey, great.' But Cargill looked skeptical. He wasn't sure about Kozicki. A few days before the strike was called he'd pulled the foreman aside and told him, 'I've heard a couple of comments about you, brother. Not complaints—just observations. Reading on the job, for one. Don't get me wrong, I think all our brothers and sisters should be informed, but if you've got questions, see your shop steward. The other thing involves your hand in your pants. You got trouble, brother, that you need your hand in your pants?'

'A little soreness,' Kozicki said. 'A pulled muscle or something.'

'Comment says you're shooting pocket pool, worrying the wire, noodling the knackers.'

'I guess it must look like that.'

'Well, take my advice, from one union brother to another. In public, hands off the nuts. Okay?'

'Sure thing.'

Cargill had clapped Kozicki on the back and told him that solidarity was forever. Kozicki had felt a surge of affection for the man, and silently promised himself that at one meeting—not soon, but at *one* meeting—he would stand up and say 'brothers and sisters' without gagging.

'Any problems so far?' Cargill was standing in the back of the truck now, hands on his hips like a general on a balcony.

'Nope,' Kozicki said.

'Terrific.' Cargill swung from the truck box to the cab, an acrobatic manoeuvre that Kozicki admired but didn't want to duplicate. He suspected that if measured on a clock gauge, Cargill's blood pressure would push the needle so far into the red that it would bounce there, throbbing like a time bomb. Even now the man's neck veins bulged like boiler pipes. 'Keep the faith, brothers and sisters!' Cargill gunned the engine and waved. 'Don't let the bastards grind you down!'

Dominico watched him go. 'Heya, Mike. Whad he gonna do when he find out we gonna work?'

'Heart attack, that'd be my guess.' Kozicki looked over his shoulder. Nearby Paterson stood grinning. 'What's so funny?'

Paterson blushed. 'Nothing.'

'You sure?'

'Well—just—*things*.' At twenty, Paterson had recently earned a degree in English Literature, and had decided that poetry was in pretty well everything. He drew sketches of trees and wrote poems about women, and his open face reminded Kozicki of himself at that age. 'Not that I was educated or anything like that,' Kozicki had explained once, 'but I was happy, just as if I *had* brains.' 'Don't you have brains now?' Paterson had asked. 'Kid,' Kozicki said, 'don't ask me any hard questions.' Once when a rainstorm forced the two of them into a warehouse to stack fertilizer bags, Paterson had confided that sometimes he woke in the middle of the night to hear the wide world calling. 'The wide world?' Kozicki had asked and Paterson had said, 'Yeah. You know—Keats? "Then on the shore/ Of the wide world I stand alone, and think/ 'Til Love and Fame to nothingness do sink"?' 'I don't know about love and fame,' Kozicki had grunted, hoisting a bag to his shoulder. 'But I got a special thing going with nothingness. What do you want to do with your life, anyhow?' But Paterson didn't know. He said he wanted to do *something*, but he wasn't sure what. Twice a week he lifted weights at the gym where Ironeagle sparred; on other occasions he jogged interminably through parks and strange neighbourhoods, as delighted with the houses as he would've been with alien domes on a lost planet. Life fascinated Paterson, and why not? He didn't know much about it.

'Where will we be working?' he asked Kozicki.

'Riversdale.'

As if on signal, the others huddled in close. 'Riversdale?' Corny Fergus touched the plaster on the back of his neck. 'Whose place?'

'Belongs to Clarence D. Rawlings.'

Corny's eyebrows shot up. 'The food store guy? The newspaper, real estate, TV station guy? The used car guy?'

'That's him.'

'He's friggin loaded,' Corny said. 'He's so friggin rich his friggin *money* makes money.'

Trischuk folded his thick arms over his chest and stood with his legs stalwartly apart. His stance reminded Kozicki of the Hercules movies he had taken his daughter to years ago. Hercules could throw javelins up into the clouds and knock down temples by wrapping chains around marble columns. Standing there, Trischuk looked like a javelin-throwing temple-knocker, in Kozicki's opinion.

'Rawlings?' Trischuk said. 'Wasn't he involved in some scandal awhile back—some government land deal or something?'

'That's right,' Kozicki nodded. 'The charges were dropped. No evidence.'

'There's never any evidence,' Trischuk said cryptically.

Anna looked at the ground. Beside her Lannie Dougal crouched on his haunches.

Kozicki's hand rubbed the no-man's land between belly and belt. Maybe it was the prostate. Maybe a little Hercules was down there heaving javelins into the soft temples of Kozicki's tissue, or wrapping chains around his prostate. Years ago his daughter Gillian had refused to go to any more Hercules movies. 'There's hardly any *girls*,' she complained, 'and Hercules is so *lumpy*.' Interested in avoiding lumps himself, Kozicki let his hand fall. 'Rawlings wants us to landscape his place. About three acres of it. He's torn it all up and wants it completely redone. He wants us to rebuild his world.'

Paterson laughed. 'You're starting to wax poetic, Mike.'

'I'm not waxing anything. Those are his words, not mine. "I want you to rebuild my world." That's what he said. Let's face it: the guy doesn't think small.'

Anna lifted her head. 'What did you tell him?'

'I told him we'd landscape the moon if he wanted us to. If the money was right.'

'Money.' Corny Fergus grinned, and something spectacular happened to his face. He gazed at the circle of faces for confirmation. 'Money. Now we're friggin talkin.'

To Kozicki, as to most people from other parts of his city, money was a tangible presence in Riversdale. He imagined that the elegant Georgian houses rested their foundations on it, that the substantial Edwardian mansions stuffed their pantries with it. Even the spanking new Dutch colonials must've been buffed with wads of banknotes to raise their aluminium siding to such a high sheen, unknown in other neighbourhoods. Money pumped the pistons in the Mercedes, BMWs and Rolls Royces. It perched on entrance gates and glittered on pebbled drives. It sang in the elm trees, glistened on the lawns. In Riversdale, Kozicki conjectured, if money was air the whole population would choke to death in fifteen minutes.

'But what a great way to go,' Corny Fergus shouted against the wind. 'You wouldn't need a friggin hard hat or nothin.' Corny clung to the toolbox in the back of Kozicki's truck as the foreman steered the battered pickup through Riversdale's sedate streets. The rear window in the truck cab was glassless, victim of a carelessly thrown crowbar, and the gaping hole provided a portal of communication between the driver and his passengers. Kozicki drove with one eye on the rear-view mirror. His truck was a clunker, a rattling nightmare of loose tie-rods and springless shock absorbers. Once at an intersection a few years before, the tailgate had popped open and his cargo of the time—two hundred rolls of lawn sod and a wino hired for the day to help lay them—had tumbled onto the pavement and into the snarl of oncoming traffic. Miraculously, the wino survived unscathed, as did most of the sod, but ever since Kozicki drove with the suspicion that disaster crouched just behind his seat. He would've liked to squeeze the entire crew into the cab, but only Dominico accompanied him there. The rest—Lannie, Paterson, Ironeagle and Corny—lay on bags of peat moss like lounging potentates. Picket duty had claimed Anna and Trischuk this first morning, and a good thing, too. How would he have fit them all into the back of this heap? In the mirror he watched Paterson stand up on a peat moss bale, teeter there with a notebook and pencil, while high overhead arching elms and maples filtered the racing sun.

'Sit down!' Kozicki yelled, unintentionally swerving. Paterson dropped to his knees.

'Whad he do?' Dominico glanced backwards.

'I don't know. Drawing a picture or something.'

In fact, Paterson was writing. Lofty trees pushed him to lofty thoughts, apparently. *Coming through light like a sun-dappled soul*, he wrote. *Like the morning-glories growing on my grannie's back gate.* The images pleased him. Writing pleased him. Writing in the back of a truck pleased him. For a moment he felt intensely bohemian, Jack-Kerouacing his observations in the notebook he kept in his workshirt pocket. Maybe writing in this way would turn him into a beatnik, or a Buddhist. Maybe it wouldn't—in which case it probably would. How did that work, anyway?

'What's the matter with you?' Ironeagle asked. 'You got pain?'

'No. I'm just thinking.'

'I tried that a few times. Could get a fella in trouble, eh.'

'What kind of trouble?'

But Ironeagle was scowling off to the side, beyond the road's edge, as if thoughts, like flurries of troublesome punches, were coming towards him. After a while he said, 'This reminds me of bein' back on the reserve.'

'What?—These big houses?'

'Not the houses. Ridin' in the back of a truck.'

Paterson put his notebook away. 'Eagle, are you a Buddhist?'

Ironeagle looked at him for a while. 'I guess you better think some more,' he said.

From the peat moss bale where he lay, Lannie Dougal suddenly sat upright and sniffed the breeze. His head, a halo of tight blond curls, swivelled until he faced upwind.

'You won't smell no dogs on the front lawns in this neighbourhood,' Corny told him. 'They're all boarded out at some spiffy kennel somewheres. Not like at my place. Friggin dog pees all over the lawn so's it looks like it's got some kinda *disease.*'

'I thought your kids made those marks.' Paterson had seen Corny's lawn, a minefield of kids' toys and dead-grass piddle spots. 'Or maybe it's you.'

Corny snorted. 'My kids know enough to use the neighbour's lawn. And you sure wouldn't catch me lettin that friggin joke outa my pants outdoors. I'd get it caught in somethin.'

Dominico, who'd been listening through the open window, called: 'Corny, he don' pull outa hisa pecker until hisa wife she say hokay.'

'Yeah,' Corny agreed, 'and she don't say that too friggin often, neither.'

The others laughed. In twelve years of marriage Corny had fathered nine children. Once Kozicki had asked how he'd managed so few. 'The rhythm method,' Corny replied. By his own admission he was a lapsed Catholic, his wife an exhausted one. Still, he laughed with the others. Stories of his pecker circulated freely among the crew. His nose, long and bulbous, inspired their speculations. Common wisdom said that the size of a man's nose reflected the measurement of his procreative organ. Given the dimensions of Corny's beak, his cock was universally assumed to be a whopper.

Peering forward from Kozicki's truck, Corny stuck his hooter out over the cab and pointed. 'You guys think my friggin dingle is special? Take a look at *that.*'

Kozicki had stopped the truck in front of a ten-foot pair of iron gates, beyond which, among the trees, loomed the home of Clarence D. Rawlings. Gothic in inspiration, art deco in execution, the building bristled with turrets, dormers, cupolas, towers, and something that looked like a crenellated balcony off the Vatican. The house had been built in the 1920s by an American whiskey runner named Shaunessy who hired convoys of prairie grain trucks to transport what he called liquid barley. 'I got a shipment of liquid barley comin down!' he used to shout into the phone to his compatriots in Minneapolis and Billings, Montana. 'More liquid barley on its way!' The end of Prohibition brought an end to Shaunessy, but his monument, known to oldtimers as Shaunessy's Folly, remained. It commanded a view of the river and the city beyond.

'Now that is one big friggin mother of a house.' Corny breathed.

Ironeagle nodded. 'I guess you know a lot about mothers, eh?'

The truck had stalled. In the silence Paterson and Lannie stood together and studied the house.

'"The splendor falls on castle walls/ And snow summits old in story,"' Paterson quoted. 'Tennyson,' he explained.

'Who's she?' Corny asked.

Dominico murmured Porco Madonne—the Madonna is a pig—repented, and crossed himself.

'Listen,' Kozicki said.

From Rawlings's driveway they heard the deep-throated rev of heavy machinery, then the whine of a lugging engine. The morning air shook; clouded in dust and diesel smoke, a six-ton back-hoe crested the drive and jounced full-throttle towards them. Considering the vehicle's speed and the angle of its bucket, Kozicki calculated that the back-hoe would smash through the iron gates and sheer his truck off at about the axles.

'Hey Kozicki,' Ironeagle called. 'Are you goin to tell us when to jump?'

Kozicki turned the ignition key and rammed the stick shift into reverse. The clutch wheezed, as if it were an old man stopping halfway up the stairs saying, 'Let me catch my breath.' Kozicki didn't listen to the old man but stomped the accelerator and popped the clutch: the truck shot backwards and stalled again, just as the iron gates slid open—electronically, Kozicki guessed—and the back-hoe hurtled through the opening, missing Kozicki's front bumper by fifteen inches before jolting to a halt.

The driver, an apple-cheeked, red-bearded man in a baseball cap that said This Is My Damn Hat! shut the engine off and gazed balefully down at the crew. 'Fucking throttle got stuck.'

Kozicki leaned out the window. 'That would explain the noise. What do you figure explains the steering?'

'I'm pissed off.'

Kozicki nodded. 'Somebody try to run over you, too?'

The driver took off his cap and wiped his forehead on a freckled bicep. He climbed down stiffly. 'Hey guy, I'm sorry about that, but you didn't have to worry. I wouldn't have hit ya. I can handle this rig.' He screwed his hat down almost to his eyebrows, then squinted along his nose at the crew sprawled in the back of the truck. 'Don't tell me you poor buggers are gonna work for Rawlings.'

'We're the landscapers.' Kozicki opened the door and set his feet on the running board. 'Is there something about Rawlings that I should know?'

'There's lotsa things about Rawlings you oughta know, but only two that matter: a) he's rich, and b) he's a peckerhead.'

'You want to expand on that?'

'I don't want to expand on nothing. Let's just say me and my brother busted our humps a whole week here and got paid F-all. How's he paying you guys—by the job?'

'A flat fee for the landscaping,' Kozicki said.

'Time limit?'

'He wants the whole thing finished by September first.'

The driver shook his head. 'Deadline, huh? Yeah, that's his style. He can kill you with them goddamn deadlines. I mean you take me and my brother. We estimated our time, put our bid in, but then we went over the deadline. With what we made on this job we can maybe buy a six-pack and a pair of bootlaces. You miss that deadline, you miss the train. Those penalty points he's got worked out will break ya.' He glanced at his watch. 'I gotta go—gotta meet my brother up at the corner there. We'll load this baby on a flatbed and piggyback 'er over to the Briarwood Mall. We're laying a sewer line over there.' He clambered up into his cab. 'We'll catch the train on that one.' He started the engine.

'What were you putting in here?' Kozicki shouted.

The driver yelled something: 'Slaughterline for a goat.'

'*What?*'

'*Water line for a moat!*'

When the back-hoe had gone, Paterson asked Kozicki if he'd ever met Clarence D. Rawlings.

'Once or twice.'

'What's he like?'

'Little man, big wallet.'

'There must be more to him than that.'

'Probably is. He calls himself an eccentric. I looked that up. Means he's a little off centre. He's a wheel with a bent rim.'

'And a peckerhead,' Corny reminded him.

Ironeagle turned his face towards Rawlings's house. 'Peckerhead,' he said quietly. 'I guess that means he's got a penis for a head, eh. A thing like that can't be too healthy for a fella.'

Dominico strode around the front of the truck, giving great, optimistic upward tugs to his belt. 'Hey, whatsa matter you guys?

Penisa head, cheesa head, pizza head—who cares whata kinda head? Mike he already tell us the guy gotta biga wallet.' Dominico held out his right palm as if he were weighing something; he hoisted his hand up and down so the crew could see how heavy a big wallet really was. 'Whadda more you need?'

'What's all this stuff about deadlines and penalty points?' Corny Fergus shifted uneasily. 'I never heard nothin about friggin deadlines. I heard of guys gettin hurt serious tryna meet friggin deadlines.' He pointed at Kozicki. 'What was all that deadline stuff?'

Kozicki spread his hands. Sometimes he wished he had a bigger dictionary, not merely to answer his own questions but other people's as well: a dictionary six feet tall and three feet thick, engraved with writing as fine as the hallmark on his dead wife's wedding ring that he kept in his sock drawer at home. Tiny letters on Biblical parchment, as light and dependable as air, full of irrefutable definitions about money and strikes and prostate glands and lost daughters and half-ton trucks. Who would write such a dictionary—God? Kozicki didn't know. He wasn't a religious man; he practised a formless kind of atheism that allowed him now and then to curse a God he was pretty sure did not exist. But—if God was to write such a dictionary, wouldn't He have already done it?—Oh not the Bible, Kozicki didn't mean the Bible. But a big *dictionary*, one you'd have to lug around in a wheelbarrow, one that would explain to people like Corny Fergus and Paterson and Gillian and Charlene and all the others—even Kozicki himself—just what was going on.

'There *is* a deadline,' he said. The crew waited. Kozicki felt as if he were a football coach about to give his team a chancy, inventive play that would make or break their entire season. The fans, the cheerleaders, even the peanut vendors held their breaths to see what he'd do next. 'Here's how it works. If we finish the job on time—by September first—we get paid the full amount. That comes to four months' wages each. If we go over the deadline, Rawlings deducts the overtime from our pay. For every day we work over, he takes off a week's wages. If we go eight days past September first, we lose every nickel.'

Understanding dawned on Corny Fergus. 'You mean we could end up doin the friggin job *for free?*'

'That's about it.' Kozicki took a breath. Something heavy, like a ball bearing, dropped out of his stomach. If he *had* been in a football stadium he would be inciting his team to a longshot field goal from the fifty-yard line, booted by a one-legged kicker. What they wanted now was confidence, a get-one-for-the-Gipper speech. Kozicki touched the dictionary in his back pocket. He wasn't sure who the Gipper *was*. He swallowed. 'I'll tell you, you gotta love this Rawlings guy. He isn't your average free-enterpriser, he's got an edge to him. If our strike ends, we'd have to work after suppers and on weekends to finish this job. Either way we got our heads in a grinder. Look, if anybody wants out of this deal, now's the time to jump. Trischuk and Anna say they're in. With them and all you guys we'd have eight workers, and with that I figure we can do it. It's a weird set-up, but the money's there waiting for us.' He paused. 'Well?'

The men sat, tentative.

'Lannie? You in or out?'

Lannie climbed into the truck box.

'Dominico?'

'You don' gotta aska me, Mike.'

'Paterson?'

'In.'

'Eagle?'

'Me too.'

'Corny?'

Corny took off his hard hat and adjusted the webbing. 'How friggin dangerous is this gonna be?'

'I don't know, Corny. It's like a football game.'

'How can it be like a friggin football game?'

Kozicki wasn't sure. He wanted to tell Corny about the ball bearing in his bowels and the one-legged kicker and the football which, he thought, was now floating towards the uprights with championship written all over it. But Corny, behind his vulnerable nose and pretence of not swearing, looked as if he wasn't interested in footballs. So Kozicki said: 'Either you play or you don't.'

Corny set his hat carefully on his head and pressed it down. 'I'll play.'

The other men cheered, somewhat self-consciously, and Kozicki thumped an exuberant fist on the truck box. 'You know what this is?' he said, spreading his arms. 'Solidarity. Jesus, wouldn't Cargill give his eye teeth for this kind of thing? My dictionary says that solidarity is *a holding together*—a whaddyacallit?—*a community of interest.*' Kozicki put his head down and did a little shuffle. 'So what do you suppose is our *community of interest?*'

The crew thought for a moment.

26

'Greed,' Ironeagle said.

Kozicki swung back into the driver's seat. 'Brothers and sisters,' he said, 'let's go and make some money.'

Rattling up Clarence D. Rawlings's curved, spacious drive, Lannie Dougal hugged himself and wondered if he would ever get off the millionaire's estate alive. With his back propped against a wheel well and his bony legs stretched in front of him like open scissors, he inspected the Rawlings house and recalled the first bughouse he'd ever been sent to. 'It's a rest home,' his mother had said. 'Not a bughouse.' But he had chanted, banging his cutlery on the kitchen table: 'Bughouse, bughouse, bughouse,' until his mother had cried and had made a phone call so that strangers came and pushed a needle into his arm. He'd been seventeen at the time.

He couldn't actually remember being admitted to the Eastview Centre but when he woke up he was wrapped in ice packs and strapped to an iron bed. That's what a voice told him had happened, anyhow, but he knew voices often lied. He knew he was a frozen sausage, and that they were just waiting for him to thaw so they could toss him into a frying pan and poke him with a fork. His bed lay under a high window, and through the screen he glimpsed a crenellated tower whose weather-vane scratched the face of the moon. During long shivering nights he watched shadows play tag over the tower's face. Gamboling puppies scampered in and out of windows and up among the eaves. They piddled among the ivy, wrestled on the shingles. Then one night the moon went out; the tower became a brooding cathedral to the god of the Everlasting Night. The puppies disappeared. On the roof behind the weather-vane a face appeared, an arm, a great big gun.

Lannie wasn't stupid. He knew the Man With the Great Big Gun wanted to punch holes in his body, that such men were sausage-shooters, puppy murderers, shadowy weather-vane scarred figures who thought nothing of puncturing boys strapped to beds. Look: look how the man raised the great big gun, squinted through the scope—

A dog had barked. Not, as Lannie would've liked, a big dog—a foaming Doberman with garden-fork teeth and a name like Zunt—but a piping little yapper, a terrier, probably called Trixie. Some-

For my mother, who taught me that all words have their own value; and my father, who showed me that all work has its own dignity.

where outside the window the dog barked: yip, yip, bowrowrow!; barked bravely into the darkness so that Lannie was hit by a panicky understanding of *straps*, *bed*, and *icepacks*. He decided to bark, too— bark and bark and bark until the door opened and the lights went on and they got him the hell out of there.

Better a dog than ground-up meat.

But the Everlasting Night. Where was the Man With the Great Big Gun now? In the years since, Lannie had seen him many times, in phone booths, on trains, once in the eyes of an old woman who begged him for a quarter. If Lannie saw the Man With the Great Big Gun too often, he would have to check himself into the centre. The staff would hand him pills in a paper cup, his eyesight would go bad, and he would stumble through clouds of puffy white cotton until a heavy-lidded doctor would coax him into a room with furniture and Lannie would talk and talk until he recognized a desk, a chair, a sofa. A little while later he would be released, with the feeling he'd just been let off a chain. But he wouldn't get very far before a phone booth, a train, the eyes of a panhandler would tell him that the Man With the Great Big Gun could find him at any time, could hide anywhere. Here, for instance, in one of those turrets, below that balustrade, behind that chimney—

Yarrroooooww!

'Take it easy, big fella.' Kozicki's voice called through the truck's rear window. He drove slowly, hugging the wheel, head turned to look behind. 'It's just a house, kid. It's not the goddamn city pound.'

The other men stared.

Lannie tried to relax. He looked up. Through glittering leaves the sky shone blue and bright. Tree branches smiled at him; a cloud, high up, mushroomed into a face, grinned, swallowed its ears and sailed away.

A hulking black raven perched on a skinny tree and glared at him through a shot glass.

Lannie sat up. Raven?

It was a camera mounted on a pole.

He started to sweat. If this was just a house, why was a camera mounted on a pole? Why did it turn to watch them as Kozicki drove past?

If this was just a house, Lannie thought, why did the owner keep ravens instead of dogs?

In his library, Clarence D. Rawlings swivelled in his chair to study the monitors on the console. Surmounted by a heron-like man in a hardhat, the battered half-ton wove up the curving drive towards the bridge. At the wheel was Korchinski or Korviski or whatever-his-name-was—Rawlings consulted the note on his desk—Mike, that was it. Mike. According to Dreedle, Mike had the constitution of a draft horse and the compliance of window putty. Well, Clarence Rawlings would see. Accept the judgement of others, but never rule out corroboration. If you hear footsteps, look behind.

Right now though, he was looking at the console: camera number five. He zoomed in for a close-up: tools in the back there, bags, crew. Truck was a nice touch: humble.

Clarence Rawlings took an abiding interest in humble; he was a millionaire of humble origins. If he ever forgot that fact, he had only to look at the profile a journalist had once written in *Business Today*. 'Clarence Rawlings: High Ideals and Humble Origins.' The article described him as a descendant of wheat farmers and Methodist lay preachers; a strong-willed lad who'd been raised on a farm in the 1930s when drought and wind scoured men's souls, when a dollar was a dollar and when those who survived did so on faith, oatmeal, and hard work.

Work was no stranger to Clarence Rawlings. While still a boy he'd stooked wheat and forked hay and, for a time with his elder brothers, managed an itinerant threshing crew that wandered back and forth across the prairies from Lake Winnipeg to the Rockies. He hated those dusty years but, as he told the reporter, 'Those years taught me something. They revealed to me a diamond in the mud.' As insights go, his was simple but inexorable; it separated power from drudgery as neatly as the part in his hair. The insight was this: somebody's got to be the boss.

'And it might as well be me,' he told his brothers, who laughed because, after all, Clarence was a runt. They kept laughing when he took his share of the threshing money and bought himself a new suit and a 1934 Chevrolet; laughed harder when he tuned up the car's engine and repainted its body. They shut up when he sold the Chev at a profit and bought two more cars.

In time the two cars begat four, the four begat eight, and so on, until it became clear to the Rawlings brothers that little Clarence was good at multiplication. At twenty-three he leased two city lots from which he hustled used cars at blinding speed, despite there being a war on and gas rationing in effect. Still in their bibbed overalls and chewing snuff, his brothers scuffed their feet in his high-polished presence and stood tongue-tied when they were introduced to prominent locals and visiting celebrities. Success rode so easily on the skinny shoulders of Clarence D. Rawlings and certainty smouldered so fiercely in his eyes that his oldest brother Dave once asked just where the heck Clarence got all his ideas.

'God,' Clarence said.

Dave swallowed his tobacco.

The house Clarence Rawlings bought contained a small ground-floor library. The former owner Shaunessy had lined one wall with paperback mystery novels and leather-bound copies of the complete works of the American western writer Zane Grey. The other shelves held multi-volumed encyclopedias: *Britannica, Americana, Funk and Wagnall's,* and a spicy, slender-spined collection called *Nudes from Around the World.* Shaunessy had read all the mysteries and westerns and had dogeared the nudes, but the encyclopedias sat untouched, and in successive sales of the house were passed from owner to owner as part of the furnishings, as if they were nailed to the bookcases.

Clarence Rawlings dumped the paperbacks and sold the Zane Grey, chucked the encyclopedias and had the nudes burned. He trucked in crates of the biographies and autobiographies of famous people, loaded his shelves with them, and consumed them at a rate of one every three weeks. 'The lives of the famous,' he told the reporter, 'are sign posts from the Almighty. Sinners and saints teach through example.' Thus in his bookcase St. Augustine shared a room with Heddy Lamar, Frank Harris rubbed shoulders with Mahatma Gandhi, Errol Flynn flirted with Joan of Arc, Oscar Wilde pooh-poohed the strongman Louis Cyr. Memoirs, diaries, journals and reminiscences jammed the library walls, and each spoke its own language. Artists, nutcases, athletes and bums—all had earned their place in the vast design of things. And what were they saying? Transmuted by the printed word, what did the immortals have to tell?—Follow the light God gave you. Question not His motives. Be blessed if thou art blessed, damned if thou art damned. Of course Rawlings didn't tell the reporter that last part about the blessed and the damned. Who wanted to look like a crackpot? All he really said was, 'Follow the light God gave you.'

He should have added, 'And never apologize.' That's what the

Exceptional Ones who lay in the arms of posterity were telling him. That's what they said. Follow the light, and never apologize. What was there to be sorry for? He'd been in business for thirty-nine years and had yet to regret a single minute of it. The deals, take-overs, mergers, acquisitions—even the losses and the failures had been meat and drink to him. At work he laboured under the constant bombardment of demand for his time, his talent, his money. And he thrived on it; he loved the energy he brought to things—the life!

Some people (the journalist was one, his ex-wife another) thought he should be lonely. They *hoped* he would be lonely. But he disappointed them. Even in his efforts to be alone (when the wrought iron gates closed behind him, and he could sit—for once completely alone—in his library), he couldn't drum up loneliness. On the odd weekend when he willed himself to relax in the library, when the servants were ensconced in their quarters, and the answering machine took his personal calls, he listened to the voices on his bookshelves and told them to wait, wait. Some day he would be right up there with them.

The truck had stopped in the courtyard. He went out to meet it.

Kozicki loved millionaires. He hadn't met many—well, just this one—but he loved them. He loved their—what was it he'd looked up the other night?—*insousiance*. That was it. Their *insousiance*. Millionaires had bucketfuls of the stuff. They could *insousiance* all over the place. Once, after he'd shipped her off to the Ontario Ladies' College three thousand miles away, his daughter Gillian had written that instead of coming home for Christmas, she'd been invited to pop down to the Bahamas with one of her wealthy classmates. Kozicki's mouth watered at his daughter's use of the words *pop down*. He saw her casually flinging a bathing suit and a towel into a string bag and vaulting into a jet that was furnished like a display window at Sears. 'Pop down' suggested levels of *insousiance* that landscape gardeners could only dream about. Landscape gardeners didn't 'pop down' anywhere; and although a spiky jealousy nibbled at his insides when he thought of his daughter 'popping down to' or 'taking a cruise to' or 'catching a flight for,' he nonetheless loved the idea that Gillian's rich friends had singled her out for such carelessly extravagant escapades. Maybe some day he wouldn't warn her, but just 'pop down' to Toronto and remind them both he was her father. Maybe he would drive over to Charlene's and they would 'catch a flight' for Peru.

In the meantime this Clarence Rawlings was wishing them all a good morning and shaking their hands like somebody selling Bibles. Rawlings wore a monogrammed blue polo shirt whose crest was a complex coat of arms that involved crossed swords on green plaid and two crazed-looking unicorns tap-dancing through a wheat field. He was a pale little guy, and Kozicki guessed that doing insouciance millionaire things didn't leave Rawlings much popping-down-to-the-Bahamas time.

'Fellas,' Rawlings began, 'before you get started I want to say a few words. Mike here should have already explained the deadline to you. Do I have confirmation on that, Mike?'

'You have,' Kozicki said.

'Fantastic. So I won't go into all that. The basic point is that if you work hard for me, I'll pay you well. Now some of you are probably wondering, why the penalty system? If he's so generous, why's he want to ding us? Well, I'll tell you, fellas: incentive. Simple as that. INCENTIVE. When I hire a body, I like to see it work. When I hire a head, I like to hear its ideas. That's the way I run things.

'Now, some of you may know that in my car dealerships I personally go over the monthly sales records of all my salesmen, and the fella with the poorest sales record, I let go. I say "let go." Not "fire." *Let go*.' The millionaire's hands fluttered, as if they were pigeons rising from a loft. Kozicki had a picture of the lousy salesman as an inflated head on a string, which Rawlings cut loose with a single slash of one of those crossed swords on his polo shirt. The salesman floated off over trees and prairies and mountains before going *phtttt* and dropping into the ocean.

Rawlings continued: 'I let him go, set him free. Why?—Because that fella's sales record tells me he is *tied down* in my employ. Selling cars *tethers* him—does not give him the freedom to fulfill himself. If I let him go, he can become whatever he wants—an artist, a violinist— whatever he's suited for. Now Mike here has told me that each of you is suited for landscaping. I've got confirmation on *that*, too—haven't I, Mike?'

'You have.'

'So I'm giving you fellas the opportunity to prove yourselves. Incentive. Freedom. That's what the game's all about.' He studied the crews' faces. 'That's all I've got to say. Any questions?'

The crew gazed at their feet.

'I got one.' Kozicki scratched his ear. 'What was the problem with that back-hoe operator we bumped into out at the gate? Was there something he wasn't suited for?'

Rawlings shrugged. 'That driver was suited for unsolicited opinions, Mike. Unfortunately at the present time I have no need for unsolicited opinions. Any more questions?'

The crew listened to each other breathe.

'Fantastic. I'll leave you to it.' Rawlings turned to go. He moved with a—what?—an *unsolicited* briskness that Kozicki guessed came in handy when a fella had a lot of salesmen to set free. 'Incidentally, Mike,' Rawlings said without looking at him, 'you said there'd be eight of you. I count only six.'

'Two of them are busy today.'

'Picket duty?'

'You have confirmation on that.'

The words simply popped out. Where did they come from, anyway? Rawlings gazed at him unblinkingly, a look that Kozicki thought he had once glimpsed on the face of a Messerschmitt pilot during the war. In 1943 at an aerodrome in Lincolnshire, Kozicki, then a pimply twenty-year-old rear gunner on night ops, had been sunbathing on a hillside one afternoon when the German plane shrieked overhead out of nowhere, strafed two Lancasters on the tarmac and wheeled away, passing so close to the shirtless Kozicki that he could see—or thought he could—a vein pulsing in the pilot's forehead. The Messerschmitt roared past and then, unaccountably, turned again, levelled off, and swooped directly towards Kozicki who, mesmerized, stood rooted to the bald hill's top, 'a sitting duck—well, *standing*,' as he would later say. Common sense told him to sprint, dive, *anything*, but instead he remained as still as a lamp-post until, coming to his senses, he turned his back, bent over and dropped his trousers. A cold blast of air surged up his nethers and flung him face-first into the grass, and though he expected at any moment to feel his rear end studded with hot nails he escaped unharmed while the Messerschmitt pilot—so he imagined, he never looked up to see— swept disdainfully back to Germany.

Rawling's eyes had narrowed. 'These other two fellas, Mike, are they good workers?'

'Two of the best. One's not a fella, though. She's a woman.'

'As long as she can work, Mike. I'm an equal opportunity employer.'

'That's good. We're equal opportunity employees.'

Rawlings narrowed his eyes a little more. 'Fantastic. And this picket line thing. A regular occurrence, is it?'

'We're each booked in for a couple of hours every day.'

'Will this loyalty to union tradition interfere with your work here?'

'Not the way we got it planned.'

'Fantastic.'

Two hours on a picket line with Rob Trischuk was two hours too long, in Anna's opinion. Walking that close to him, certain vows she'd made—to hell with men, to hell with love, to hell with dark chocolate and red meat—were dangerously close to being thrown right out the window. Already she'd told him about the tumour she'd had in her fallopian tubes and how in her office younger, better-educated women had jumped right over her head into the plum promotions. She'd complained about Alex, her unemployed structural-engineer husband who'd sat watching an all-day news channel on TV and had once scribbled a list twenty-seven items long that proved life was essentially a waste of time. She'd admitted that many women worried far too much about their appearance and that having children was not as important as most people said it was, though if she'd had the choice she would've happily turned that tumour over to someone with more appreciation for sterility. She wasn't at all sure that being a vegetarian and a student of karate was contradictory, and yes she enjoyed doing her *katas*, not because it reminded her that she could kick someone's nose right around his head but because the movements recalled for her a happier time in her childhood when she studied modern dance. No, she didn't mind his asking her all these questions; no, she was not ready to shoot the moon with him—she thought he might have the wrong expression there, anyway. No, she didn't object to telling him how old she was; thirty-eight. Dreams? Yes, she entertained dreams. But not ambitions. In her family boys had ambitions. Girls had dreams.

'What was your dream?' he asked.

'It's not important.'

'The hell it isn't. I have two daughters, and they have dreams. When you were a little girl, what was your dream?'

He could look so earnest. It drove her crazy, all this earnestness.

'Okay,' he said. 'You want to know what my dream was?' He glanced down at her shyly, from behind mounds of pectorals, deltoids and all those other muscles she didn't know the names of. He was like a Greek hero, hiding behind rocks. 'Guess.'

'Muscles?' she asked.

'Naw. Perfection. Balance. The old ideals. When I was a builder, know what I had pasted on my ceiling? Above my bed, so I'd see it first thing in the morning? EAT BIG, TRAIN BIG, THINK PERFECT. Can you believe that? THINK PERFECT. Now come on. What was your dream?'

They walked an elliptical path in front of the greenhouse compound. Her picket sign demanded JOB SECURITY; his FAIR WAGES. As a picketer she felt like a dancer in an empty theatre, running through a demanding routine of pirouettes and *jetés*, and all she was getting for it was the janitor wringing out his mop in a bucket. How could she not talk to Trischuk? The compound lay on the campus fringe, an outpost of willows and elms on the edge of a vast prairie that opened beyond the city like a sea. None but they and a handful of management people would read their picket signs. If they'd been selling something, they would've been through bankruptcy and into receivership.

'When I was a little girl, I dreamed that someday I would be my Auntie May.'

'Who was Auntie May?'

'My mother's older sister. An antique dealer—ran a business in Edmonton, I think. She smoked cigarillos and wore dresses that showed her cleavage. That was a big deal in those days—cleavage. One time at an auction the auctioneer was late, so she put on one of my grandad's old suits and directed the bidding herself. She wore gobs of make-up and was married three times, once to a Hungarian everybody said was a count. My mum said the guy was a Romanian chicken-farmer. I think my mum thought Auntie May was a tramp.'

'What did you think she was?'

'I don't know—a goddess, I suppose. The happiest person in the world. She drove a white convertible that had a secret pocket the size of a twenty-six of whiskey built into the door.'

'Is that what you want? Whiskey and white convertibles?'

'Of course not.'

'What *do* you want?'

'I'm not sure yet. Auntie-May-ness.'

They walked slowly, arms touching. 'So,' he said. 'Did your dream come true? Do you have any Auntie Mayness now?'

'Auntie May swallowed a bottle of sleeping pills when she was fifty-three. They found her with her feet stuck up on the dashboard and her shoes in the glove compartment.'

His face tugged at itself. She guessed his heart was contracting. His heart was always contracting at something—his daughter's crooked teeth, his wife's loyalty and patience. It endeared him to her, all this contracting. Or was it just a pose? Was everything he did some kind of muscle-flex? Maybe he had biceps in his soul, maybe his heart was all pectoralis major. Once he had told her he wanted to will away her sadness, he wanted to love his wife and children, he wanted to pump the world with strength. Now she wondered, did he want to drive a white convertible and drink whiskey and have people think he was the happiest person in the world?

He asked, 'What about your husband?'

'Alex is in Vancouver.'

'Are you still afraid of him?'

'Not at this distance.'

'Would he attack you again if he found out you were having an affair?'

'But I'm not having an affair.'

'I'm thinking of having one. You can share mine.'

'Thank you, no. Didn't you say think perfect?'

'What would Auntie May do?'

'*That* was Auntie May.'

He stopped. 'Listen,' he said. 'I had polio as a kid. My mother used to wake me up at four in the morning to do exercises with a bean bag. She used to make up songs about Malvolio Polio. Doctors told her my arm would never grow. Well, guess what?' He flexed a bicep the size of a grapefruit. It jumped around inside his skin like a kitten in a bag. 'Twelve years of gym work. Tough Times Don't Last, Tough People Do. Strong Enough to Bear the Strain, Man Enough to Take the Pain. I got a hundred of them, but the point is this. Be your own hero.'

He believed what he said. She could see that. His eyes clouded over, eclipsed by barbells or something. He stood in front of her with his arm flexed and, though she felt silly—giddy, if she told herself the truth—she couldn't refute his own creation. His arm *was* big. And something else, too: a fineness had shaped him, a symmetry that went beyond the narcissism of his muscles, a tenderness that had sucked away most of her breath and a good deal of her judgement the first time he kissed her.

As he did now.

And now.

And now.

Soon she would need oxygen. 'You're so warm,' she murmured. 'Sometimes I think of you as the sun.' Her lips were getting lost, her fingers, with no instructions from her, grazed his shoulders, his chest, his stomach and, because neither of them mentioned the word stop, the rocket aimed at the moon.

'Malvolio Polio,' he crooned in a strangled voice, 'your time is almost done.'

'Oh, God.'

'Malvolio Polio,' his words were muffled in her neck as their picket signs clattered to the pavement, 'we've got you on the run.'

A week after the crew started at the Rawlings house, Kozicki came home one evening to find old Mrs. Burkmar from down the street ensconced on a fold-up aluminium lawn chair on his front step.

'That dog of yours,' she said.

'Churchill?' Kozicki was tired. He'd spent most of the day on a miniature tractor harrowing topsoil in grand, smooth circles around the Rawlings house. Now a dumptruck was backing up behind his eyelids, raising its box to release its load. Already, thick loamy sweeps of topsoil were sliding under the tailgate, piling up in his forehead. 'What about Churchill?'

'He went and died in my begonias.'

Kozicki left his lunch kit on the step and followed Mrs. Burkmar through the dusk to her house. He offered to carry her lawn chair, but she refused, asking him if he thought she was useless.

'No,' he said.

'Well, I'm not.'

Churchill lay on his side, his legs outstretched as if he were in eternity chasing perpetual rabbits that never got any closer. His eyes were open and muddy-looking, and his pink tongue poked out the front of his mouth in such a way that Kozicki was reminded of his daughter as a child tasting garlic for the first time. The dog was a morose cross between a Cairn terrier and a bulldog, with pop-eyes, an overbite and a roll of flab on him like a beachball. Even so, Kozicki thought, he didn't deserve to be laid out in Bonita Burkmar's begonias.

'There's ants all over him, Mrs. Burkmar.'

'I need to be told that? What do you think I am, blind?'

'No.'

'Well, I'm not.'

Kozicki brushed away the ants from the dog's wiry fur as best he could; it was a rainforest in there except for the pink patches of skin that Kozicki had always considered Churchill's armpits. Kozicki noticed the dog's legs were skinny as pencils. Churchill had never been an enthusiastic runner, even as a puppy. Growling and a lot of bow-legged defiance had been more Churchill's line. One Halloween when Gillian had been flung to the ground by two bigger kids in sheets, Churchill stood his ground over the fallen child and made bow-legged, overbite lunges at the sheet-boys' ankles until Kozicki exploded out the front door and chased them away. Picking him up now, Kozicki was surprised at how small the dog was; he weighed no more than a large cabbage. Kozicki started to walk back towards his own house. He wished the dog *was* a large cabbage. 'I've got to bury you now, boy,' he told the stiff little animal in his arms. 'I'm sorry, but I've got to put you in the ground.'

'Those begonias will have to be replaced,' Mrs. Burkmar called after him.

'Not now, Mrs. Burkmar. Maybe later.'

'Don't think I'll forget,' Mrs. Burkmar called.

'You won't forget, Mrs. Burkmar.'

'Because I *won't.*'

Kozicki carried the dog across his lawn and around the side of his house—in reality a mobile home that plywood skirting and strategically placed shrubs had disguised as a bungalow. He and his first wife Emily had done all the work themselves—poured the cement, raised the garden shed, built the brick patio upon which Kozicki now laid the rigid corpse of his dog. Darkness was falling and, although he only meant to sit on the patio for a minute or two,

Kozicki found he was still sprawled there when the streetlights flipped on and gathered clouds of moths and mosquitoes.

He was thinking about Emily. Tall and slender, she had developed breast cancer when she was forty-two. 'And look at me,' she'd said. 'I don't *have* any breasts to start with. How can you get cancer in *these?*' The things those doctors did to her: first one breast, then the other, then they talked about going in after her lungs. Kozicki remembered standing in the doctor's office—he didn't want to sit, but preferred to stand—while the surgeon talked about mastectomies and the lymphatic system. Talk about big words: Kozicki didn't understand half of what the surgeon said, but he studied the weeping birch on the hospital lawn (lime deficiency, and it needed to be pruned), and shook the man's hand when the time came. He even signed the papers. In the end they cut Emily open. She lived long enough to make a couple of brassiere jokes—'Why buy hammocks when the old folks have moved *away?*'—and then she died.

Gillian was eleven at the time, already taking a run at puberty with a bust bigger than her mother's had ever been. The sight of bumps on his daughter's sweater frightened Kozicki terribly; he knew it could never happen, but what if Emily's cancer had somehow lodged itself in the walls of their home—they were just fibreboard, after all, sandwiching cheap insulation between them and the aluminium siding—what if the disease liked to hang around low-rent housing and knock off its female members, or at least disfigure them? Gillian was a beautiful girl who could play the piano and do long division in her head. What good were those talents when they could be snuffed out by a shameless affliction that slashed at something as defenceless as a woman's bust—a disease that didn't even have the courage to attack a *man?*

Gillian's bust. After Emily's death Kozicki and his daughter had constructed whole arguments around her bust. No sooner did the girl's chest begin to swell than Kozicki pushed her to wear a bra.

'You need support up there,' he'd said.

'They're just boobs.'

'Don't talk like that.'

'Well they are.'

'You gotta take care of them.'

'Because of *Mum*? Daddy, that's so *stupid*.'

'You just gotta take care of them, that's all.'

How could a man tell her? A girl's breasts were cancer's resting place, death's open door. If it would've protected her, he'd have riveted her in bra-armour, packed her into stainless steel undershirts. He approached her bra-buying—dragging her into the bargain basement at Eaton's and aiming her at a well-endowed saleslady who he figured knew her business—as he would've outfitting a son with a jockstrap. Gillian had wanted nothing to do with brassieres, and until she went away to school suffered under their yoke by walking around with her thumbs hooked in her shoulder straps like a contemplative farmer hitching at his overalls. Well, boarding school had taken care of her bra-wearing and, although at moments like this he wondered if there wasn't some unfinished you-weren't-there-when-I-had-to-wear-my-bra business between him and his daughter, he reasoned that now she was a grown woman she could probably take care of her bust herself. He thought that sometime—when they were alone—he'd ask her if she went in for those whaddayoucallits—boob check-ups.

Eight months after Emily's funeral, he had registered his daughter at the Ontario Ladies' College near Stratford, Ontario. He used the insurance money to settle the tuition and boarding costs. Why not? What did he know about raising a little girl? At the college they would teach her Shakespeare and physics and how to sing in a choir. He imagined his daughter in a blazer and jumper, rosy-cheeked and sturdy on field-hockey legs, winning piano recitals and speaking French. She would paint complicated oil canvases full of reds and philosophical ideas, and go on field trips to museums with Egyptian mummies in them. She would join the college swim team, she would cross the autumn-leaved campus in a crowd of laughing girls who would be her friends for life and phone her in later years from places like Jakarta or Tucson, Arizona. And somewhere at the college a gracious, intelligent woman, probably tall and elegant but not necessarily so, would teach Gillian gracious, intelligent woman-things that Kozicki, who'd taken to nipping at a bottle of White Horse whiskey after suppers and then falling asleep face down on the kitchen table, would have a hard time putting into words.

'But Daddy, I'm not sure I want to go.'

'Of course you aren't, sweetie. Who's ever sure about anything? Get me a glass, will ya?'

He delayed sending her away for another year. Instead of autumn leaves and museums she got a mobile home that was hard to heat and looked as if it had been taken over by a band of hobos on a hunger march. The living room became a minefield of dirty socks, soiled underwear and White Horse empties. In the kitchen, stuff that was green and furry grew under the sink, and every time Gillian moved the garbage pail a herd of silverfish scuttled under the stove. The bathroom was spattered with little hairs and shaving soap and, although on occasion Kozicki pushed aside crumpled newspapers, hugged his daughter close and told her everything would be all right, most of the time he gave her household tips that he'd heard on the radio on the way home from work. 'To get rid of odours, pour some vinegar in a saucer and leave it on the counter,' he told her. 'You want that ink out of that blouse, rub it with toothpaste.' She was in grade six. Sometimes she cried; once she threw the double boiler at his head. In the end, he came home one day to find the house spotlessly clean and Gillian standing in the living room next to her suitcase.

'You win, Daddy,' she had said.

Later, a few days before she left, she led him to the kitchen where, under the table and nestled in a cardboard box lined with old clothes, lay the sleeping puppy.

'That's my sweater in there,' Kozicki had said, peering.

'His name is Churchill, and the lady said you don't have to worry, he's already been fixed.' Gillian had ruffled the puppy's ears with her fingertips. 'You'll have to take care of him, Daddy.'

Now, seventeen years later, as he sat on the patio stroking his dog's cold and stiffening muzzle, Kozicki felt his daughter's words like a barbecue skewer through his liver. How had he taken care of Churchill?—He couldn't even get the poor beast's tongue back between the coldly grinning lips. Churchill was saying nya-nya from the afterlife, if there was one, and Kozicki could do nothing to help. Sighing, he got up and went to the garden shed to get a spade.

Above him the night sky glittered with stars. Kozicki's house trailer was near the airport, and at regular intervals enormous jets roared over the chimney tops, sounding like colossal vacuum-cleaners whose sole purpose was to Hoover the sky. One passed overhead as Kozicki's hand felt for the spade along the garden shed's dark wall; the tin roof rattled, and the musty scent of spiders reached him, as if they all had bailed out of their webs at this first sign of an air strike. When he stepped back out into the moonlight, he half expected to see the sky swept clean, starless and unwinking. But the heavens shone on as they always had, giving him enough light to shape Churchill's grave among the roses along the back fence.

He dug deep, sweating and mosquito-ridden. When he finally laid the dog in the bottom of the hole it occurred to him that Churchill would be uncomfortable down there, so he went inside and got the old wool sweater the dog had slept on for all those years, lined the hole with it and laid Churchill on top of *that*. In the wan light he could see the tufts of fur along Churchill's flank, looking pale and vulnerable. He couldn't drop stones and dirt on all that exposed fur, so he lifted the dog out again and wrapped him *in* the sweater. In the process of being bundled up, the dog emitted a tiny groan, due no doubt to some gaseous retention but to Kozicki a whimper from beyond the grave, so that he spent several anxious moments on his knees trying to coax the dog back to life.

By the time he had buried the dog he was crying; nothing loud and blubbery, but still a few slippery tears that accumulated on the end of his nose and made him wish he'd never given up drinking. Considering the occasion, he thought a few words might be in order, but all he had on him was the dictionary so, from it, under the porch light, he read: '*Dog, noun; a carnivorous quadruped of genus Canis, of many breeds wild and domesticated.*' The definition fell far short of the meaning he was trying to get at, and he stood over the grave in shame, like a defeated baseball pitcher on a mound, wondering what to throw next. In fact, as a kid Kozicki had played a little baseball— never the infield, but always out near a fence somewhere, where the grass was deep. As a hitter, he was never one to wallop the long ball; oh he could lay down a bunt, or maybe punch through a one-bagger or even a double, but the triples and homers had always eluded him. Now here he was at the old dog's graveside and all he could come up with was one lousy definition, the verbal equivalent of a pop fly. He filled in the grave and covered it with a heavy stone. Then he put the spade away.

Back in the house he waited awhile before making the phone call. He wasn't surprised when he heard the answering machine; after all, Toronto was in a different time zone—it was one in the morning there. He thought of hanging up; however, when his daughter's voice asked him to leave a message at the sound of the tone, he did so for the first time in months.

'Hi Gillian, this is Daddy. I'm sorry, but I've got some bad news. Churchill died tonight.' He waited, wondering if the tape allowed more time. When it did, he said, 'He was a good friend, Gillie. I'll miss him.'

Later that night in bed, the little ball bearing in his innards dropped again, only this time it felt different. If Kozicki was a house, the ball bearing had just bounced down a flight of stairs. From the way it hit the floor and rolled up to his basement door, Kozicki guessed the ball bearing wasn't a ball bearing any more. It was a baseball.

PART TWO

FOR THE NEXT TWO WEEKS KOZICKI LOST HIMSELF IN THE RHYTHM of the Rawlings job. Forty-five years a labourer, Kozicki had concluded the work was work, all right, but it was something else besides. All work had its own rhythm. Work had a pattern, work had a beat. Work was music.

'Oh I don't mean it's got a string section and drums and a singer and a pile of brass and all that,' he told Paterson one day. They were in Kozicki's truck, racing to the greenhouse on a clandestine mission to pick up a rototiller. 'But it's music, just the same.'

'What kind of music?' Paterson asked.

'Depends on the job. You take a girl waiting on tables in a crowded restaurant. Running for this, running for that, hopping around like a fart in a net. What's she got?—Clickers on her heels. Tap-dance music. Or take a guy painting a house. Long smooth strokes, sun on his neck like liniment. What's he got?—A slow waltz on an accordion. Music.'

Kozicki wasn't sure where he'd gotten this idea. His own musical ability extended to a couple of folk songs on the guitar and, during infrequent bouts of celebratory inebriation, the bawled-out lyrics of show tunes and singalongs from World War II. During his White Horse days, he'd often scared Gillian half to death by wallowing in maudlin renditions of 'When the Lights Go On Again' and 'Lilli Marlene.' He came by singing honestly, though; in the 1930s his Welsh mother had early besieged him with voice lessons, only to be brought to her knees when he persistently screeched off-key.

'The child has a tin ear,' she once lamented to Kozicki's father, a tailor who liked to play Glenn Miller and the Dorseys on the Victrola while he stitched together cheap suits in the shop downstairs. The word *tin* had sent Kozicki to the back step for ten minutes, where he'd rapped on the side of his head to see if it pinged like a can of baked beans. When he finally understood what his mother meant, it was too late: he already loved music, even though he had no talent for making it—even though a week later the Victrola had to be pawned to pay the rent.

But the music: put a shovel or a rake in Kozicki's hands, point to gravel that had to be screened or soil that had to be graded, and his blood sang the lugubrious air of labour. Forget strikes, groin troubles, forget everything. The lift and fall of a shovel, the rise and stoop, rise and stoop of what most people called drudgery played in his heart like a symphony. Once he discovered a job's rhythm he fell into step with it, emptied his mind so he could become that dumb thing—the tool for the job. No language was needed there, no words, no dictionary. Movement defined him. In the rise and stoop of labour he was a slave, and in his slavery, free.

'I don't understand that last part,' Paterson said.

'Me neither.' Kozicki wove his truck through the traffic. 'I'm tired. I think I just made that up.'

It was 9:00 A.M. They'd been working since 4:30 that morning and wouldn't finish until the sun went down at 9:30 that night. According to Kozicki, early starts and late finishes were the rhythm required to complete the Rawlings job on time. 'This is an all-night number,' he'd told his crew. 'A marathon on a dance floor.' As a boy in the thirties Kozicki had attended a dance marathon, not as a participant but as one of many ragged kids who thought they'd pick up a few pennies selling chunks of ice out of a bucket. Dance couples clung to each other under the dim lights of the old Armoury building, dragged each other across the sawdust floor like corpses with nowhere to lie down. Kozicki remembered one woman with thin, brittle legs and sharp breasts who during a break had flopped in a chair and said, 'My feet are salamis, my eyes are two peeholes in the snow.' Her partner, a soft, peach-coloured man, suggested they quit. She pushed herself up off the chair, pushed and pushed. 'Just let me get the nails out of my ass,' she'd said, 'and then point me in the right direction.' Kozicki never learned if the woman and her peach-man won but, whenever he had grown tired—even in his gun turret during the war—he imagined her coming after him with a crowbar, prying his ass loose, and shoving him in the right direction.

Which at the moment was east. The route to the campus greenhouse led him through the shabby fringe of downtown, along a street that ran a gauntlet of bike shops and cafés, pawn shops and second-hand clothing stores, auction rooms, pool halls, and crumbling red-brick hotels with names like the King George and the St. James, whose beer parlours offered safe haven for every crook and straight shooter in the city—in Kozicki's opinion, everybody. Even this early in the day, when the heat and exhaust were just beginning to rise from the pavement, people were shouldering their way into the street. Winos stumbled towards the benches under the trees on Station Corner; flat-footed women in pale veiny legs and summer frocks dragged baggy-eyed kids into discount stores; teenagers on roller-skates played chicken with city buses. The place reminded Kozicki of his old neighbourhood in the city of his childhood; his father's rented frame house where a gilt-etched 'Kozicki the Tailor' shone from the front room window. The people of this street were his kind of people. He swam in them. If Cargill had been there, Kozicki would have poked his head out the driver's side window and hollered, 'Brothers and sisters!' and come pretty close to meaning it. He loved their persistence, their sweatbox houses, their hand-me-down shoes. They were just like him. They stood outside the Warehouse Furniture Store to see what Crazy Louie was up to today; in Excel Drugs they bought Milk of Magnesia tablets and little plastic sandals with see-through toes. At Rawlings Payless Foods they—

'Holy shit!' Paterson shouted. 'Are you trying to kill us?'

Kozicki had slammed on the brakes in the middle of a long line of flowing traffic. His truck stalled; he had to grind the nagging starter until the engine caught, while around him horns blared. Somebody called him an asshole.

'What's the matter?' The force of the truck's halt had catapulted Paterson forward, flung his hands protectively at the dash and shot his nose within inches of the windshield.

'What's the name of that Inca king, Attaboy or something?' Kozicki asked.

'What Inca king?'

'The one that got his head cut off.'

'How should I know?'

'Give me the name of an Inca king.'

'What for?—Atahualpa, I think. What for?'

'You need a drink?' Kozicki asked. 'A Coke? I gotta go into Payless Foods.' He eased the truck to the curb and parked it. 'I won't be long,' he said. 'Write a book or something.'

At first he hadn't recognized Charlene. She was tanned, and something drastic had happened to her hair; it had been cut, curled and possibly tinted, and now flounced jauntily on her well-shaped head as if one trip to a hairdresser could trim and sweep away fifteen years of middle age. Had he been a stranger, Kozicki would have put her age at thirty-six; forty, tops. She was dressed in a cashier's uniform, a turquoise dress edged in purple piping, and white shoes that made Kozicki think of athletic nurses and tennis instructors. Watching her bound into Payless Foods with two other uniformed women, Kozicki suddenly felt arthritic, basket-footed, one hundred and two.

Payless Foods was a cinderblock fortress, a bunker whose utilitarian design was meant to reassure customers that here was not an effete market constructed for profit, but a warehouse whose sole purpose was to distribute food to the thrifty. A no-frills parking lot squatted on the roof. Groceries were set out in plain cardboard boxes on unpainted metal shelves. Fruits and vegetables were dumped in splintery, mirrorless barrows; the customers themselves packed their purchases in brown paper bags at checkout stands so unglamourous that Kozicki sometimes wondered if the cash registers were an afterthought—some legal requirement forced on the store's management who would really rather give everything away. At Payless Foods Kozicki imagined he was in a quartermaster's store or a food bank; no matter what he bought, the dim lights and unfinished cement told him he was getting a hell of a deal and, even if he knew that the store's chairman of the board, Clarence D. Rawlings, was as rich as King Farouk, the possibility remained that Kozicki and thousands of other Payless shoppers were sliding one by the little fella. They were scooping up tons of groceries at cost.

At the checkout counter Kozicki pushed two cartons of soft drink cans ahead of him.

'You look good, Charlene.'

'How did you know I was here?'

'Detective work. I saw the uniform, and I followed you in.'

'You followed me? You've been following me?' Charlene's nose got big.

'I haven't *been* following you. I just *followed* you. In *here.*'

People were lining up behind him. An enormous man with a stomach like a sack of water nudged him with a grocery cart. Kozicki lowered his voice. 'Couldn't I just see you?'

She punched the cash register. 'Have you seen Dr. Brandell?'

'I been busy.'

She herded the cans along the counter with her arm, and handed him his change. 'Pack your own.'

'Atahualpa.'

'Pardon?'

'Atahualpa. The Inca guy you said the Spaniards beheaded.'

'Some people think the king was Huáscar.'

'Who?'

'Huáscar.'

'I don't know him.'

'Hey,' the man behind waved a bunch of celery. 'You gonna pack your stuff or what?'

'Maybe we should leave the Incas out of this, Mike.'

'Let's leave everybody out of this,' the big man said. 'Let's leave me out of this, you out of this, let's leave the whole world out of this. Let's leave my pork chops out of this, my bananas, my ice cream—'

'Churchill's dead,' Kozicki said.

Charlene stopped. 'Oh. Oh Mike, I'm sorry.'

'Hey,' the man behind said, 'so what? Churchill's dead?—So's Roosevelt. So's Mackenzie King. Hey, even fucken *Stalin's* dead!'

Charlene touched Kozicki's hand. 'Are you using your dog to get at me?'

'Would it work?'

'Have you seen Dr. Brandell?'

'I'm in the middle of a job.'

'Guess what?' The man behind thumped his groceries on the counter—bunches of celery, bananas, and a package of pork chops as long as a hockey stick. 'I'm in the middle of a fucken nervous *break-down.*'

'We're on a deadline,' Kozicki said hurriedly. 'Me and the crew. We gotta finish this job by September first.' He paused. 'Do you think a couple of old Incas could have until September first to see if they'll rise again?'

She considered, then nodded. 'But no later. And don't call me until you've seen the doctor,' she added as he headed for the door.

'Don't even *call*!' the big man hollered.

Back at the truck Paterson was scribbling furiously in his pocket notebook. Kozicki climbed in, slid the Coke cans over the gearbox and onto the floor at Paterson's feet. 'Help yourself.'

Paterson obliged, popping the can's tab and swigging great throaty gulps while his pen never slackened its vicious sprint across the page. Kozicki recalled his hospitalized wife once being attached to an electroencephalograph; there had been talk of a brain tumour. 'I feel like an island,' Emily had said as her brain patterns were being printed out, 'with waves washing on my beaches.' Kozicki didn't know about beaches but, compared to Emily's languid thoughts, Paterson's pen appeared to be involved in a hurricane.

'What do you write in there,' Kozicki said, 'if you don't mind my asking.'

'Observations.' Paterson's pen was really going after the page now. Kozicki wondered if the boy's hand controlled the pen at all. Maybe it had a life of its own; maybe once it ran out of paper it would leap out of Paterson's fingers and attack both of them, write all the things it knew about them all over their faces.

'That's some writing,' Kozicki said when Peterson had finished.

' "What oft was thought, but ne'er so fast expressed," ' Paterson said. He sat guzzling his Coke, expended, like a runner who'd just dodged through traffic and couldn't believe he hadn't been flattened. The truck was moving again; they were on the University Bridge, overlooking the river.

'Where are we going?' Paterson leaned his head against the seat back.

'Come on—you *really* forget sometimes?'

Paterson grinned wearily. 'Oh yeah—the greenhouse.' He took another drink. 'Yeah, sometimes I forget.'

'Must be a big kick having all those words pour out of the end of your arm like that.'

'No bigger kick than you carrying them around in your back pocket all day.'

'That's different,' Kozicki said. 'I look 'em up—I can't *write* 'em.'

Paterson was watching him now.

'What would you write, if you could?'

'Cheques.'

'Seriously.'

'Seriously?' Kozicki turned off the bridge and drove under the stone-arch entrance to the campus. The sudden shade from a row of maples obscured Paterson's face, which was all right with Kozicki. The kid was staring at him too hard. 'Letters, for one thing.'

'Letters? You mean like the alphabet?'

'I mean like the post office,' Kozicki said.

The greenhouse looked deserted, as if it were a border outpost whose guards had been smacked on the head with a ballpeen hammer, gagged, and tied up on the floor. Kozicki had never seen a border outpost, but during his time in the air force he'd often dreamt of one. In his dream, his plane plummeted from the sky trailing plumes of black smoke; he would bail out and drift on his parachute into a woods, where a beautiful woman in a trenchcoat would supply him with civilian clothes, false identification and a ballpeen hammer. Of course, Kozicki never got the chance to bail out of his plane; over Berlin shrapnel slashed his parachute into string underwear and studded his arm with little bits of German metal that looked like the heads off finishing nails. The cold, lonely hours crouching in his rear turret as the bomber limped home drove all thoughts of women and hand tools right out of his head. He'd rarely thought about border outposts until now.

'I wonder where everybody is?' he asked Paterson. 'Trischuk and Anna are supposed to be on picket duty this morning.'

'There are two picket signs leaning against the fence,' Paterson pointed out. 'Maybe they went for coffee.'

Kozicki grunted, steered the truck through the compound's gates, and swept around to the back of the greenhouse. He reversed the truck out of sight into the loading bay, where Dreedle's assistant, Mr. Bistritz, met them.

'We gotta hurry,' Kozicki said, jumping out of the truck. 'You alone here?'

'Alone, but not lonely.' Mr. Bistritz tossed his coiffed head. In the subtropical climate of the greenhouse, Mr. Bistritz was himself a rare flower. Flamboyant, maybe—he dyed his hair alarming shades of strawberry blond and wore his trousers so tight Kozicki worried that one day the man would bend over, cut off the blood supply to his torso, pass out and suffocate face-first in a flat of geraniums. Whatever Mr. Bistritz's sartorial proclivities, he was a good worker; he had a gift for making things grow, as if he sensed humidity and temperature through his pockmarked skin. 'Since this strike began,' he told Kozicki, 'I've been working precisely like some great hairy sweaty *Trojan*.'

'Where's Dreedle?'

'In conference at the Maintenance Building. Some strategic tête-à-tête whose details I'm not privy to.'

'And the picketers — Trischuk and Anna?'

Mr. Bistritz brushed the soil from his fingertips and lowered his considerable lashes. 'A brief sojourn, perhaps. I'm not one to tell tales out of school.'

'Has Cargill been around today?'

'Not yet.'

'Jesus Christ.' Kozicki paced in a little circle. 'Paterson, you go out to the gate, grab a picket and walk the line. If Cargill shows, tell him I had to go away for a while. Tell him — tell him I had a doctor's appointment.' Paterson nodded and rushed off. Kozicki was sweating. He pictured Cargill bursting a blood vessel, or arriving with a truckload of strike-enforcing maintenance goons, all armed with crescent wrenches and old oil filters. 'Okay,' he told Mr. Bistritz. 'Let's load up the rototiller. What else you got for me?'

'Cement, sand-screen, finishing trowels, cold chisels.'

'Dominico's been on my back about those chisels.'

'Dominico's so *cute*.' Mr. Bistritz dropped the tailgate and together he and Kozicki wrestled the ramp into place. The rototiller was an orange-coloured, self-propelled behemoth whose cowling hid lethal, toe-slashing blades. Once Corny Fergus had started the tiller when it was in reverse. The machine had bounded backwards, chased him to a wall and slammed his kidneys against the bricks so vigorously that Corny had peed beet juice for two weeks after. Mr. Bistritz cranked the engine and steered it, roaring and without incident, into the back of Kozicki's groaning truck. They threw the ramp in after it.

'Let's load the cement, and cover the whole thing with a tarp.'

A loud sharp whistle split the air.

'That'll be Paterson,' Kozicki said. 'Take a look out front.'

Mr. Bistritz flew through the door to the front of the building.

Moments later he returned, panting. 'Cargill—out there.'

'Coming in here?'

'Talking to Paterson.'

'Tarp.'

They unfolded a heavy canvas tarpaulin and flung it over Kozicki's truck box. The rototiller's handles stuck up like moose antlers under a tablecloth.

'Jesus.' Kozicki said.

'No time.' Mr. Bistritz looked rattled.

'Where should I go?' Kozicki felt trapped. For nineteen years he'd come to this building in the morning, at noon, and at the end of every working day. He knew its tool boxes, lunch room, the garage where engines were tuned. Suddenly the place was different; the rooms were skewed, as if the walls weren't set at right angles. It was too well-lit; the ceiling was naked. Where were you supposed to hide from a shop steward? How were you supposed to avoid a guy who only had your security and fair treatment at heart? Holy Hannah. Where could you go?

'*Bathroom!*' Mr. Bistritz pointed, and Kozicki started to run. 'I'll knock when the coast is clear.'

Inside the bathroom Kozicki clicked on the light, locked the door, and sat on the toilet seat with his head in his hands. What a waste of time! Time, time! Over two weeks gone already, so that left—he counted on his fingers—five weeks and three days. Out of that, two hours per person on the picket line per day. That was sixteen man-hours a day, five days a week. That would make . . . fives times sixteen . . . eighty hours a week! Eighty hours a week pissed up against the wall and here he was crouched in a john wasting *more* time! He looked at his watch. Damn!

'Nnnuhhhh, nuh, nuh,' he heard.

He lifted his head.

'Ah, ah.'

'Nuh, nnnuhhh, nuh.'

'Ah. Ah.'

The words weren't in his dictionary, but Kozicki knew the language of love when he heard it. Holy Hannah, they were doing it. With Cargill right outside at the gate and their picket signs leaning against the fence and himself hiding like a thief in the crapper they were busy *doing it!* He got up and paced around the room, amazed at their passion, their stupidity. *Jesus.* He touched each wall, as if he were blind. What if Cargill walked in? What if humping was against union policy? What if humping on management property was breaking a union by-law? What if humping a fellow union member on management property during a strike was not only anti-union, but was against the *law of the land*? Kozicki was hazy on the law of the land, but weren't there codes of moral decency, wasn't there some kind of God-thing that applied to humping? And what if Clarence Rawlings got wind that two of his landscape gardeners liked to hump each other at the drop of a hat—he was a God guy, wasn't he? He'd fire them, and then the crew'd be down to six people. Six people at what—three hours a day on the picket line? Eighteen man-hours per day—

Kozicki told himself to take it easy. Calm down.

'Nuh, nuh, nuh.' And now a thumping noise. Humping *and* thumping? Were they trying to *advertise*?

He held his breath and tried to locate the sound. Behind him the door led to the loading bay. Too obvious, he would've seen them. The wall to the right, behind the sink? That was adjacent to the greenhouse. Too much glass, they might as well be on TV. The back wall, behind the towel dispenser?—The warehouse. Bingo. The warehouse. Humping heaven. Seed bags, fertilizer bags, piles of folded gunny sacks. They were humping on sacks of Kentucky Blue, screwing in the Russian Rye, hiding the salami in the Creeping Red Fescue.

He tiptoed to the back wall, cupped his hands around his mouth, and pitched his voice low.

'Hey.'

'Ah, aaahhhhh!'

'*Hey!*'

'*Yes!* Oh yes yes yes yes yes!'

'HEY!'

Silence.

'Keep the noise *down*!'

Silence.

He pressed his ear to the wall. Nothing. He made a tube with his hands and listened. Nothing. Had he killed them? Fatally shocked them at orgasm, so that now they lay, naked as onions, dead as fish, socketed together in such a way that ambulance attendants would have to haul them out like tree roots under a single sheet, while Kozicki explained to the police and everybody else that he hadn't meant it?

He cupped his hands around his mouth again and whispered: 'Sorry.' He sat down and glanced at his watch again. Time, time. In places like this, Kozicki thought, if time was a person it'd be on a motorcycle.

He was more used to seeing the hands crawl around a clock's face. When Emily was in the hospital he had sat with Gillian in the waiting room for a hundred years, playing solitaire, reading kids' books, teaching his daughter twenty-one or bust. If Anna and Trischuk were still alive back there—he thought he heard rustling and giggles—he ought to tell them what love was. Love was time. You waited and waited, and drank coffee and showed your little girl how a red queen went on a black king, and all the while beauty faded and got skinnier and skinnier until you thought there'd be nothing left to love. But there was. There was.

Ten minutes passed; then Mr. Bistritz knocked: 'Cargill's gone.'

Kozicki opened the door. 'What about Trischuk and Anna?'

'Who?'

'Don't give me that. I just heard them screwing their brains out in the storeroom. How long have they been doing that?'

'A week. Maybe two.'

'You better get them out of there.'

'They're back on the picket line.'

Kozicki raised his eyebrows. 'Are they even *dressed?*'

'Don't be so hard on them.'

'If they get caught, what they're doing could be hard on all of us.'

Mr. Bistritz swept a lock of hair off his forehead. 'They needed a place—but I understand. Your point is well taken. My only defence is a soft heart; my only request that Large One not be informed.'

'So Dreedle doesn't know?'

'Of course not. He has an aversion to sentimental whims.'

'Aversion. Now there's a word.'

Kozicki and Paterson finished loading the truck and roared out to the gates. There the two lovers walked slightly apart, picket signs in hand. Anna's cheeks were splotchy, Trischuk's hair peppered with pale, dusty flakes.

'Some information,' Kozicki told them. 'We got forty-four and a half days left to finish the job. That's a lot of time for somebody to catch you guys in the Hotel Paradise and mess up the whole deal. I'd say do it on your own time, but you don't have any of that. So I'm asking you—be reasonable.'

Trischuk gazed at him steadily and curled his lip. 'Anything else?'

'Yeah. You got grass seed in your hair.'

As Kozicki drove away he watched them recede in the rear-view mirror. They walked contritely, it seemed to him, as if their experience had purified them, shortened their steps to a chaste daintiness that was all higher purpose and reflection. As if they had an *aversion* to lust.

On the other hand, Kozicki thought, maybe they were just resting up.

'What did you talk to Cargill *about*?' Kozicki asked Paterson.

'Arteries.'

'Whose arteries—his arteries?'

'Union arteries.'

'And what did you decide about union arteries?'

'Union executives are the arteries. Union members are the heart. They pump the blood to the arteries.'

'That's it, huh?'

'That's it.'

'What about veins?'

'We didn't talk about veins.'

'I'd sure like to know about veins.' Kozicki turned a corner, eased into a line of traffic behind a taxi. 'How'd you get on the subject of arteries, anyhow?'

Paterson glanced at him. 'I told him about yours.'

'My what? My *arteries*?'

'I told him you had trouble with your arteries—you know, *down there*.' Paterson pointed *down there*. 'I told him you had to see a doctor.'

'*I* don't have trouble with my arteries down there.'

'I told him you did.'

Kozicki drove intensely for a while. 'So what did he say—when you told him.'

'He said he hoped you didn't have what he's got.'

'He's got trouble with his arteries—down there?'

'No, he's got trouble with his heart.'

'I suppose,' Kozicki said, considering, 'that the union has trouble with *its* heart, too.'

Paterson shrugged. 'He didn't say any more about hearts. Or arteries, or the union. He just said he hoped you didn't have what he's got. Then he left.'

Kozicki steered the truck along Riverside Drive, where the river flashed between the trees. He thought of Cargill worrying about hearts and arteries, he thought of Cargill's red face, he thought of union hearts and union arteries. 'That Cargill,' he told Paterson. 'I bet he doesn't make love in the middle of the day. We better keep an eye out for that guy.'

On the third Saturday in July, Kozicki gathered his crew around the architect's blueprint that he'd spread out on the hood of his truck and pinned down with a rock at each corner, and considered the Big Picture. He held such briefings at the beginning of the project, of course, but a fella never knew when the Big Picture might slide away from him, because the Big Picture was more than just a line on a scroll. Oh, a blueprint could spell out the details you needed to do your work, all right; those lines could show you where waves of soil had to taper off into plateaus of lawn, where junipers and rock pines had to be planted, where shrubs and hedges and flower beds and irrigation pipes had to be laid out—but a drawing was nothing more than lines. It didn't give you the *feel* of a place. Kozicki didn't want to sound gooey, but you had to admit that every place had a feel to it. Landscape a hospital grounds and you couldn't help but imagine peacefulness—right, Lannie?—like you were a patient in pyjamas bum-warming yourself on a sunny bench. And Paterson—plant shrubs around a university residence and in your head you were kissing a co-ed in the shadows under the maple trees, weren't you?— Well, maybe not. But you got the point. Every place had a feel to it, and this one was no different.

'Yeah?' Corny Fergus listened to Kozicki with his mouth open. 'What kind of feel does this place got? Friggin weird, if you ask me, like it's evil or something. First day I got here a gull flew over and shit on my shirt.'

'That's supposed to be *good* luck,' Paterson said.

'What's so friggin good about birdshit in your pocket? If that'd been an elephant, it woulda killed me.'

Trischuk moved in, draping his arm over Anna's shoulders. 'Meet the challenge, buddy. Pay the price.'

'I ain't payin nothin,' Corny said. 'I wanna *get* paid before I get killed or some friggin thing. We got a new kid at our house and she needs shoes.'

Dominico hooted. 'Whaddayou mean—youra wife she'sa make another bambino? Corny Ferg, Corny Ferg, whadda guy, Dio canne! Makea da bambinos, makea da bambinos, a *binga binga bing*! I think maybe you don' aneed apay, Corny Ferg—I thinka you need asleep!'

'Corny,' Anna said gently, 'a baby won't need shoes right away.'

'She ain't a baby, she's nine years old. We adopted her, okay?' Corny fiddled with the tensor bandage on his elbow. 'All's I'm sayin is it's fine and friggin dandy to talk about the feel of a place but talk ain't worth chicken spit if we don't finish on time. I mean, you take me and Eagle gradin that soil, up by the house. Other day Eagle cranks up the bobcat and moves a couple of loads and what's this Rawlings guy do? Comes out like the friggin Pope and tells us to shut 'er down because the machine's shaking his friggin *windows*. What kinda guy puts stainglass windows in a friggin *house*?—A screwball, that's who. I tell you, that guy's got more friggin bends in him than a coat hanger.'

'He's paying the piper,' Kozicki said. 'He's calling the tune.'

'I don't know about tunes,' Corny grumbled, tucking in his chin. 'I do know I don't see no gullshit on *him*.'

'And you won't, either. That's what I'm getting at.' Kozicki spread his big hands over the blueprint as if he were a pants-presser getting ready to lay on the steam. 'This guy is finicky, but that shouldn't bother us; it shouldn't matter if he's so tight-assed that he uses a shoehorn to get into his underwear. That's okay. All it means is we got to do the job right *the first time we do it*. There's a word for that: *meticulous*. That's the feel this place has got:—weird, maybe, but *meticulous*. So we're going to out-*meticulous* this guy, we're going to *meticulate* him right into the ground. Now look here.' The crew bent close over the blueprint. 'Here's the irrigation line. Trischuk and Anna have nearly got it hooked up already. These lines over here are the slope I made with the tractor. Some hand-raking and it'll be done. The grading around the house here needs to be finished, and a couple of trees need to be pruned back. Corny, that'll be you and

Eagle. Dominico, how you coming with that rock work, on the moat?'

'That astone I don' like.'

'I know you don't like it—but how's it coming?'

'One—maybe atwo load. That astone, she don' likea to be cut. I puta the chisel on the astone and the astone she say "No, no, I don' makea the cut, I makea the piece!"'

'You need someone to help you?'

'Hey, Mike—whaddyou think?—I need *God*.'

'Paterson will have to do.'

'Sure. Patersoni, God, whad's the difference?'

Kozicki straightened. 'Anybody else bothered by talking rocks, talking trees, talking—' His eyes fell on Lannie Dougal. '—whatevers?' He grinned, but no one else did. Their faces were somber. They were looking at the white lines on the blue linen. In three weeks they'd already filled in some of those lines. But the drawing was a spider's web where every strand would have to be spun out of days, hours, minutes, even seconds, while the deadline hunkered off in a corner like some god-awful black widow, ready to tear them apart the minute they got stuck on the web. 'Any questions?' Kozicki said anxiously.

Trischuk laid his hand on the drawing. 'Are we on schedule?'

'I think we're a little behind.'

'How much?'

'A couple of days maybe. It all depends on how you look at it.'

'Let's look at it straight,' Trischuk suggested.

Kozicki sighed. 'Okay. We're behind about two days. We gotta step up the pace. But once we get the grading done, we can make up time while we're planting.'

'If the friggin union don't catch us. If the friggin weather holds.' Corny Fergus cast an eye upwards. For nearly three weeks the sun had risen every morning and travelled unobstructed across a sky any normal person might have taken for a painted ceiling. Lately, though, clouds had begun to build up in the evening, like thugs gathering on a corner—grey, suspicious-looking clouds with big shoulders and their hands in their pockets.

Ironeagle stood off to one side. 'Could be we should get to work,' he said quietly.

'Meticulous work,' Kozicki reminded them. As they walked away to collect their tools, he regretted the remark. What good was putting a dictionary in your mouth when you already had your foot in there? They were worried, and how could he blame them? At best, his judgement of how long the job would take was an estimate. Sure, Corny was a doom-crier—the guy saw disaster under every bush; but he was right too. Sometimes things went wrong. What had Paterson said the other day about the best laid plans of mice and men? They went a-gley. Whatever that was.

Kozicki rolled up the blueprint, slid it into its cardboard tube and noticed, not for the first time, that sometimes the Big Picture could be a damn tight squeeze.

Up near Rawlings's house, every friggin day for over three friggin weeks, Corny Fergus and Ironeagle worked like friggin convicts shovelling and raking enough dirt to build a friggin highway to friggin Mars. Holes? You never seen so many holes; holes where trees used to be, holes where trees were goin, holes as empty as your wallet, holes full of sewer pipe; holes for catch basins, holes for irrigation pipes, holes for what you didn't know what they were for; holes, holes, more friggin holes than a friggin graveyard at friggin midnight; that's what Corny Fergus told his wife every night when he got home and all she you could say was, 'When are you going to bring him over?'

'When the friggin time is right,' he'd answered.

'There's never a *right* time,' she said, 'and you watch your friggin language.'

And then one of the kids—usually one of the little ones but the big ones weren't much better—would heave a boot at his brother or another one would chase her sister with the cat or set fire to the grass by the garage or yell WHAT HAPPENED TO MY JEANS—or some other friggin thing—and there went another conversation. Up in noise.

'But at least fillin in all these friggin holes is *quiet*,' Corny said.

Ironeagle grunted, bent over and touched the ground with his fingers.

Corny stopped shovelling. 'See? You went and done it again. I tell you, you're doin it all the time. That's the kinda thing I mean, that's what the wife's been talkin about. You'd be a friggin natural. Now tell me—what was that?'

'What?' Ironeagle paused in his work to unbutton his shirt. His hairless chest glistened with sweat.

'That thing you done with your hand, touchin the ground and that. What was that about?'

'Touchin the ground.'

Corny planted his feet apart and speared the earth with his shovel. 'I ain't shovellin until you tell me.'

'Well that's a good idea, eh. We're goin to make a lotta money on this job if you stop shovellin. Not that you do much anyhow.' Ironeagle's shovel had started again; he was known as a steady worker. Once, when Kozicki had asked how he came by such extraordinary endurance and single-minded purpose, he'd replied, 'Brain damage,' did a ringside shuffle and then threw a couple of left-right combinations. 'Anyways,' he advised Corny, 'I think you just cut your toe off.'

Corny danced backwards; a piece of leather, like chafed skin, dangled from his boot. His first instinct was to check for blood; even with steel-toed boots you could never be sure. Ten years before he'd seen a guy twist the steel toecap right off a pair of Kodiaks with a gas engine posthole augur and the fella never even knew he'd lost anything until the auger jammed and he found five of his own toes mangled in the screw. 'Don't change the subject,' he warned Ironeagle, who was grinning. 'Tell me.'

When he was working, Ironeagle's speech tended to match the action of his shovel; he would pile up a few words, fling them out, then poke around for a few more. In the ring he'd been notorious for a similar technique that involved whistling through his broken nose while hammering body shots into his opponent's stomach, then during the clinches muttering through his mouthpiece such words as *asshole* and *weewenosis*, the latter a Cree expression meaning 'little dink.' Without a hitch in his shovelling, he explained to Corny, 'When you—tell me—your sob story—you give me—bad thoughts—bad spirits—so I—give them back—to Mother Earth— by touching—the ground.'

This information prompted Corny to forget about shovelling altogether. 'Who taught you this stuff? The elders?'

'—No—'

'Medicine man?'

'—Uh—uh—'

'Where'd you learn it, then?'

'—I go to—the movies—eh.'

Disappointment shut Corny up for a few moments, left him

leaning one-handedly on his shovel thinking thoughts too friggin black and deep for a guy whose wife had just last year had all her plumbing taken out. He remembered the day Marion came home from the hospital, every friggin kid in the family out on the porch with the flowers they'd ripped up from the neighbours' gardens and Elsie and Edna the twins with the friggin brownies they'd burnt, all of them waiting, the little ones expecting another baby and howling blue bloody murder when she told them she'd had a miscarriage and wouldn't be having babies any more. Christ, the noise, it was like a fire in a turkey barn. You'd think nine friggin kids was enough but when you plan on one more and it don't show up it's like you missed a friggin bus or something. All on your lonesome in the depot. So then you jump through all the friggin hoops for adoption and you get this new kid and the guy you work with won't even friggin visit her.

'Hey,' Ironeagle said. 'Maybe you want to use my shovel. I got it warmed up, eh.'

Bending, Corny matched the pace of his shovelling to Ironeagle's. The guy was a friggin gearbox. 'It don't do no good to work fast in heat like this,' Corny grumbled. He had an uncle who'd built roads in Burma during the war, as a guest of the Japanese army. Uncle Sol had come home hollow-eyed, a hard-drinking walking bone-rack who once a year cooked up a big pot of rice, mixed it with tempura and tofu and then flushed the whole mess down the toilet while singing 'God Save the Queen.' Uncle Sol knew about heat exhaustion, heat stroke, heat rashes, prickles, nosebleeds, and several jungle disorders Corny didn't like to hear about. Whenever Uncle Sol visited Corny he gave him a big bottle of salt tablets and some free advice: heat can kill a man. If Corny were to drop dead, how would his new daughter Rosalee find someone like Ironeagle on her own? A fella *had* to wear a shirt and long pants to protect himself from scratches and bumps and friggin skin cancer, but what if those same friggin clothes overheated him and he fainted, and maybe split his friggin face open like a zucchini?

Ironeagle lifted his head. 'Hey, where you goin?'

'I gotta change,' Corny said.

He ducked around the corner of the house. In the shade of a cedar he quickly stripped off his boots and pants, tucked his Hawaiian shirt into his boxer shorts and laced his boots on again. Uncle Sol said a guy had to allow his skin to breathe. Corny felt a cool draft shiver the length of the old sausage under his skivvies and decided Uncle Sol sure knew what he was talking about. He rolled up his pants, checked to make certain he wasn't hanging out of his shorts, and stepped back into the sunlight. Hard-hatted, hairy legs protruding like pipe cleaners out of his baggy boxer shorts, Corny resembled a surplus-store mannequin on a cheap flight to Bermuda. The shorts were blue, dotted with dollar-sized palominos.

'Ho,' Ironeagle pointed. 'A Man Called Horse.'

'Shut up.' Corny kicked the shovel blade into the soil. 'You don't sweat much, do you?'

'I like—to save—it up.' Ironeagle was already in rhythm. It was hard to keep up to the guy.

'I sweat like a friggin beer glass.' Corny admitted. 'In this weather I'm butter on a stick. That's because of all the friggin scars I got. Them scars ruin the pores. I bet I got acres of pores blocked up by friggin scars. Got one on my back from when a tar-bucket fell off a roof. Must of cost me seven hundred pores at least. This one here on my forehead? Two hundred anyways. My hands and arms don't even bear friggin thinkin about. Then them doctors swiped one of my kidneys that time the rototiller hammered me against a wall. Who could even count how many friggin pores that's worth?'

'I didn't know—you lost a kidney.'

'Four years ago. I'm peein on one tank.' Corny rubbed his back reflectively. He shovelled for a while before he confided: 'That new kid of ours, Rosalee? She's got scars.'

Ironeagle worked and said nothing.

'Like I told you before,' Corny went on, 'she was born on a Cree Indian reserve, just like you.'

Ironeagle scowled and stopped shovelling. 'Yeah, but I got a Lakota name: Ironeagle. How come you think that is? A kid with a Lakota name gettin born on a Cree reserve? Ironeagle's my mother's name. How come I got my mother's name? Could be that Indian Agent couldn't tell us apart, eh? Could be my mother didn't know my father's name, eh?'

'Come on, Eagle, I don't mean nothin like that.'

'What *do* you mean then? How am I sposed to find out what a man means when he's workin in his underwear?'

'You think these look like friggin underwear?'

'They *are* friggin underwear.'

'If it bothers you maybe I oughta go change again. Maybe I oughta let the sun boil my friggin brains. Maybe you oughta go tell

Kozicki I took my friggin pants off if it bothers you so much.'

Ironeagle lifted his head. 'What would I tell Kozicki for? What would he care? He's a moony-ass—a whiteman. Not like you. You adopted one of my people. You'll be teachin that little Cree girl all about shoppin malls and the Pope and Elvis Presley. Racial equality. That makes us blood brothers, eh? Could be I'll bring a pipe over to your place and we'll have a smoke. Or could be you could give me a jug of wine and a rusty used car, eh, blood brother?'

'You don't hafta say stuff like that, Eagle. You don't hafta get mad.'

Ironeagle took a breath. 'Everyday this week you tell me about this girl of yours. She does this, she does that. Every day. Well, I tell you something. I'm not mad, I'm just tired.'

He *did* look tired. Loose skin hung below his eyes like wet laundry. He started shovelling again, in silence. Then he said: 'These scars on your Indian kid. What do they look like?'

'Burns on her arms and stomach. All puckered up. She must of fell on a stove when she was little.'

'So they're not Sun Dance scars?'

'What're Sun Dance scars?'

'Those are the scars you get when you stick rabbit bones through your chest and tie them to a pole. You lean back and dance until the bones jump right through the flesh. Those scars look like this.' He flipped his shirt open. Two short scars like jagged white worms lay embedded in his chest. 'If you want your kid to be a real Indian, could be she might have to go through that sometime. Mostly it's boys, but I seen some girls do it too. My grannie had those scars.'

Corny's shovel hung in mid-air. 'You got them scars at a Sun Dance?'

Ironeagle closed his shirt. 'I got those scars from a hooker in Soho.'

'Get outa here.'

'I had to wander around there three nights before I could find one with the right kind of teeth.'

'You got a hooker to bite you?'

'Twice.' Ironeagle tapped his chest. 'One on each side, eh.'

'Bull. Even a hooker wouldn't bite a man like that.'

'She will if you pay her to give you Sun Dance scars.'

The hole was full. Corny leaned his shovel against the house and went to get the hose. They'd have to soak this friggin soil to make it settle. He oughta soak Ironeagle while he was at it. Friggin liar. A hooker!—On the other hand, maybe Ironeagle was telling the truth. Corny had seen the photo the ex-boxer carried in his wallet: a much younger Ironeagle with a bone in his nose, dressed in silk trunks and taped fists and posed in front of that big friggin London clock tower. But a hooker? Corny could just hear what his wife would say when he told her. 'Silly man,' she'd say. 'He was himself before that woman tried to tell him who he was, so what did he accomplish besides wasted money and a mortal sin?' Marion would work in that mortal sin, somehow; she never went to mass, but she was big on mortal sins. Hadn't she got him to stop saying fuck every five seconds? It was friggin handy having somebody like her around, somebody that knew the twists and turns of religious thought. God knew Corny's knowledge of the subject was pretty murky—in a dark room he couldn't have told you the difference between a mortal sin and a friggin chairleg. Well, his wife was a deep one. Everybody said so, and they were welcome to their opinion. She was good and she was tough, and that was enough for Corny. She'd straighten him out on the Sun Dance scars because frankly stickin bones in a little kid didn't sound like a friggin good idea, if a fella wanted the truth. Of course, Eagle was probably jokin—but it would take Marion to figure that one out for sure.

He returned with the hose, let it trickle over the hole. Ironeagle had stalked off with his shovel and rake slung over his shoulder. From the back, Corny thought he looked mad enough to carve Sun Dance scars in everybody, mad enough to carve scars in friggin old Mother Earth *herself.*

Kozicki didn't like the idea of a man marching toward him carrying sharp tools, especially when that man was an ex-boxer and had a face that could have been used to split wood, but lately that's what Ironeagle had been doing, stalking away from Corny Fergus like a man about to embark on a long journey if only he could find the right road. Where Ironeagle's road would lead Kozicki couldn't guess. Although much of the boxer's biography was supposed to be a mystery—intentionally, since Ironeagle practised an amnesia of convenience, selectively forgetting his past the way most people forget Saturday's excuse for Sunday's hangover—Kozicki knew enough about the man to feel a tingle of nerves each time the guy got something in his hands that could be used as a weapon. On several occasions Kozicki had joined Ironeagle at a table in the Queen Anne Hotel , a watering hole that specialized in people who considered drinking a serious business, and between beers he had understood Ironeagle's life to be one battle after another in a war that had no armistice and few surrenders.

As the only Lakota Indian on an all-Cree reserve, Ironeagle had spent his boyhood dealing out black eyes and bloody noses. Jokes directed against him dealt mainly with Lakota intelligence, or the lack of it: 'Two Lakotas ride deep into Cree territory because a white man has told them that they will get a dollar for every Cree scalp they take. One morning one of the Lakotas wakes up and there on the hills surrounding them are seven thousand Cree warriors on horseback, each in warpaint and carrying a spear. The Lakota who's awake counts the warriors for a few minutes, then nudges his friend. "Hey," he says. "Hey, wake up. We're rich."'

Ironeagle didn't get rich, and though he lived with the Cree he was never accepted as one. So when a teacher at the school offered to coach boxing, he jumped in with both fists pumping. He jogged, skipped, shadowboxed and sparred, beat up the heavy bag and hammered the shit out of just about everything else. 'I liked fightin,' he told Kozicki. 'It gave me a focus, eh.' Eventually it gave him something else: a Golden Gloves championship, and a shot at being a professional.

'So when I was eighteen I moved off the reserve. I went down to Regina and I thought now I'll get away from those Crees. But then I ran into the moony-asses—your people. And they were worse than the Cree. You tell a moony-ass you're a Lakota and he thinks you can't talk right, he says "Dakota," or "Sioux," or "Dumb Fucken Indian." So then I started drinkin a little—not much—but a little, and my coach says, "Eagle, I got to get you out of here," and he gives me to this other coach, this Englishman, and *he* says, "We're goin to London." So I went there. Almost four years I was there, in that Whitechapel district, where those Cockneys talk funny and they always want their tea break. My coach Morrie Green goes to synagogue on Friday nights and calls himself a tin lid—a yid, a Jew, eh—and always pays the Burton on time. Burton, that's Burton-on-Trent, that's rent, eh? And before I know it I'm talkin like him and everybody's callin me Eagle. You can hear them yell that—"Ea-gle! Ea-gle!" when I step in the ring. And my name is Moses and those tin lids like it that I got the name of the real Moses, and on the street they say Shalom, Moses and I say Shalom and I figger I'll be a tin lid too. It's like I got a tribe for the first time, eh. I fight twenty-seven bouts and win twelve on knockouts and seven on points, and then one night at a bout up in Sheffield Morrie Green has a heart attack. It's like I lost my father, eh, but I never had a father, so Morrie was him. And then he went and died. So I'm in London with no coach and I try this other coach for awhile but he's not Morrie. He wants me to wear feathers and I want to wear a skullcap, eh. He says you can't be a tin lid and a Lakota too, you're a Red Indian, and I tell him I am not and he says are you fucken blind and I hit him. One big mistake you can make if you're a boxer is if you break your coach's nose: it doesn't make him co-operative, eh. So I came home, but where is home? That's one question I still got, eh. Where is home?'

Kozicki had no answer to that question, nor did he have an answer every time Ironeagle strode towards him waving a shovel or a pick and demanding to know what Corny Fergus expected of him.

'I don't know,' Kozicki said. 'Why don't you go over to his place and find out?'

'Sure, go over to his place, that's real easy, eh? What am I sposed to do over there? Tan a few moosehides? Put on a sweetgrass ceremony, pound the drum and Ai-yi-yi all over his back yard? Build a sweatlodge maybe, drag his ten kids in there, give that new kid of his an Indian name? Why not give them all Indian names? Why don't I call them all Kemo Sabe and move into their rumpus room? We could dry fish on their clothesline. Corny could buy me a pinto pony so I could ride it to the mall.' Ironeagle paced back and forth fuming. 'You'd think that kid was mine, eh. I showed Corny those Sun Dance scars I got but they don't scare him.'

'They would if he thought about them long enough.'

'How long is that?'

'I don't know, three years.' Kozicki scratched his neck. Talk was pleasant, but it didn't rake the stones. 'Look, you work with Lannie here for the rest of the day. I'll get Corny to check the irrigation lines for leaks and fill in the trenches. We gotta get that front section graded and ready for Monday. There's a load of lawn sod coming in then.'

At the words *lawn sod* Lannie uttered a noise that sounded like 'boof.' Lawn sod had the pungent odour of fresh-turned soil and the minty whiff of green grass and Kozicki knew that when it came time to lay it, Lannie would carry the rolls high on his chest, snorting and sniffing surreptitiously, on the trail of the good clean earth. At the moment, however, Lannie worked on a mound perhaps twenty feet high, a ruined desert hill the colour of dust and littered with rocks, weeds and scraps of broken branches. The bunker mound, Kozicki called it, an arid waste whose destiny involved a rock garden, trees, a carp pool and a bomb shelter.

'Bomb shelter?' Ironeagle asked.

Kozicki led him to the foot of the mound and showed him the door, an unfinished cement slab set back under a rocky overhang. The door was locked but, had it opened, Kozicki said, the two men would have entered an underground den whose walls were three feet of reinforced concrete lined with lead that was outfitted with its own water and air supply.

Ironeagle ran his fingers over the door. 'What's that fella expecting?'

'The worst.' Kozicki was not sure he was telling the truth. What could the worst be, an atomic bomb or a prostate the size of a bowling ball? He should have asked Clarence Rawlings that question, but the little millionaire was too intimidating. The man's eyelids had no nerves; he never blinked. Whenever Kozicki looked into those eyes—as clear and blue as ice water in a tinted jar—Kozicki remembered a CO he'd briefly served under during the war, an immaculate half-man, half-lizard the air crews dubbed Lidless Lavigne. Lidless had been keen on bombs, too, and rumours at the aerodrome credited him with volunteering the ninth squadron—Kozicki's group—to drop bombs every chance they got. Where other flight crews at other bases flew twenty-five missions, Lidless sent an endless stream of communiqués to Bomber Command requesting that his group be allowed to fly more. Lidless Lavigne was, apparently, a crackerjack pilot in his own right and during the early days of the Battle of Britain had sent a score of German pilots for their last drink in the North Sea. But that steady gaze, full of unswerving courage and dedication, had given Kozicki the willies.

Clarence Rawlings gave Kozicki the willies too.

'As for the shelter,' Rawlings had said, the first time he showed it to Kozicki, 'I want it camouflaged. An integral part of the rock garden. No one should know it's here.'

'I'll know it's here,' Kozicki said. 'My crew'll know it's here.'

'True.' Rawlings turned his unblinking eyes on Kozicki, and that was when Kozicki thought Lidless Lavigne. 'Naturally, absolute secrecy would be impossible.' Rawlings had sounded disappointed as if, what with all the other millionaire things he had to do, secrecy was the one thing a man with money and eccentricities could count on. He lidlessly thought for a few lidless seconds, so that Kozicki was forced to look away. 'Discretion,' Rawlings had decided. 'Discretion, bolstered by legal obligation, would not be out of order.'

' 'Meaning?'

'Affidavits, I could get my lawyer to draw up some legal affidavits for your crew to sign, swearing they will not reveal the whereabouts of the shelter.'

Kozicki had shrugged. 'Once the Bomb hits,' he said, '*every-body*'ll know.'

'Once the Bomb hits,' Rawlings had said, 'I won't care.'

Kozicki had wanted to say, 'I'll care,' but the truth was he didn't actually believe in the Bomb, even though from his turret he'd watched with exhilarated horror tons of explosives drop from the belly of a Lancaster, the bombs metal fish that swam groundward, diving to become little minnows with twitching tails, then tadpoles, finally dots, and at last shattered blossoms of flame that, as the war went on, scared the hell out of him. Once on leave in London an air raid siren sent him scampering out of a pub with a crowd of other people and down into an underground station where they huddled together like sailors on a raft and told jokes and sang songs until the all-clear sounded. When they emerged, little bombs had levelled their neighbourhood into a harrowed field, and Kozicki had no doubt his own little bombs had done the same thing to Hamburg. It was those little bombs a fella had to worry about, Kozicki decided, the daily grind could nickel-and-dime you to death. The Bomb would just be one almighty fart on God's thunderpot followed by the wind whistling over the sand. Think small, he wanted to warn Rawlings, but didn't, because he was himself too busy thinking small. The more he looked around, the more little bombs he saw.

The bunker mound was just one of them. Corny and Ironeagle were another. Who knew what casual remark or imagined insult would set Ironeagle off, so that one day he would brain Corny with a shovel once and for all, pound out a death chant on the dead man's hard hat and disappear into Lakota country forever? Then there was Anna and Trischuk, day after day hooking up the irrigation line, kneeling together over the trenches as if they were welded to each other at the hip, pushing pipes into couplings, easing valves into T joints, sliding things in and out, around and around—they must be ready to explode. And Dominico culling piles of grey stone that Paterson wheeled up from the river bank, fussy little *paisano* calling on God the dog and Madonna the pig to help him deal with this ungodly shit that in Italy wouldn't have been used to pave the path to an outhouse, let alone the banks of a big shot's moat. How long before Dominco boiled over, blew the top of *his* head off? And Paterson, scribbling, always scribbling, so it wasn't a habit, it was a *tic*. And Lannie whining and whimpering when Kozicki mentioned one morning, confidentially, because when you spoke to a person who only made animal noises you *had* to speak confidentially, that Kozicki's own dog, his own Churchill, had died. 'I had him seventeen years,' Kozicki said, 'so I think I know how you feel about those hounds at the experimental station.' Lannie's eyes had brimmed with tears and for a few embarrassed moments Kozicki was afraid the kid was going to clutch him in long spidery arms and sob uncontrollably in his neck. Kozicki appreciated sympathy but could do without sappiness. To his relief Lannie patted him on the shoulder and left it at that, although since then every time Kozicki looked at the kid he had to face those sad brown eyes and that halo of curly hair. Uncomfortably, he was reminded of a drawing of St. Francis of Assisi he'd seen in one of Charlene's textbooks—a cassocked young man with a vacant smile on his face and a bird on his shoulder, barefoot, a simpleton. Not the kind of sweet-natured guy who could take a lot of little bombs.

And the whole time the clock was ticking and Cargill was probably nosing around, so that every time you climbed into your truck you had to look over your shoulder to make sure he wasn't hiding back there, ready to pull the whole project down around your ears. Jeez, Kozicki was glad when the day was over, happy when the sun finally sank behind the city towers at nine-thirty or ten o'clock, so he could drive home along cool windless summer streets where normal people stretched out on their lawn chairs or sipped from tall glasses in their back yards, murmuring over the day's events. A guy could almost forget about work and unions and deadlines. The lawn sprinklers chic-chicked in sleepy rhythm and the only things a fella had to do were throw a couple of wieners in a pot, sit out on his patio drinking beer, stare at his dog's grave and wonder why the telephone didn't ring.

Kozicki had several theories about the telephone, one of which was that such an instrument should be used only in case of emergencies. As a child, he'd been raised in a household that survived for years without a phone, except for a giddy period of prosperity in 1928 when his father had a wall-crank model installed in his tailor shop. That telephone was connected to a party line, and only his father was allowed to answer it when it rang one long, two short. Once when his parents were out, Kozicki had crept downstairs into the darkened store, past the big Singer treadle machine, lifted the receiver and cranked one long, two short, hoping he would be able to talk to himself. Nothing much happened, although after an hour during which he experimented with other combinations of cranking, a man's voice came on the line and told him to stop fucking around, a telephone wasn't a fucking toy, and if he kept cranking the man would be over to rip his fucking tongue out. Kozicki never touched that particular telephone again, and felt a vague satisfaction when, two years and several unpaid phone bills later, a worker from the phone company arrived and unscrewed it from the wall.

Whether Gillian shared his phobia about telephones, he didn't know. Certainly she didn't call often. Like her mother, she was a chronic letter writer, although in recent years her letters arrived further and further apart—at Christmas, mostly. Kozicki, of course, rarely wrote back. His handwriting resembled worm tracks under a rock and his vocabulary wasn't up to snuff, either. For a while Gillian was living with a man—well, from the photographs a buzzard with no chin—who apparently found Kozicki's letters 'a real hoot.' Rick, the guy's name was, a graduate student in economics and political science, who eventually waltzed out of Gillian's life and into the labour dispute mediation business. There he met and married a pale, elongated Swedish woman whom Gillian described as 'strong, but refined' (whom Kozicki imagined to be a buzzardette). Kozicki sometimes wondered if his infrequent attempts at literacy, those scrawled letters on yellow lined paper that he could never fit into envelopes without ironing flat with his fist—had scared off *Rick*, made *Rick* a little jumpy about what sort of father *Rick's* true love was lumbered with. Since *Rick*, Gillian had 'seen' several men; was 'seeing' one now, in fact. A guy named Noberto who had something to do with oceans or seaweed or fish. *Noberto.* Kozicki had never met anyone named Noberto.

He'd never finished the last letter he'd started to write to Gillian, either. He'd begun it over a year ago but put it aside when he discovered that life was tough enough *living* with a woman who was smarter than he was, let alone *writing* to one. Besides, now that the baseball in his groin was growing, he wasn't sure that a letter would be sufficient. What he should be doing—what he *had* been taking a crack at—was writing a farewell speech and a will. The thing was, a fella needed a pretty big stock of words to attempt a thing like that; you could no more write such a thing without words than you could fix a Mack truck with a penknife. The dictionary was a help, and Kozicki had almost filled two spiral notebooks with whole lists of definitions. But when it came right down to writing, he realized that a person had to have a plan—a blueprint—to give him an idea of how to separate the shrubs from the trees.

The letter he'd begun writing to his daughter was in reality half a dozen letters whose lengths varied between three lines and four pages, depending on the season in which they were written. In Kozicki's view, a good way to start a letter was to discuss the weather; in the fall a guy could go heavy on the autumn colours and the harvest and how the air smelled like snow and so on; winter offered lots of remarks about the cold, storm windows, failing furnaces, bird feeders, a whole range of letter-fill that the recipient could sit in front of a fire with and fall asleep to. In spring you could spend a full page on birds alone; but summer, what was summer but hot weather and mosquitoes? Summer you had to punch up a little, throw in a little politics and a visit from the Royal Family; a tornado would be good, but you had to have the right conditions for one. Kozicki spiced up some of his letters with generous sprinklings of ten-dollar words; three of his false starts included the words *efficacious, salubrious, pertinacious,* and *mendicant,* while another trotted out *exculpation,* as in *Dear Gillian, It's been a long time since I wrote you'd think I was pertinaciously trying to get out of it but I do ask for your exculpation. The weather here has been pretty near salubrious what with the sun out pertinaciously every day burning the hide off of my arms. I'd be a dyed-in-the-wool mendicant if I—*and so on. None of his letters rang true, he knew that much, but if he wrote them following the advice of anybody who knew something about writing—Paterson, for instance—his thoughts came out flatter than a farmer's wallet and about as interesting. 'You have to be yourself when you write,' Paterson had told him. 'Write what you know.' Judging by the six half-finished letters he kept in a basket on top of the fridge, Kozicki's self was a certified moron and what he knew was doodly. Until he got this baseball thing checked out, he was operating on a hunch. *Operating*—there was a word. Who the hell needed it?

Dear Gillian, I've got some bad news well it might not be bad but it sure isn't efficacious but I won't know for sure until I get a doctor to check me out, which I can't do just yet until I finish this job hopefully by September. Well I know you want to know what the condition is I've got, but as I don't know as yet I can't tell you, suffice to say it's plumbing troubles I'm leaking like a wet sponge at times but that's as per usual for a guy my age so Charlene told me once. Now I know you'll want me to get examined before Sept. but I'm tenacious about this, really impassive. In the meantime we've got to consider what has to be done if this medical news turns out to be a lethality. What follows is my last will and testament well more like a list of things I want you to have which is mostly everything. Starting with the house you can have that, actually it's a 40 ft. trailer and you could sell it as is or move it off the pad. To do that you—

From there the letter deteriorated into a series of technical instructions of how house trailers could be disconnected, dismantled and transported—information that dribbled on and on, much like Kozicki's full bladder over the bowl at midnight, a thin anaemic stream of urine with no pressure behind it, no pizzazz, as if someone had turned off the valve and the only thing that let the water through was a leaky O-ring. The burning sensation was gone, and the baseball no longer thumped around his bladder's floorboards, but sat lower, on his water bag, like a fat lady on an air mattress, pressing, pressing. He would return to bed disillusioned, only to be jarred awake again in the wee hours of the morning, blissfully trapped in a dream in which he peed gallons, buckets, oceans, loosed waterfalls of urine that turned out to be, on inspection, merely teardrops of moisture on the bedsheet. Even so, he rushed down the hall to the bathroom where he stood huffing, dangling his startled penis over the bowl and watching the limp old trooper gamely squeeze out a few drops followed by—jeez, what luck—a reluctant drizzle. After a while he would shuffle back to his bed, unrewarded, unsatisfied, to lie awake with his heart pounding, 'Deadline, deadline,' into the bedsprings until the alarm went off at 4:30, at which time he would get up, make some coffee, and watch the sunrise, silently vowing that he'd give up coffee and sunrises for one good piss.

Two days later, several tons of lawn sod were delivered at the Rawlings estate—mats of still-living carpet piled four feet deep on pallets—while Kozicki and Paterson slouched along the picket line in front of the university greenhouse, their lethargic sign-waving and funereal pace all they could muster as a daily contribution to union fervour. Their picket duty began at 12:30 in the afternoon, fully eight hours after their alarms had kicked them out of bed and shoved them through a full day's work at the millionaire's house. As Paterson, who was composing an ode to sleep deprivation pointed out, the end of their picket-duty shift at 2:30 allowed them to begin a *second* work day at the Rawlings place at three o'clock.

'What are you saying?' Kozicki asked him. It was a game they played.

'I'm knackered.'

'What body part?'

'My eyes.'

'Okay,' Kozicki ventured. 'Eyes: this morning when I drove to work, my eyes were hanging off the end of the hood.'

'Mine were fish-shit in an aquarium,' Paterson countered.

'If I'd opened mine any wider,' Kozicki said, 'I'd've bled to death.'

'One point for you,' Paterson said, but stopped short when the Monkey Man arrived.

The Monkey Man was a thick-torsoed individual whose limbs reflected those simian impossibilities that Kozicki, the son of a long-deceased tailor, recognized immediately as *short in the pants* and *long in the sleeve*. He could see his father shaking his head as he thumbed the tape measure down *this* specimen's leg. 'A real tree-swinger,' his father would have told Kozicki and his mother later over the supper table. 'A vine and banana man. I should've asked him if he wanted gloves to keep the pavement off his knuckles.' Downy red fur covered the Monkey Man's head and neck, disappeared into his T-shirt and emerged again on his long sinewy arms so matted that Kozicki believed every square inch of the guy's body was as hairy as a baboon's butt. 'Don't get me wrong. I got nothing against hair,' he told Paterson later. 'I let it grow wild on my ass. But you put that guy's hair together with those eyes and you got yourself a scary proposition. Did you notice those eyes? Most places you'd need a licence to own eyes like that.'

The Monkey Man loitered on the hood of a small white sports car for about ten minutes before he dropped to the pavement and loped towards them.

Kozicki muttered, 'Uh-oh.'

'Afternoon,' the Monkey Man greeted them.

'Afternoon.' Kozicki agreed on the time of day but didn't push for anything further. The Monkey Man had eyes like BBs. Kozicki had only seen one pair of BBs before, and they had glittered in the face of a Regina cop in 1935. Kozicki had been fourteen years old then and on Dominion Day had ridden his bicycle to Market Square because his father was going to listen to the speeches. Slim Evans was giving a talk, his father said. Kozicki wasn't sure who Slim Evans was, but he knew the ragged quiet men who climbed down off the boxcars at the railyards were the trekkers and that they were going to Ottawa to tell Mr. Bennett they were starving. He knew too that when the furniture vans blocked off the sidestreets leading to the square where the men had gathered that something was going to happen. From his bicycle in an alley he heard a shrill whistle, at which sound the furniture van doors slapped open and mobs of helmeted policemen swinging baseball bats spilled down the ramps. To Kozicki they had looked like mad ballplayers in their Sunday suits, on the hunt for wayward home runs. The crowd scattered. Women picked up children and sprinted, men scampered around looking for weapons. The police waded forward. Kozicki heard a shot, then several more, and then a great shout went up and a kid was crying and a woman pushing a baby carriage stumbled past him sobbing that somebody had been killed, but Kozicki knew that was ridiculous because the shots weren't loud explosions but only sharp pops, like planks being flopped over wet cement, and who had ever died from that?

Daddy, he'd thought.

But his father had appeared, and pushed him on the bicycle. 'Get home!'

'What are you going to do, Daddy?'

'I'll be all right, tell your mother I'll be all right. Get home!'

'What should I tell her?'

'Jesus Christ, Michael, tell her I'm playing *baseball! Will you get home!*'

So Kozicki pedalled wildly down the alley for a half a block, while behind him glass shattered and something metal shrieked as it was dragged across the pavement. Ahead, on a brick wall, giant lips puffed a giant cigar, and words as big as the voice of God told him WHITE OWL: THE TASTE TELLS. Then he heard a clatter like boulders on a tin roof and fifty mounted policemen spurred their horses down on him, as if they were late for some fantastic steeplechase that required they trample as many kids on bicycles as possible in as little time as they had. Kozicki had swung off his bike and jerked it behind two listing garbage cans in the recess of a doorway just as the horses surged past him, a wind of pungent sweat and creaking leather. The last rider, trailing the others, had leaned from his saddle in his glittering tunic and uttered the first words Kozicki had ever heard one of His Majesty's policemen say: 'Get the fuck out of the way, kid.'

Under his helmet the man had BB eyes and, when he saw another pair just like them on the Monkey Man, Kozicki decided it was never to late to heed a policeman's advice.

'What can we do for you?' he asked the Monkey Man.

'I'm looking for a woman.'

'I've done that quite a few times myself.' Kozicki shifted his picket sign to the other shoulder. 'Maybe you should try a different neighbourhood.'

The Monkey Man stood very still, long arms swinging. 'Do you guys work here?'

'We do not.'

'I mean normally. When you're not on strike.'

'Only on weekdays.'

'Do you work with a woman named Anna Berenson?'

'We do not.'

Paterson found a rock on the ground and with his toe dribbled it this way and that.

The Monkey Man hooked his thumbs in his back pockets and lifted his chin. Neck muscles fanned out of his T-shirt collar. 'Anna Creighton then. She's probably using her maiden name. I'm her husband.'

'We know an Anna Creighton, but I think she has an ex-husband.'

'Husband, ex-husband, I'm it. Does she come on picket duty here?'

'Not when we're around.'

'I mean at some other time.'

'Does she belong to the union?' Kozicki asked.

'I don't know.' The Monkey Man scowled until his BBs almost disappeared. 'You work with her. Does she belong to the union?'

Kozicki turned to Paterson. 'Does she belong to the union?'

'I guess so.' Paterson dribbled the rock expertly. 'She would have to, wouldn't she? I mean if she works with us, she'd have to belong to the union.'

'She probably belongs to the union.' Kozicki told the Monkey Man.

The Monkey Man growled impatiently. 'Where does she live?'

Kozicki turned to Paterson, who turned to the rock. 'Where does she live?' Kozicki asked.

'In a house,' Paterson said. 'On a street.'

'In a house," Kozicki said, 'on—'

'What house? What street?'

'Well?' Kozicki looked at Paterson.

'The one in the phone book.'

'The one—'

'She's not in the phone book.' The hairs on the Monkey Man's arms stood on end. 'She's not in the goddamn phone book, she's in your goddamn union and if you can't tell me where to find her I'll find somebody who goddamn *will*.' He pointed to the greenhouse behind the gates. 'Who's in there?'

'Administration,' Kozicki said, 'but you can't go in there.'

'Why not?'

'Because this is a legal picket line.'

'What's that got to do with anything?'

'People shouldn't cross legal picket lines.'

'This person's going to.'

'Crossing a legal picket line interferes with our collective bargaining rights,' Kozicki said.

But the Monkey Man was already loping towards the greenhouse. 'Eat shit,' he called over his shoulder.

'Pardon me?'

'Eat shit.'

'No, thanks,' Kozicki shouted back and muttered, 'I'd rather have a banana.'

Mr. Dreedle sat in the greenhouse office with the door closed and the blinds drawn and wondered what to do about the red-haired man outside who looked like a monkey and who said he was Anna Creighton's husband even though his name was Berenson and he didn't know where his wife lived. There was a chance—not likely, but a slim possibility—that the red-haired man wasn't Anna Creighton's husband Berenson at all, but a union man from some other department whom Cargill had sent over to spy on Kozicki and Paterson and Mr. Bistritz—and Mr. Dreedle himself. On the other hand, Mr. Dreedle thought, the red-haired man might really be a member of that league to apprehend war criminals that he'd recently read about in the papers. Not that Mr. Dreedle was a war criminal, but he had belonged to the Hitler Youth in 1942 when he was twelve, and did have an uncle who'd driven a Panzer tank in North Africa. Mr. Dreedle's real name was Von Deitl, but he was a Canadian now and he couldn't understand what a man who looked like a monkey would want with him.

'That's all he wants?' Mr. Dreedle whispered to Mr. Bistritz. 'Are you sure?'

'Just her address, O Large One.'

Mr. Bistritz whispered too. The office door was a notoriously thin one, and on several occasions people in the outer room had overhead private conversations. Once when Mr. Dreedle's toupee had come unstuck, he and Mr. Bistritz retired into the office to wrestle the thing back into place. When they emerged, they confronted the grinning faces of Kozicki and his crew, who'd driven back from a job for an early lunch because it was raining. Surrounded by smirking cretins, Kozicki had solemnly handed Mr. Dreedle a hammer and a spike— 'Just in case,' he'd said.

'What was he yelling at Kozicki?' Mr. Dreedle whispered.

'"Eat shit."'

'"Eat shit"?'

'"Eat shit."'

Mr. Dreedle chewed his thumb knuckle. 'Do you think he's a union man?'

'I think he's a cuckold,' Mr. Bistritz whispered.

Mr. Dreedle held his head in his hands. 'Send him over to the Administration Building.'

'He's been there.'

'Send him over to Payroll.'

'He's been there, too.'

Mr. Dreedle raised his head with exaggerated weariness. 'And?'

'They informed him that it is not the policy of this institution to give out the addresses of its employees without the employee's consent.' Mr. Bistritz hunched confidentially over Dreedle's desk. 'Alan says that *everyone* in that office has fallen in love with red tape. They have oodles and oodles of red tape over there. They have so much red tape, Alan says, that they could tie birthday bows on half the population of *China*.' Mr. Bistritz was sniggering. His friend Alan worked in the Payroll Office and apparently spoke in nothing but hyperboles. Mr. Dreedle had met Alan once, at a party; he was a tall, slender young man in accountant's horn-rims and pleated trousers, whose sense of humour centered around investment portfolios, trading opportunities, and new industries. When he shook hands with Mr. Dreedle for the first time, he aimed his glinting horn-rims at the top of Mr. Dreedle's head and said, in a rather loud voice, 'Bisty tells me you're deeply involved in the rug trade.'

'What does Alan suggest?' Mr. Dreedle was not above putting his trust in people who wore horn-rimmed glasses.

'Alan says that we should simply lend the man a copy of the student directory.'

'What student directory?'

'The one that lists Anna Creighton.'

'She's a seasonal employee. Is she a student, too?'

'She's a seasonal employee *because* she's a student. Don't you remember how Kozicki wanted to hire her because she was a mature student? Don't you remember him saying that his own daughter had at one time been a mature student? He made such a *glorious* fuss about Anna.'

'I thought he made a glorious fuss about Anna because she's a woman.'

'She's a mature student woman. If we give her husband the directory, we're not actually giving out an employee's address without the employee's consent. We're giving out a student directory.'

Mr. Dreedle frowned. 'Why didn't Alan give him a student directory?'

'The Payroll Office isn't authorized to hand out student directories.'

'Who is?'

'The Student Union Office.'

'So why didn't Alan send him there?'

'The Student Union Office is closed. It's on strike in sympathy with the maintenance and grounds workers.'

'How is it Alan's not on strike?'

'He's management. Like us.'

Mr. Dreedle pressed his palms together and thought. 'So this man in the other room is not a union man?'

'Hardly.'

'But he's a cuckold.'

'So it would appear.'

Mr. Dreedle had a terrible thought. 'Has Kozicki got something to do with this man's being a cuckold?'

'Absolutely nothing.'

'Because I don't want this man yelling, "Eat Shit," around here. If Cargill gets wind that we've got a cuckold around here yelling, "Eat shit," he might get suspicious.'

Mr. Bistritz crossed his legs and draped himself so far over Dreedle's desk that his elaborate hair fell over his eyes. He looked like a sex symbol impersonating a sheepdog. 'Why on earth would he get suspicious?'

'Because he's a union man, that's why. Union men take one look at administrators and get suspicious. If we drink coffee they want to know why it isn't tea. Union men remind me of Nazis. Union men remind me of that league they've got to apprehend war criminals.' Mr. Dreedle lifted the corners of his toupee and flattened them down again. 'Union men hear a guy holler, "Eat shit," at a picketer and before you know it they're over here with a lawyer and a court order and they're taking inventory of the tools and auditing the books and asking where their fellow union members are. Union men hear a name like Clarence D. Rawlings and they want to cut our livers out. You forget, I used to be a union man myself.'

Indeed, Mr. Bistritz had forgotten that fact—just as he had nearly forgotten the red-haired man in the outer room. He tossed his hair in a gesture towards the door. 'So what should I do with him?'

'Give the man the directory.'

Mr. Bistritz raised himself from the desk and tugged at his tight pants. 'Do you want to talk to him?' he whispered.

'I don't want to talk to anybody. Even Kozicki—especially Kozicki. Who knows if Cargill is watching? You say this man in the waiting room isn't union—fine. But why take chances? If Kozicki wants to talk to me, tell him to write me a note. Better yet, tell him to phone me.'

Mr. Bistritz moved to the door. 'Anything else?'

'Yes,' Mr. Dreedle said. 'Tell Kozicki to use the stones he's got. Dominico phoned me again last night—nearly *midnight*—and whined about those river rocks. He's doing a door now and wants lapis lazuli or granite or something, I don't know. I can't understand the man. Just tell Kozicki to tell Dominico to use the stones he's got.'

'Is that all?'

Mr. Dreedle fidgeted with his hairpiece. 'No. When that guy leaves, come back in here and give me a hand with this damn thing.'

The door closed. Mr Dreedle held his toupee in both hands and told it a secret. 'We need a holiday,' he said.

As a child in a northern Italian village whose name, San Lorenzo e Santa Lucia di Massarossa, was longer than its main street, Dominico had padded adoringly behind his stone mason grandfather, a square, bellowing, fireplug whose raging white hair and pencil moustache was welcomed in bars as far away as Milano and whose work— convent walls, fountains, flagstones, and once the cornice on a recon-structed cathedral in Genova—was universally admired as the labour of a master craftsman. Dominico had carried the old patriarch's lunch-bag and leather apron over his shoulder, following the clanking lumpy canvas tool sack that swung across his grandfather's own broad back. Since Dominico had come to Canada twenty-five years before, he was still trying to match his stumpy steps to the long confident strides of old Babbaluche, the stone mason.

But mio Dio, what would Babbaluche have made of this job? For three weeks Dominico had planted stones along the sloping banks of what the millionaire called a moat but which was actually a half-moon-shaped pond, shaded beneath weeping birch trees and willows, and headed for stagnation, algae and plenty of mosquitoes if Anna and Trischuk didn't get the filter system connected and working. Each morning when he drove his aircraft-carrier car over the moat's bridge, Dominico flushed with proprietory satisfaction that below him, at least, was stonework of which old Babbaluche would have approved, even though the rocks used weren't fit to throw through a fascist's window. Once at the end of the war, Dominico *had* thrown a rock through a fascist's window—a wizened little woman who, the boys of the village claimed, hoarded crates of Swiss chocolate sent by her son, a filthy Blackshirt bastard who painted MUSSOLINI IS ALWAYS RIGHT on Padre Disanto's dustbin. When she learned what Dominico had done, Dominico's mother boxed his ears and called upon God, the Madonna and the spirit of Babbaluche the stone mason, by then deceased, to punish such a disgraceful peasant *animale* who did not know a *fascisti* from a plate of fetuccini. Dominico was forced to enter the woman's house and sweep up the glass and stones, while the old woman herself huddled near the fireplace, and offered him tiny glasses of *grappa* from a miniature flask.

But those stones! How ashamed he was to have to pick them up, fired as they were from his disgraceful peasant arm; not even well-shaped stones, but disfigured, grey, as common as mud. As he loaded them in the box he'd brought along for the purpose, he thought he heard old Babbaluche's voice telling him what the stones were *not*: they were not *giallo antico* yellow marble, or *rossa antico* red marble, or even the crumbly marble full of sand.

On a job, before working with a rock, Dominico first cradled it in both hands, hefting its weight and shape. At the Rawlings site, the grey stones were not marble, *giallo* or *rosso* or even *verde*; scrounged from the river bank, wheeled in a barrow to the hill's lip and hauled off in the bobcat's bucket, they possessed a cast-off, desultory air that tempted Dominico to throw them back in the river, like undersized fish. With marble, Dominico could feel a stone's centre, could judge its beauty and permanence by the way it tipped between his palms. With marble he could sense the stone's final shape before he put the chisel to its surface. But with these stones?

'These astones,' he announced to Paterson, 'are ashit.'

'I've heard this before,' Paterson said wearily, because he had. The only time he hadn't heard Dominico's opinion about the stones was when the two of them weren't working together. Picket duty offered Paterson a respite from Dominico's geologic criticisms, as did more immediate projects such as the arrival of another Big Load of Lawn Sod. A Big Load required all hands, since the strips of grass had to be laid, peat-mossed and watered before the midsummer heat dehydrated them into patches of singed burlap. For awhile Paterson had become engrossed in stone masonry, and had scribbled in his notebook information about mortar, chisels, and plumb bobs. But several days of fighting a rock-filled wheelbarrow up duck planks from the river bank dimmed his fascination, and in the midst of mixing mortar he uttered silent prayers for another Big Load to trundle through Rawlings's gates and spring him loose for a couple of hours. Now that they'd begun the door on the bomb shelter, Dominico's critique of river rock showed no signs of abating; on this day, however, his conversation took a metaphysical turn.

'Every astone has got a centro,' Dominico said, vigorously scrubbing a rock with a wire brush. 'Justa like people. People, they got a centro.'

Paterson, screening sand, grinned. 'What now, Dominico—philosophy?'

'Sure, philosophy. Why not?' Dominico stiffened. 'Whatsa wrong with philosophy? Everybody got a philosophy. You, me, Corny Ferg, Kozicki—we all got a philosophy. Leonardo da Vinci—he got a philosophy.'

'Leonardo da Vinci's dead.'

'He still got a philosophy.'

'He was a painter, mostly.'

'He was *everything*, amostly. Whatsa matter, you don' believe? Leonardo he do *everything*. He paint, he sculpt, invent the complicated machine; he makea the beautiful things. He believe in the beautiful things. He got a philosophy of the beautiful things. Dio canne! He was a genius, that Leonardo.'

Paterson, who secretly hoped *he* was a genius, and secretly knew he wasn't, squatted in front of the bomb shelter door that was studded with shit-stones. Dominico had abutted the stones into place by means of notched two-by-fours. 'This cement's hardening, Dominico.'

'Okay. All right. You getta the stick. I fixa the astone.'

'You'd better hurry up.'

'Eh, you think they gonna rush Leonardo? You think they gonna say, "Thatsa nice, Maestro, the lady shesa beautiful, but quick, painta the smile on hera face. Don' take too long, Maestro, any smile itsa gonna be okay." Holy cow, Patersoni, whaddayou think?'

Gently, Dominico set the stone in the cement, tapping it in place with the butt of his trowel. When the prop had been fixed securely in place, he straightened and nodded approvingly.

Tradition, pride, old Babbaluche—what did these people like Patersoni know about such things? He was too young, his country was a baby. 'In my country,' Dominico reflected, 'sometime the astone mason he put hisa mark on hisa work. Hisa *firma*, hisa *segno*.'

'So put your mark on your work.'

'Not on this astone.'

'Why not on this stone?'

'Porco Madonne!' Dominico implored the sky. 'Don' I already told you? This astone is ashit. I don' put my mark on ashit.'

Paterson kicked the pile of stones at his feet. 'That's all we've got here, Dominico. All these stones are shit.'

But a light had entered Dominico: the spirit of the maestro and old Babbaluche flared in his soul. He stood with uplifted head, gazing at the cornice which jutted below the balcony on the Rawlings mansion.

'What are you looking at?' Paterson edged closer.

The blocks forming the cornice glowed in the afternoon light. Against the golden sandstone bricks, the marble shone serenely pure, polished, divine. Mio Dio, Dominico thought, that marble is from Carrara; that marble is like a piece of heaven, God's holy line. So white, so smooth! Holy cow, that Carrara marble is some astone.

'What are you looking at?' Paterson asked again.

'Philosophy,' Dominico whispered.

All but invisible, moving in wordless canine stealth, Lannie dug holes for the winterberry bushes that were to be planted along the sloping ridge of the bunker mound, and eavesdropped on the conversation between Paterson and Dominico. The two men moved below him, unaware that his keen ears sifted through their words and picked out in their voices the notes of wonder and curiosity and decision, all those qualities that Lannie had weaned himself away from, a milk-toothed puppy untimely ripped from life's teat. Philosophy? What good was philosophy when the instruments of this world—leashes, collars, knives, ropes, various brands of toilet cleaner, poisons, carbon monoxide, carbon *di*oxide, airplanes, cars, diseases, burglars, hobgoblins, psychiatrists—all ended in one thing: the Man with the Great Big Gun. Who needed philosophy? Better to have protection. Better to run with a pack.

Oh, he knew. He knew what these philosophers would say. That you had to brave it alone, stand on your own two feet, pull your own sled, bury your own bone. And he knew who they'd serve up as examples: those lone souls steeped in unpampered courage, Rin Tin Tin, Lassie, White Fang—all the solitary heroes. No frilly basket behind the kitchen stove for them. No gravy on their kibble. He knew what he *should* be, but he only had two legs. Only two. They were easy enough to count, all you had to do was look down and there they were. One, two.

He and Tall Bennie had worked out this leg number thing the day after Lannie's mother and father had visited their son on Ward Five. His mother had wrung her hands while his father asked him if he was a faggot. 'What the hell's the matter with you?' his father had shouted several times, so loudly that two attendants came running with their coffee mugs still in their hands. 'Are you some kind of faggot?' Lannie didn't know the answer to that question, but then it wasn't even one he'd considered. The question that interested him was *Who is trying to kill me?* Watching the veins throb in his father's temples, a fleeting answer occurred to him—faggots—until he realized he didn't know any faggots, and even if he did their faggotry didn't mean anything to him, it was their business, not his. Faggots, or anyone else for that matter, were nothing compared to the Man with the Great Big Gun.

After the ward nurse and Dr. Gowda had led Lannie's parents away and Lannie had been given a pill in a paper cup so that his lips turned into two furry mice and his head bumped the ceiling, Tall Bennie sat beside him and said, 'I been thinking, you know, thinking conjecturing visualizing about limbs legs appendages and what they mean in the evolutionary warp and you know woof, woof, woof and two legs is the problem. You know, who's got the problem?—Two legs have got the problem. You don't see any cows in here, do you? Do you?'

Lannie's mice tried to say, 'No you don't see cows in here,' but what they said instead was, 'Woof, woof, woof.' And Tall Bennie said, 'Right right right. Maybe not cows; maybe dogs.'

Dogs were obvious, Tall Bennie said, dogs were, you know, universal cosmic infinite. The oldest domesticated four-footed quadruped. Look around, Tall Bennie said; dogs are, you know, everywhere, like they survive, last, experience longevity. It might be a dog's life, you might, you know, be a dog in the manger, a mad dog, sad dog, gay dog, stray dog, straw dog, sundog, lucky dog. Wear a dog collar, be as sick as a dog, put on the dog, be dogged. Dog your footsteps. Look hangdog. But listen, Tall Bennie said, listen: every dog will have his day.

His day was what Lannie was waiting for. He nearly had it once: his almost-day. Kozicki had presented him with his almost-day nearly a year ago. On a clear, frosty Saturday morning in October when the leaves rustled underfoot like old newspapers and the freshness tingled in Lannie's nostrils so sharply that he wanted to stand up on his hind legs and howl, Kozicki had picked him up in the beat-up half-ton, handed him a red woolen mackinaw and a yellow baseball cap, and plumped a smelly, overweight terrier in his lap.

'This is Churchill,' Kozicki had said. 'If he farts too much, put him on the floor.'

The little dog had shivered delightedly, its sharp ears cocking and uncocking in mute semaphore to the cadence of Kozicki's voice. 'I want you to keep an eye on Churchill. When we get out in the bush, he leaves his brains on the front seat. He loves it out there. Well, you'll see. He already peed three times before he climbed in this morning—didn't you, you little peckerhead?'

Churchill had crouched on Lannie's lap and licked his face with rancid, slobbery enthusiasm each time his name was mentioned.

Kozicki drove north out of the city, where the flat prairies ambitiously heaved themselves into low rolling hills that blazed with autumn colour. 'Churchill's fat, sixteen years old and as blind as an umpire,' Kozicki said, 'but when he sees me pull that rifle out of the tool box he's got more juice in him than an orange.'

At the word *rifle* Lannie screamed, jerked the door open and rose from his seat. The dog leapt in terror at Kozicki, clawed up his face and entangled its rear end in the steering wheel. 'Jesus Christ!' Kozicki shouted, swerving from one side of the road to the other. Lannie rested one foot on the running board, clutched the flailing door in his left hand and the door frame in his right, like a chuteless sky diver about to jump the big one. Knobbled pavement whizzed less than a foot below his boot, and it occurred to him that even if he survived the fall he would scarcely make it through the ditch and over the barbed wire fence before Kozicki plugged him between the shoulder blades. As for the dog, what chance did Churchill have against a raging maniac who was telling him to get the fuck off his face and who was wearing him like a ski mask while the tires squealed and the smell of burnt rubber filled the cab? The truck snaked across the highway, vaulted the road's shoulder and came to rest on all four wheels in a ditch that smelled of dust and grasshoppers. The trembling dog whimpered and licked the raw gouges that scored one side of Kozicki's face.

'Let me get this straight,' Kozicki told Lannie, who was leaning out of the truck, busy being sick. 'You don't like my dog.'

Lannie accepted the rag Kozicki proffered him and wiped his mouth thoughtfully. He wanted to say, 'I don't like rifles,' but his throat wouldn't work.

During his regular stays in the hospital he usually spoke to three people only—Nurse Pritchard, Tall Bennie, and Dr. Gowda—and those compassionate listeners were to be eventually whittled down so that only the gentle, enigmatic and seemingly comatose Dr. Gowda would remain. Nurse Pritchard would become engaged to an ear, nose and throat man and would transfer to pediatrics; Tall Bennie would eat his own face and would be removed to Ward Six; and Dr. Gowda would continue to murmur commiserations but would cease to look Lannie in the face, opting instead to keep his eyes lowered and to pick lint off his trousers. Like his employment, Lannie's reticence was seasonal: during the spring, summer and fall he worked on Kozicki's crew and remained essentially tongueless except for the occasional doggie noises or sentient grunt; during the winter he checked in as a voluntary outpatient at the Eastview Centre for the Emotionally Disturbed, at times sedated and as batty as a weasel, at others as chatty as a politician. It was an arrangement he'd settled into for five years now. The money he earned in the warmer months paid for his hospitalization during the cold, and the pattern of his existence shaped his perennial vigilance against the Man with the Great Big Gun, for how could the Man blow a hole in his skull when there were witnesses all around him? Lannie had posed that very question to Dr. Gowda, who grew more and more uncomfortable, and having run out of lint on his gabardine sought more on his Argyle socks. Dr. Gowda had suggested Lannie could use his savings for a winter's holiday in Arizona or Auckland, New Zealand, and might have pursued that preposterous line had Lannie not pointed out that *one needed people who knew one in order to have reliable witnesses to one's own demise.* How could strangers be expected to scare off the Man With the Great Big Gun if they *didn't even know the person he was after?* Really, Dr. Gowda's naivety was laughable; he seemed completely unaware of Tall Bennie's theory of appendages and the cosmology of dogs, and tried to tiptoe around the subject by luring Lannie into discussions about other animals—cats, for instance. Lannie fended him off—might've fended everybody off—until that crisp fall day when Kozicki dumped the whole dog and gun thing in his lap.

'Maybe you don't like rifles,' Kozicki had said.

Lannie nodded.

'Churchill loves the damn things, that's why I bring him out here.' Kozicki had pointed to the pale trunks of white poplars and the looming shapes of spruce trees on the other side of the fence, undeterred that his truck was parked in a ditch. He had turned off the engine and drew Lannie's attention to certain botanical and topographical features that were good news for dogs and men with rifles. 'See how sandy the soil is in there?' he asked. 'Look at the ground cover—those shiny leaves on the crest of that side hill? Low-bush cranberries. Know what likes them? Ruffed grouse. Know who likes ruffed grouse? Me and Churchill.' They had climbed out of the cab and Kozicki jumped up into the truck box, where he opened the coffin-sized tool box and lifted out a .22 single shot. The gun's barrel was long and blue-black, its worn hickory stock a dull satin sheen. At its appearance Lannie had stepped backwards and momentarily snagged his mackinaw on the barbed wire behind him. 'You don't have to be scared,' Kozicki said. Churchill frisked in ever-widening circles, hurled himself at Lannie and rebounded, chased his tail and yipped in imbecilic hysteria. Kozicki jumped down, grinning. 'See what I mean? Once he gets out here he's got more bounce than a golf ball.'

The hunt had led them along arid jackpine ridges and under birch trees whose leaves fell like gold coins and into steamy gullies that skirted a muskeg's spongy margins. Tamaracks and shoulderless black spruce stood knee-deep in moss, and periodically the impenetrable undergrowth exploded to a whirr of wings that Churchill dementedly attacked and obscurely pursued, yapping, 'Alph! Alph! Alph!' with such professional zeal that Lannie had to subdue an impulse to strip to his gotchies and bound after him. Later they drank tea from a thermos and ate cheese sandwiches and, although the gun was never fired—'With that dog around I'm lucky to see the tail feathers waving goodbye,' Kozicki grumbled—the day remained one of Lannie's favourites, full of fearful exuberance and exquisite terror.

But now Churchill was gone. And lately others had followed. At the experimental station the collie had disappeared, replaced by a goofy Alsatian with freakish blue eyes; the poodle had been trucked away; so too the chihuahua. The spaniel with ears down to his knees knew something was up; he cowered in a corner, like a saloon gambler with his back to the wall. In kennel eleven the Australian heeler Bluey lay resignedly with her head on her paws, next to feathery-tailed Muttley who only knew how to yowl. Of the original eighteen dogs, fourteen remained. Death had fingered them, science had put out a contract on their lives, and the Man with the Great Big Gun had bid low and won. He was in a hotel room now or behind a tree or crouched in a clock tower, screwing together the parts of his specially designed 30.06 with its night scope and silencer. The dogs were being picked off one by one, blown backwards into the Everlasting Night, tagged for laboratories that would electrify their hypothalami, blister their skin, notch their ears, puncture their eyes, inject cancer into their pancreases, play fast and loose with their genitals, spritz up their nostrils scents most people wouldn't tolerate on a compost heap. Dogs needed meadows, Lannie decided; they needed muskegs, jackpine ridges and whirring wings in the undergrowth. Poised on the bunker mound with his shovel in mid-air, wavering between which tool would best serve his purpose—tin snips or a bolt cutter?—Lannie ascertained clearly what those hounds would need once he set them free. They would need Lannie.

'I need plants,' Kozicki growled to Mr. Dreedle over the phone. He sat in the Rawlings kitchen in his work socks, having left his boots at the back door, despite the cook's insistence that he come in and make himself at home. Kozicki had explained that by removing his muddy work boots he *was* making himself at home, had taken one step on the polished white tiles and promptly scooted across the floor like a figure skater doing the splits. For a moment something horrendously elastic occurred; the anatomical baseball dropped into a slingshot that immediately stretched from groin to clavicle, paused, then snapped back into place, propelling him forward into the arms of the cook, a massive woman with many chins and stomachs, who led him solicitously to a chair. 'The maid waxed this morning,' the cook said. 'Here, have a cup of coffee.'

'What's wrong with your voice?' Mr. Dreedle asked. 'Are you gritting your teeth? Are you digging around in your pants again?'

'I stopped that a long time ago,' Kozicki lied. The cook had left the room, freeing him for exploratory probing. 'I need thirty junipers and four flats of shasta daisies and five runners of that ivy we used on the chancellor's house. I need a half dozen climbing roses, some phlox if you've got it, and a dozen ferns. I need three Swiss rock pines, lily-of-the-valley, and marble.'

'Marbles?'

'*Marble*. One marble, a chunk of marble. Dominico's in the middle of a masterpiece here and he wants a chunk of marble.'

'Rawlings won't go for marble. Look, *are* you gritting your teeth?'

'I'll talk to him then, he'll go for marble. And I'm not gritting my teeth. Listen.' Kozicki unclenched his teeth and clicked them three times. 'Does that sound like I'm gritting my teeth?'

'He won't go for marble,' Mr. Dreedle said. 'He wants the rock work to be indigenous.'

'Hang on.' Kozicki clamped the telephone between his shoulder and ear and twisted to retrieve the dictionary from his hip pocket. His back crackled, and he imagined he felt better. 'Indigenous. How do you spell that?'

At the other end of the line Mr. Dreedle took a deep breath. 'He wants rocks that are common to that area.'

'Common?—That's it, that's the problem. Dominico says these rocks are too common.'

'Tell Dominico to use the stones he has. I thought I already told Mr. Bistritz to tell you to tell Dominico to use the stones he has.'

'Bistritz told me and I told Dominico but Dominico wants marble.'

'He can't have it.'

'We'll see.'

'We don't need trouble, Mike.'

'Don't we? What this I hear about Anna's husband?'

'What do you hear about Anna's husband?'

'That when he came to see you, you gave him her address. Are you nuts? Did you take a good look at that guy? He's got eyes like bird shot, he's a rodent in a box. He used to beat her up, for Chrissake.'

'What are we, Mike, marriage counsellors?'

'I don't know. Is the pay any good?' Kozicki swallowed a mouthful of coffee and scalded his tongue. The day he'd told Anna that he'd met her husband her face closed up like a shop on Sunday; no tears, no smiles, nobody home. 'Where?' she'd asked guardedly, and Kozicki was reminded of Gillian: 'You win, daddy.' In shame, Kozicki realized that some people you could beat up without raising your hand.

'While we're on the subject,' Mr. Dreedle said.

'What subject?'

'Trouble. The trouble subject.'

'Have we got a trouble subject?'

'We've got Cargill,' Mr. Dreedle said, lowering his voice.

Kozicki lowered *his* voice. 'Why are you lowering your voice?'

'Because you never know.'

'What don't you never know?' Kozicki imagined Mr. Dreedle pressing the telephone to his wet, nervous lips and tugging at the toupee that draped over his head like a dead hamster. In front of Kozicki Rawlings's spanking bright kitchen hummed efficiently, a tribute to modernity and electrical appliances; stoves and ovens gleamed above the sparkling floor, refrigerators and an upright freezer burbled contentedly near the pantry door. A gas range cowled in an exhaust hood dominated the kitchen's centre, and when he'd first seen the room Kozicki had the impression that what people said about the twentieth century was true: owning stuff was good. But now Mr. Dreedle's tone suggested sinister plots and dire consequences, as if saboteurs were hunched in the ventilation system, spies tucked away in freezer compartments. 'What about Cargill?'

'He knows.'

'What?'

'At least I think he knows. At least Mr. Bistritz's friend Alan over in Payroll thinks he knows.'

'How would Mr. Bistritz's friend Alan know that Cargill knows?' Kozicki was getting a headache. It was as if the baseball had been catapulted up between his ears and was stuck there, pressing on his eyelids. He recalled a similar feeling in the London underground during the war when explosions crumped interminably overhead like a crazed jackhammer and he expected the curved tiled roof to shower a slagheap of crushed bricks on him and a crowd of cheerful Cockneys who expected the worst and would've been delighted if they'd got it.

'Alan overheard Cargill talking to a couple of Payroll secretaries

on the picket line in front of the Business Administration Building.
The secretaries complained about the meagre strike pay, and Cargill
laughed and told them to take up gardening.'
'Gardening? So what?'
'Landscape gardening. And he's been singing.'
'Who, Alan?'
'Cargill.'
'What do you mean, singing?'
'He sings to me over the phone. Every morning. The phone
rings, I pick it up, and somebody sings, "You can't fool me, I'm part
of the union/ The union makes us strong."'
'Isn't that "touch"?'
'What is?'
'The *song*.' Kozicki sang, '"You can't *touch* me, I'm part of the
union."'
'How the hell should I know,' Mr. Dreedle asked irritably.
'"Touch," "fool," what difference does it make? He *sings*.'
'How do you know it's him?'
'Who else would it be? Who else would say what he says?'
'You mean he speaks?'
'Of course he speaks.'
'What does he say?'
'He says, "Let my brothers and sisters go."'
'That's it?'
'"Scab,"' Mr. Dreedle said.
'Scab?'
'That's how he ends it. "Scab."'
Kozicki chewed his lip. 'Cargill,' he agreed. Little bombs,
nickel-and-diming you to death. But if Cargill knew, why didn't he
do something about it? Tell the executive, or the strike committee?
Was the guy wacko? Sadistic? Kozicki tried to see Cargill's face but
got instead a tomato with veins like pumpkin vines. 'Maybe he
knows, but doesn't take it seriously. I mean, who *would* take it
seriously? We're just a few guys doing a landscaping job.'
'A few *strikers*,' Mr. Dreedle said.
'Okay, a few strikers.'
'Using their employer's equipment, their employer's materials.'
'Okay, equipment and materials.'
'That they pilfer by means of illegal entry of their employer's
property.'

'I've got a key, for Chrissake! You gave it to me.'

Mr. Dreedle fell silent for a while. Kozicki could hear him breathing. 'If the wrong people ask me about that key, Mike, I'll have to say I know nothing about it. If they ask me about rototillers and sod-cutters and tree-spades and rakes and shovels, I know nothing about them either. If they ask me about ferns and shasta daisies and Swiss rock pines—'

'You peckerhead,' Kozicki said. 'You numb-nutted badger's ass. What are you saying here? You know nothing? Well, guess what I know—guess what I *have*?—the blueprints. Who drew up those blueprints?'

Mr. Dreedle sighed. 'I did. But Mike, who *signed* the blueprints?'

'Not me,' Kozicki said.

'Nor me.' Mr. Dreedle chuckled apologetically. 'I'm just the middleman, Mike. If the union demands an investigation or if the university wants to audit my books—I'm just the middleman.'

Kozicki had more to say, but when he opened his mouth the words weren't there. Even his dictionary didn't help. He pulled the receiver from his ear and stared at it, recalling that other telephone long ago, the little tinkling noise it made when the man from the phone company unscrewed it from the wall and caught it in his arms. Kozicki's father had stood silently in the corner, a businessman gone bust, his one mark of prosperity now just an unpainted patch on the wall. Kozicki knew he himself should've stayed away from telephones.

'What about the plants?' he asked lamely.

'Mr. Bistritz will see to the plants. Mike, I'm due to go on holiday.'

'When?'

'Next week.'

Kozicki hung up. When he put his boots on and stepped outside the air was steeped in ozone, the garish light in copper. A cool breeze flipped a black poplar's leaves belly-up while malevolent grey clouds brooded over the city. Kozicki sniffed the nitrogen in the air. At the bunker mound he was met by Dominico who jabbered about somebody named Corraya or Carrara who was related to Leonardo da Vinci. Corny Fergus stumped over with a bandaged knee that he'd wracked on the side of a wheelbarrow and demanded to know when friggin Ironeagle was going to do his share of the dirty work in the friggin horse manurin rose beds. Ironeagle smiled thinly and Kozicki told Corny to put on his pants. Lannie waved from the top of the mound and gazed at Kozicki like a moonstruck collie. Paterson stood to one side scribbling and, next to the truck piled high with leftover scraps of black plastic irrigation pipe, Trischuk wrapped his arms around Anna and wouldn't let her go.

For the first time in days, Kozicki slid his hands down inside his pants. It was August already, less than four weeks until Rawlings's deadline. What if Cargill really knew? What would he do?

Crew, Kozicki thought bleakly. *An associated body, company of persons: set, gang, mob.* He called them together and told them what Dreedle had said about Cargill. 'And you know what Cargill's like,' he said. 'He eats union Wheaties for breakfast. So let's keep our heads down and our mouths shut.'

'Hey,' Trischuk said. 'We're not stupid.'

'Stupid's got nothing to do with it.'

Anna said, 'What do you think would happen, Mike?'

'Unemployment,' Kozicki said, just as it started to rain

At first the fat drops splatted meekly on Kozicki's bald spot and trickled inside his shirt, but soon the drops fell harder and faster, until within minutes the crew was shouting and scampering through puddles to gather up tools and roll up car windows. They sought shelter in Rawlings's open garage, where Kozicki told them this is what they needed, a little summer storm to clear the air. But the rain kept falling, one hour, then two, until finally, by the time Kozicki gave in and ordered them all to go home, the rear courtyard was awash like the deck of the *Titanic*, and there were no lifeboats in sight.

It rained for three days, a deluge so unprecedented in Kozicki's experience that he was hard-pressed to call it simply 'rain,' but instead ransacked his dictionary for a word that would satisfactorily encompass all his fears about washed-out lawn sod, flattened plants, crumbling rockwork and general mayhem that such a pile of goddamn water would cause if it didn't goddamn *stop*. Seated in his living-room window, he gazed at the street that flowed past his house and tossed around the words *monsoon, typhoon, alluvion* and *torrent*. He was about to head for *cataclysm* and *cataract* when the telephone rang, the first of several calls that diverted him from the Big Piss, as he would later call the storm. On the line was old Mrs. Burkmar who, since Churchill's death, had cheered up considerably to the point that she sometimes waved to Kozicki in a vague, neighbourly fashion but who was now apparently drowning.

'It's happening,' she shrieked. 'Oh God, it's happening!'

He pulled on his rubber boots and yellow-hooded slicker and stepped smartly along to her house, where he discovered brown water seeping furtively into the basement. He spent an hour and a half heaving the old lady's freezer, steamer trunks, boxes of books and canning jars up onto cinder blocks, transforming her cellar belongings into a South Seas village on stilts. Afterwards she offered him a cup of tea—'But don't ask me for biscuits, I hate biscuits.' When he got home it was nearly noon and the phone was ringing again, so insistently that he nearly flung the jangling instrument out the back door, knowing full well that later he would wander out and contritely salvage it from the quagmire that was forming on his back lawn.

'Daddy?'

'Gillian?'

'Daddy, what kind of message is that to leave on my answering machine?'

'What do you mean, what kind of message?'

'About *Churchill*!' Gillian lowered her voice in imitation of his. '"Churchill died tonight, he was a good friend."'

'Well, it was true.'

'It doesn't tell me much.'

'That machine of yours doesn't give a guy any *room* to tell you much. I hate those things. Anyhow, what else was I supposed to say—"Churchill croaked after he squashed all of Mrs. Burkmar's begonias"?'

'Oh, he *didn't*.'

'Sure he did. He was lying in them already stiff when I got home.'

'Poor Churchill. Where is he now?'

'Gillian, that was weeks ago.'

'I *know* that. I just got back from Cape Breton. Where did you bury him?'

'What were you doing in Cape Breton?'

'I went with Peter. Daddy, did you bury him under the roses?'

'Who's Peter?'

'He's a man, Daddy.'

'I thought it was Noberto, the whaddayacallit—the seaweed guy.'

'Noberto was an oceanographer. It's Peter now. If you'd been reading my letters, you'd know it's Peter now. If you'd *answered* my letters, you'd know it's been Peter for the last six months. Daddy, did you bury Churchill under the roses?' As a child, Gillian had turned part of the rose garden into a cemetery for a series of deceased pets— hamsters, gerbils, budgies, and a turtle named Knuckles.

Kozicki looked out the kitchen window, in front of which rain poured like an opaque curtain. 'He's under the roses. Well, if you want the truth he's under two feet of water and *then* he's under the roses. It's been raining steady for two days here.' Raining cats and dogs, he might've added, but the thought occurred to him that should the rain continue, the rising tide could exhume Churchill and float him to the surface, along with the turtle, gerbils and, he now recalled, a bad-tempered alley cat Gillian had befriended until it succumbed to some mysterious, alley cat disorder.

'Poor Churchill,' Gillian was saying. 'Remember when we used to take him skiing?'

Kozicki remembered, although the ski trip happened only once, when Gillian was in her final year at high school. She came uncharacteristically home for Christmas, and in a fit of insane gratitude Kozicki rented a winterized cabin up at Lake Wasagam, a beautiful, frigid resort set among sprawling pine hills and a million miles of cross-country ski trails. As a member of her school's cross-country ski team, Gillian wore her own skis and dressed in fashionable gaiters, corduroy knickers and an intricately-coloured Fair Isle sweater that she had knitted herself on circular needles. Kozicki, who'd never skied before in his life, dressed in longjohns, green khaki, and a Montreal Canadiens' tuque that gave him the look of a sweet but vacant mental defective on his way to the bus stop. With two rented boards strapped to his feet and two sticks that were supposed to hold him upright, he floundered through magically frosted forests that he hardly noticed through the sweat. Behind him, Churchill struggled over the soft snow that on one particularly mild day collected in icy chunks between his paw pads and hind legs, so that he hobbled forward valiantly, like an absurdly well-hung ram, until the weight and bulk of his snowballed genitals drove him to an exhausted halt and he lay panting on the trail, a fairly good picture of how Kozicki felt himself. Gillian, a mile ahead, scissored back to them in long sylphlike strides and bundled Churchill into her backpack, from which the dog's head and front paws smugly protruded as they skied the seven miles back to the cabin. The feelings Kozicki had towards his daughter then were the same ones that nagged him now: pride, love, annoyance.

'Who is this Peter?' he demanded.

But Gillian had questions of her own. 'What happened to Charlene?'

Kozicki didn't know the answer to that one. What happened to anyone? Get it seen to, Charlene had said, but he saw now she was talking about more than the ball bearing in his bowels. She was talking about *him*. Get yourself seen to. Well, maybe she was right. His own father hadn't got himself seen to, and look what happened to him. 'Charlene and I had a parting of the ways.'

'For good?'

'We're not sure yet.' He wondered at the truth of that statement.

Gillian said nothing, but he could hear little bubbles snapping at the other end and realized that she was chewing the inside of her cheek.

'Your face will freeze like that,' he said.

'Oh Daddy.'

'And you'll spend the rest of your life—'

'—with a mouth like a goldfish.' She laughed.

Over the phone she was still only twelve years old, and long distance, he'd discovered, could keep her that way. But she was also his twenty-seven-year-old daughter, and there were things he should tell her. He wanted to tell her that something was rolling around inside him, and whatever it was not only had him shooting at the world record for most number of pees committed during bedtime hours, but also had his right hand falling in love with everything below his belt buckle. He meant to tell her that he was leaving her a forty-by-sixty mobile home that was paid for, but whose insulation factor was a lousy R2. He yearned to tell her what a kick it was that despite her years and Ph.D., she still called him Daddy.

'Daddy? Are you still there?'

'Yeah, I'm here.'

'Daddy, Peter and I were thinking we'd come for a visit.'

'A visit? Here?'

'Well, there—or we were thinking of going up to Wasagam.

Peter has a canoe and I have that tent and all that gear—remember? If we drove out, you could come with us. We thought we'd canoe through the Bagwa Lakes and visit Grey Owl's cabin. You know, for a week or so. Do you think you could get time off?'

Kozicki paused. 'Actually I got a job going right now, Gillie. And we're on strike, too.'

'You're on strike but you're working?'

'It's one of those private deals; you know.'

'Oh.' He heard the bubbles again. 'Look,' she said, 'we were thinking of travelling now, but we could delay for a while. How about—how about two weeks from now?'

'How about the second week in September.'

Gillian rustled paper. 'We're both back teaching then. How about the first week in September? The Labour Day weekend? We won't camp. Just visit, maybe go fishing.'

'Sure,' he said. 'Gillian?'

'Yes.'

'What does Peter do?

'Oh,' she laughed. 'he's a horticulturist. You know—plants?'

Plants, Kozicki thought after he'd hung up. Plants. As a gardener he was always flattered when someone crowned his vocation with academic dignity, but the notion embarrassed him too, as if all those published articles and Ph.D. theses were a con job, mountain-building out of molehills. At the university he'd seen horticulturists of all types, bluff men and women with hands like farmers and faces like old saddles, or pale, sickly people, their skin like the cap on a mushroom, their talk no meatier than spores. Plants? He walked around the kitchen cradling his lower belly, probing it with spade-shaped fingers while the rain drummed on the porch roof. Plants? Well, he hoped Dr. Peter Plants would grow on his daughter better than Noberto the crab man or Rick the whatever-he-was. Plants. If this rain ever stopped, he would have to get Bistritz to deliver the plants to Rawlings. Maybe Bistritz could use that white van he and his friend drove around in. Kozicki would slip Bistritz a couple of bucks about which Dreedle, that carpeted dipshit, would know nothing. Right now, though, Kozicki had to go to the bathroom.

When he emerged he remembered he was scheduled for picket duty at 12:30, rain or no rain, so he threw together a ham and pickle sandwich and plugged the kettle in for tea. He turned on the kitchen radio to tune in the weather forecast, and learned from the news reader's sombre tones that early that morning disaster had struck the 20th Street Payless Foods store. Excessive rainfall, the newscaster reported, had caused the store's rooftop parking lot to collapse, plunging at least two vehicles through the ceiling and into the store proper. A handful of customers and staff may have been trapped in the rubble, although police reports had not yet confirmed this fact. Firemen and rescue crews were presently at the scene. For a more detailed report—

But Kozicki didn't wait for details. He ripped the kettle's plug from the wall socket, pulled on his raingear and dove out the door.

Although Kozicki had long ago decided there was no God, that God was dead, he periodically talked to Him anyway, just in case he could startle the Almighty back to life, or at least into casual conversation. As he drove through the streaming rain, through intersections so flooded that kids rafted across them in fibreglass canoes, he offered God a few pointers. 'Don't be such an Asshole,' he told the deity. 'Don't be such a Cheapskate. You took my father and brother too early, my wife too early, and You didn't do so well with some of those lads during the war, either. What've You got up there, some kind of Youth Club? You got enough young ones, for Chrissake. Charlene and me might not be as close as we could be, but what chance have we got to be closer if You want her? What is it with You, anyway? She's only fifty-eight. She's got a lot of years left in her *whoever* she's with, so You don't need her now—' And so on. Kozicki noticed that even when he insulted the Lord, called him a Big Bugger, for instance, the Big Bugger never answered. 'Smarten up,' he told Him.

God had never been very smart, in Kozicki's opinion; or kind, or compassionate, or even *awake*. Certainly not fair. The war taught Kozicki all God's shortcomings but, even then, the war only provided the final few nails in what for Kozicki was already a well sealed coffin. Kozicki's mother had been an Anglican and had dragged her young son to incomprehensible church sermons at which he thumbed through the prayer book, picked his nose, and screechingly bellowed out the words to the two hymns he loved, 'Onward Christian Soldiers' and 'All Things Bright and Beautiful.' While still in short pants,

Kozicki announced that he might some day be a priest, at which revelation his atheistic father said, 'Over my dead body.'

In his charitable moments, Kozicki's father admitted to being what he called a 'bush Baptist,' a term he winked at rather than explained. Politically, he leaned to the left, having once as a pattern cutter in a Montreal sweatshop had his head split open for signing a union card. After he moved out west, he boisterously supported the CCF whom he called the Confederated Canadian Farmers, even though he couldn't tell wheat from a hayrick and was an entrepreneur whose own shop would remain forever unionless because he couldn't afford to hire anybody but himself. Kozicki's father read pirated copies of the *Daily Worker* and clipped news articles that reported the socialistic views of Nellie McClung and J.S. Woodsworth. Hope in the brotherhood of humankind led him optimistically to the trekkers and Market Square in 1935, but the ensuing riot there not only curtailed his political activity but his breathing as well.

Whenever Kozicki was drawn into catastrophe, the evening of Market Square returned to him as if he were still pumping his bike along dusty alleys, dry-mouthed, heart-hammered, while behind him horses shrieked and men shouted and gunshots slapped flatly against the buildings. His father had told him to go home, and the idea seemed a good one until the back lane he rode down suddenly opened up into a vacant lot beside the Chinaman's corner store. The store's owner, Mr. Keow, a slender man whose upper lip was too long for his small teeth, rushed back and forth from his shop with cardboard boxes that he handed out to kids Kozicki's age and younger. The kids shoved the boxes into their wire bike-carriers, then scuttled among the lot's weeds and rubbish heaps like gnomes on a scavenger hunt, picking up bottles, rocks, tin cans, iron scraps and broken bricks. Thick dust and bloody anticipation had hung in the air and had pulled Kozicki in: he loaded his bike-carrier, too. He'd been thrilled. Maybe he would get to club a cop with a beer bottle, or bean a Mountie with a rock. The opportunities were infinite. The riot would be more fun than a ball game, more exciting than the roller-coaster at the exhibition grounds.

But at Market Square a seriousness had overtaken the combatants. Overturned cars blocked the streets that opened onto the square, and the trekkers and their supporters, including Kozicki's father, cradled ammunition in their arms, quick-marched through an opening in the barricade, threw brutal, rattling volleys at the advancing police, and then marched back again, as orderly and grim as soldiers. To Kozicki, it'd seemed they weren't having any fun at all.

He would never be sure how many loads of rocks and bottles he'd delivered that night. Mindless, he rode a desperate, continuous circuit to the barricade and back again, as a wire of terrified exuberance twanged between his ears. He saw only what lay under his nose: someone's blood dried like rust on his bike's handlebars, the flash of brick buildings on either side of the alley, other kids' bikes, broken glass, a woman's shoe. Maybe he actually saw more; maybe he saw the blue-coated policemen advance, maybe he heard them driven back in a smattering of rocks; maybe he saw a gun, maybe he glimpsed the Mountie's horse as it reared confusedly in front of the overturned bus; maybe he saw his father in a vest and shirtsleeves lift his skinny arm to fend off the hooves. Maybe Kozicki saw it all—or maybe he saw nothing.

Behind the barricade his father lay with his head resting on someone's rolled-up leather jacket. His father's knees were pulled up towards his chest, as if the old man had stomach cramps. Kozicki wished his father had been born with thicker legs—how had the old man ever expected to stand up to a horse on those rake handles? His arms were too thin, his nose too big, his hands too fine; he should have been at home letting out a pair of pants, taking in a suit jacket. A man with a moustache knelt beside Kozicki and told him, 'Don't lean on him like that, kid. A horse stepped on his chest.' To another man he said, 'We've got to get him out of here. Is there any way Willie can bring the truck around?'

'Willie's truck don't have no gas,' the other man had said.

'What do you mean, no gas? I gave him gas money.'

'You might of give him gas money, but that don't mean he bought gas with it.'

While they argued, Kozicki had sat beside his father and held his hand. His father's face was the colour of cold porridge and his breath puffed out in raspy burbles. Once he opened his brown apologetic eyes and whispered, 'I should've played more baseball, son. I can't throw worth a damn.' He'd coughed a little, until red bubbles foamed along his lips. And then, because he seemed to be unable to do anything else, he had died. Kozicki decided right then that he did not like being with people when they died, and that God was a Big Bugger. In later years, his opinion of God wouldn't change much; but he learned from the war, from Emily, and even from Churchill, that the only thing worse than being with a person when he or she died, was *not being* with a person when he or she died.

Girded for tragedy, Kozicki was unprepared for the festivity that surrounded the ruined Payless Foods store. The place bustled like a circus after the big show was over. Firetrucks and police cars blocked the street; inside a blue-ribboned cordon an army of firefighters in bright yellow rainsuits and glistening firemen's hats strolled over the rubble like junk dealers. Another squad of people in blue coveralls and fluorescent vests shifted cinder blocks and sodden groceries with that cheerful assistiveness that Kozicki had witnessed among British fire wardens, Home Guardsmen and civilian volunteers during the London Blitz; in the presence of disaster, their faces dropped and their spirits lifted. Unqualified benevolence animated them, and they wouldn't stop being helpful until someone threatened to shoot them for it. Kozicki stepped over the cordon to join them.

'Where do you think you're going?' A policeman wearing a fluorescent vest and carrying a walkie-talkie hooked him under the arm. The cop was young, friendly, the size of a Coke machine.

'I'm going to help.'

'You're not a member of the DRV.'

'What's the DRV?'

'Disaster Relief Volunteers. Those guys in the coveralls.'

'I can still help.'

'No you can't.' The policeman tugged on Kozicki's arm. 'Those people are trained.'

'I'm trained too.'

'But you're not wearing DRV coveralls,' the cop pointed out.

A second policeman approached. He too carried a walkie-talkie and wore a fluorescent vest. 'Where does he think he's going?' the second cop asked. Kozicki wondered if the two men were brothers.

'He thinks he's going to help,' Kozicki's cop said. Both policemen smirked.

'Look.' Kozicki tried to pry loose from the first cop's grip. 'I know somebody who might be trapped in there.'

'Who's trapped in there?' Startled, Kozicki's cop raised his walkie-talkie to his mouth. His fingers sought Kozicki's armpit, found it, and dug deeper. 'Where is somebody trapped in there?'

'I don't know *where*.' Kozicki said. 'She *might* be trapped in there.'

The cop relaxed. 'Who's she?'

'Charlene Mendelhauser.'

Without relinquishing his hold, Kozicki's cop said over his shoulder. 'You got that?'

'Got it,' the other policeman said. 'Mendelhauser. Is that "e-l" or "l-e"?'

' "E-l," ' Kozicki said. 'She's a cashier here, she works in the mornings, I think, and—'

' "—hauser," ' the second cop said. 'Is that "a-u" or "o-w"?'

' "A-u!," ' Kozicki was shouting. 'Look, was anybody pulled out of here this morning? I mean was there anybody hurt?' Kozicki squirmed under the big policeman's grip and squinted at the ruined building. The roof had collapsed inward, funnelling debris towards the store's centre, as if a giant index finger had poked the soft spot on the building's head. Smashed or crushed cans, loaves of bread, fruit and bottles lay strewn on the floor. Yards of toilet paper were draped like sodden streamers over the shelving. In the dairy section, like a piece of garish sculpture, a red sports car winced under a twisted steel girder, its hood spattered with Neapolitan ice cream. A black pick-up truck had slid into a meat cooler and was parked serenely up to its axles in frozen chickens.

'One man was hurt,' Kozicki's cop admitted.

'Meat-cutter,' the second cop confirmed. 'Had to come to work early. Got his head stuck in a fridge.'

'Cooler,' Kozicki's cop corrected.

'Yeah,' the second cop said. 'Cooler.'

'Listen,' the first cop told Kozicki calmly. 'Take it easy. This roof caved in more than five hours ago. The store hadn't even opened yet. They've had a scent dog through here from Search and Rescue, heat sensors, all the precautions. They found one male individual with his head caught in a meat cooler. That's all. The ambulance took care of him immediately. To the best of our knowledge, nobody else is in here. The store manager confirms that opinion. The firemen and the DRV are just checking things over. They're a little worried about freon gas. If any of the refrigeration equipment is still leaking, they'll have to contain the freon gas. Now this lady you know, this Hindelhauser—'

'Mendelhauser.'

'Mendelhauser. Is she a relative?'

'No. She's a friend.'

The two policemen glanced at each other.

Kozicki's cop relinquished the hold on Kozicki's arm. 'I suggest,' the cop said, 'that if you're worried about her, you call her at home. Or,' he pointed to a crowd of people who loitered outside the cordon further along the street, 'you might ask someone down there.'

As he walked, Kozicki recognized the call letters on a local TV van that was parked on the sidewalk. A small crowd clustered in front of a man with a shoulder camera as he filmed a woman in a red suit brandishing a microphone. The crowd was made up of ghouls, Kozicki decided, and was about to turn away when he glimpsed a turquoise Payless Foods uniform under a raincoat.

'Excuse me,' he asked the jittery, acned girl who had trouble keeping her feet still. 'Do you work at this store?'

'Isn't it great?' the girl squeaked, as if someone were choking her. 'I won't make it on the noon edition, it's too late, but I'll definitely be on at suppertime. And the late-night final too. Definitely the late-night final.'

'Do you know Charlene Mendelhauser?'

'Who can tell,' the girl giggled, 'maybe this will go on "The National." Like, we're a national chain, so it could go on "The National," couldn't it?' She looked at Kozicki. 'Who?'

'Charlene Mendelhauser.'

'Charley?'

'Charlene. Mendelhauser.'

'Yeah, Charley. She *was* here, but she's gone now. She should've waited, though. Like I told her, she could've made it on the news too, you know?'

'Is she all right?'

The girl frowned. 'Sure, yeah, she's all right.' She placed her hand on Kozicki's arm and peered myopically into his face. 'She's all right. Hey,' she said gently, 'did you think she was like *crushed* or something? No, she's all right. She went home with her boyfriend.'

'What boyfriend?'

'Oh shit.' The girl chewed her bottom lip. 'You're the other boyfriend, aren't you?'

'*I'm* the boyfriend,' Kozicki said. 'The *other* boyfriend's the other boyfriend.' Kozicki felt dizzy; he started away. He was going to be late for picket duty.

'Hey,' the girl called after him. 'it sure says something about Charley though, doesn't it? I mean like two boyfriends worried about her? That says something, doesn't it?'

'It sure does.'

'Like I hope I have two boyfriends to worry about me when I'm that age,' the girl called. 'Hey! Hey, look for me in the news, okay?'

Half a block behind in his rented car, Berenson trailed his wife to the shopping mall. She walked ahead in yellow vinyl boots, a yellow raincoat, under a red umbrella. A flame in the downpour. Once inside the mall she wandered in and out of the shops as though she were a woman free of all ties.

He kept his distance, obscured in a leather jacket and soft-brimmed golf cap.

At one point on the mall's upper level, she leaned so suddenly over the mezzanine railing that he had to duck behind a pillar to avoid being seen. She was staring at the crowd below, feet together like a palace guard's, pert rump high. What was she looking at? He strained to see.

A commotion of some kind. Crowd of people around a vintage car display, a Stutz Bearcat it looked like. Outside the restraining rope a big blond guy flanked by a sturdy blonde woman and two blonde girls. All holding ice cream cones. Beside the car a photographer giving a spiel. The big blond draping his arm around the woman's shoulders while the smaller girl's contriving to tuck her head under his other arm. The photographer cajoling the older girl, who gawkily slips under the restraining rope to pose on the car's running board, adolescently hip-jutted, an anorexic Mae West. Smiling. Camera flashing. Girls' family hooting like gibbons.

And Anna? She'd turned away, face to the ceiling. From the tilt of her head and hunch of her shoulders he knew what look he'd find there. He should've slapped it off.

But he stayed behind the pillar and whispered to himself.

'Kapow,' he said.

As soon as he parked his idling truck across the street from Charlene's son's house, Kozicki succumbed to the weight of spontaneous cowardice and sat immobile in the cab, head cocked to one side like the RCA Victor dog, ostensibly tuned in to the racketing pistons under the truck's hood, but surreptitiously surveying the house, its doors, windows, eavestroughs, chimneys, driveway and lawn. His neck ached from craning. The rain had stopped, the clouds broke into greasy clots, and the sun steamed from the pavement a clammy heat that forced Kozicki to roll down his window and shrug out of his raincoat.

In his heart he was disappointed; oh, on the surface he was grateful that Charlene—*Charley*—had escaped the twisted beams and fallen cement, but inside he felt let down that she hadn't been buried alive, terrified but intact under tons of Payless rubble, trapped in a cubby-hole of teetering slabs, heavy steel, and not much oxygen. Had she been cornered, he could have used his own hands to free her, murmured encouragement and promises, demonstrated love and masculinity through his strength and determination. He could have *saved* her. Instead, she hadn't even gone into the building, and then ran off with a goddamn boyfriend. *Boyfriend?* She was fifty-eight years old, for crying out loud. Where did a woman that age get off having a *boyfriend*—especially one that wasn't *him*?

He swung out of the truck and slopped across the sunny street in his gumboots. His fingers barely touched the bell when the door opened and a man with a baby under one arm confronted him. Kozicki recognized Charlene's son Roger, a harassed, fair-haired man whose protruding eyes made him appear forever on the verge of blowing a gasket. He worked somewhere in the bowels of the police department doing God-knew-what, and the only time Kozicki ever saw him was when he was off duty.

The baby cried plaintively, and inside the house two other youngsters tortured each other.

'Make it fast, Mike,' Roger said, jiggling the baby. 'This guy's shit up to his eyeballs.'

'Charlene here, Roger?'

'Not today, Mike. Actually—she's not here much. I thought you knew that. Spends a lot of time with the new guy, Maurice.' He pronounced the name *Maw-reece*. 'Maurice the priest.'

'He's a priest?'

'Yeah. Well, he was. My mother defrocked him. Aw, don't look like that. I'm *kidding*. Look, it wasn't you. It wasn't her—it wasn't anything. Except maybe the hair colouring. She coloured her hair. And the exercise class. A woman colours her hair and goes to exercise class, and her priest leaves the church. Hey, I'm kidding.' The baby hollered. Roger slung the child over his shoulder and bounced him a couple of times. Kozicki caught a whiff of milky, harmless excrement. 'Look, Mike, Jeanette's at work right now, and Mum—well, Mum doesn't come around much any more. If it's any consolation, we're not too happy with her either. But what can you do? She's a big girl, she can take care of herself. Not like Dumper here.' The baby thrashed its pudgy legs and jerked its torso up and down over the man's back like a fish on a dock. 'Look, if there's nothing else, I gotta go. I'm sorry. Really. I gotta go.' He paused as the child continued to bellow. Two little girls ran screaming into the hallway, saw Kozicki and turned to stone, mouths gaping. 'Do you want to leave her a message or something?'

'No, no thanks. Roger, does she—does she ever come home?'

'Sure. Sometimes.' Roger looked embarrassed. 'Wanna buy a kid? Wanna buy three kids?'

'You keep 'em, Roger.'

The truck started first try but, as he drove away, Kozicki thought the pistons sounded bad, like old bolts in a coffee can. He rolled his window the rest of the way down to listen to the noise, leaned his head out to hear this junkpile on wheels rattle Maw-reece, Maw-reece, Maw-reece, until he considered stopping the truck right there, lifting the hood, and attacking the valve cover with a tire-iron. But what good would that do? She'd left, he'd done nothing, and now she was almost as good as gone forever. Having assessed the situation accurately didn't make him feel much better. Then at the end of the street he wheeled around the corner and was confronted with a magnificent mountain ash loaded with orange berries and alive with birds. Cedar waxwings swarmed over the tree's branches, a carnival of feathers and chatter, warbling so loud Kozicki fancied he could see their tonsils. He stopped the truck and listened to the birds trill their euphoric triumph over the Big Piss. Idiots, Kozicki thought gratefully, and wished he could climb up in the tree with them.

Clarence D. Rawlings eased back in his leather chair and contemplated the man in front of him. Korchinski, Korchaski, Kor-whatever-it-was, he'd never get the name straight. What sort of name was it anyway—Polish? Lithuanian? Ukrainian? One of those garlic sausage, hair-in-the-soup names. Not that Clarence Rawlings could fault a man for his name; there was his own, for instance: Clarence. He would have much preferred something less archaic. Clarence conjured up an addle-brained Edwardian in a starched white collar—Clarence Rawlings's paternal grandfather, as a matter of fact, a sometime farmer who had combined Bible-reading in the parlour with whiskey-drinking in the barn to construct a vociferously evangelical career in lay preaching and whoremongering. On the other hand, Clarence also suggested milkwagon horses with backs like broken bedsprings and muzzles buried in feedbags. Clarence Rawlings might have gone further, he sometimes thought, or at least gone more polished if he'd been christened Harrison Rawlings, or Montague Rawlings, or even—after his mother's maiden name—Macgregor Rawlings. He might have changed his name, as this man Korchinski's boss had: Von Deitl to Dreedle. But such a move would be dishonest, and Rawlings preferred cunning and shrewdness to dishonesty. Another alternative might have been the D of Clarence Rawlings's middle name, but that D stood for Dudley, two syllables he could scarcely pronounce without gagging. Dudley was almost as disheartening as Korchinski.

'So what are you saying here, Mike?' Rawlings interrupted this Korchinski, who'd been sitting in the library for the past ten minutes whining. 'What exactly is the problem?'

'The storm has thrown us back a few days,' Kozicki said. 'Most of the bedding plants look like they've been run over. Run-off from the house caved in about fifty square yards of sod, the lawn looks like a mine shaft. The topsoil on the mound slid down to the bottom and covered the rockwork Dominico was doing. A few trees came down too, big branches. They'll have to be pruned back. We got a big clean-up ahead of us.'

'And so? Let's bottom-line this thing, Mike.'

'We need an extension.'

Clarence Rawlings pressed the tips of his fingers together and made a little cathedral. Extension suggested limitation. In the old days, when the banks pursued him for their loans and mortgages, had he snivelled about an extension?—He'd sold more cars. When his eldest son had galloped off to McGill and then to Ontario after wasting four years at the University of Saskatchewan, had Clarence Rawlings flung open his wallet and offered an extension?—The kid had gone and got a job. Say 'extension,' and you were spitting on sacred ground. Say 'extension,' and you were saying 'failure.' Rawlings tilted his recliner back further so he could see the spines of the biographies standing in judgement on his library shelves. Napoleon Bonaparte—extension? Sarah Bernhardt—extension? Rawlings smiled thinly, a black line on white paper.

'No extensions, Mike.'

This Korchinski, who sat opposite him on the other side of the desk, did not move. 'Where was that written down?'

'This isn't a written agreement, Mike.'

'Exactly. Was it carved in stone?'

'It's on tape.'

'Pardon?'

'It's on tape. When you and I and Dreedle first met to arrange this deal, I taped the meeting. I don't mean just sound, Mike. I mean pictures, everything.' Rawlings opened his hands ingenuously, like a Christian martyr carrying an armload of beatitudes. 'We live in a modern age, Mike. Visually oriented. You've seen the remotes on the poles outside. I have them everywhere. In here, for instance.'

He waved at the corners of the wood-panelled room: where the carved mahogany cornices met in the high corners of the ceiling, bracketed cameras stared like cyclopic birds. 'The videotape is superfluous, of course,' Rawlings continued expansively, 'And the sound, unfortunately, is inferior. But these remotes are my diary— you might say—the rough-cut lumber of my daily commerce. In time they may become the stairways and newel posts of my personal archives, but I doubt it. If I wanted a film made, I'd hire professionals.'

Kozicki grasped the arms of his chair. To Rawlings, this Korchinski looked as though he thought the floor would start on fire. 'I'm not too sure my crew wants to be posts.' Kozicki said.

'Mike, I was speaking figuratively.' Rawlings laughed. 'But don't sell your crew short. Already they've provided some fascinating diversion. Those two lovebirds, for instance—they seem to need constant reassurance from each other, don't they? The clumsy guy with the big nose and his Indian friend who doesn't want to be his friend—do you know that for one complete day the big-nosed fellow worked in his underwear, and the Indian was so disgusted that he refused to work with him? And the silent lad, the one who never speaks—a steady worker there, Mike, a good solid employee. The other young lad spends too much time writing. I detect in him another diarist, although to be frank, Mike, if he were under my immediate supervision, I'd kick him and his notebook out of here so fast he wouldn't have time to dot his i's. The bricklayer is unintelligible, but his physical gestures alone convey worlds of meaning and frustration. And you, Mike. The hand in the pants is disconcerting, but—I've seen you consult a dictionary—what's the word? Colourful? Likely symptomatic of something, but fantastic nonetheless. Local colour, a filmmaker might call it. Fantastic.'

'Jesus,' Kozicki said.

'What's that, Mike?'

'Jesus Christ.'

'I'm not fond of people in my employ taking the Lord's name in vain, Mike.'

'If I'm going to be in a movie, I might as well talk.' Kozicki's face was red. 'Look, I missed the boat somewhere. I thought you hired us to do a job here.'

'So I did.'

'Is the job for landscaping, or play-acting?'

'Landscaping, Mike.'

'Then why all this bullshit with the cameras?'

'Let's watch the language, Mike.'

'Why all this shit with the cameras?'

Clarence Rawlings sighed. Was it true what someone had written about people in the world: that ninety per cent of them were stupid? 'The *shit* with the cameras, Mike, is my relaxation. I'm not home very often, and I'm not one for relaxation. My doctor would be thrilled to see me lounge around like this.' Rawlings sat up now; he fixed this Korchinski with his gaze. 'Let me ask you something, Mike. Have you seen many of my servants?'

Kozicki thought. 'I met the cook once. She said there was a maid. A guy showed me in here this morning.'

'Andrews, the butler.'

'Yeah. Andrews, the butler.'

Rawlings watched Kozicki closely. 'Where are my gardeners, Mike?'

'What gardeners?'

'I have a large tract of land here—full of plants and lawns, even before you got here. Where are the gardeners who take care of all that?'

Kozicki was really confused now. 'I don't know,' he muttered. 'I never thought of them.'

Rawlings shook his head. 'Never thought of them, Mike? A man who belongs to a union, a man who religiously walks the picket line, even while he violates his union's regulations?—Although you missed your picket duty the other day, didn't you?'

'How do you know that?'

'One of my television crews filmed the aftermath of the roof cave-in at one of my supermarkets—and there you were, trying to pick up one of my cashiers.' Rawlings shook his head again. 'Mike, do you honestly believe that I hired you and your crew simply as background for a home movie? My interest in my employees goes deeper than that. The gardeners I don't have Mike, the gardeners you didn't think about, have all been transferred to other properties for the summer. You and your crew have replaced them.'

Kozicki was sweating.

Rawlings rocked gently in his chair. 'You're a dictionary man, Mike. You probably already know what an entrepreneur is, but let me refresh your memory. An entrepreneur is a person who undertakes a commercial enterprise with the chance of profit or loss. Am I right?'

'Okay,' Kozicki said.

'He's a gambler—though he likes the odds in his favour. Now, let's consider the job I've set for you and your crew, Mike. I've given you a time-frame—a structure—within which to landscape my estate. If you finish on time you will be paid in full. If you don't, you lose money. But leave that aside. You've just asked me for an extension. What's changed here? What docs an extension change, Mike?'

'The time-frame,' Kozicki said. 'The structure.'

'Precisely.' Rawlings leaned forward in his chair.

Beads of water glistened on Kozicki's forehead. 'I'm giving your crew the opportunity to work under pressure, Mike. I've giving them the chance to test their strength and will. A chance to gamble. Basically, I'm giving your crew—your union crew—a chance to be entrepreneurs.'

'You're a big-hearted guy, Mr. Rawlings.'

'Don't be facetious, Mike. Dreedle's already been paid for his contribution, and if I remember correctly you were given a little advance for bringing the crew in.' A thought teased Rawlings for a moment. 'Tell me, Mike, how would your crew feel if they knew their foreman had already received money for a job they might not even get paid for?'

Kozicki stared at him. 'You know, you're something right out of a can, aren't you? My dad had names for guys like you.'

'Oh?' Rawlings tried to feel interested. 'What were they?'

'You told me to watch my language. It's your house, after all.'

Rawlings smiled, for a fleeting instant aware his dentist had insisted on capping those incisors. 'Was your father a union man, Mike?'

'He liked to think he was a socialist.'

'What does he think now?'

'Not much. He's dead.'

'That's too bad.'

'Yeah, I think he thought so too.' Kozicki got up to leave. 'They told us the official cause of death was a punctured lung. I think now maybe it was a broken heart.'

Rawlings stood as well. 'I'm sorry to hear that, Mike.' And he was. In the silence and subdued light of his library, Clarence D. Rawlings felt genuine sympathy for this Korchinsky. He wanted to give the man something.

'Let me give you some advice, Mike, of which possibly your father might even have approved.'

'What's that?'

'Finish the job.' Rawlings sought Kozicki's eyes and held them. 'Finish the job. Because, believe me, broken hearts are nothing. I've had a few and caused a few and survived them all. Everything's a risk and a gamble. Finish the job. That's what I plan to do. I've got my books and my bunker, my business interests and my caved-in food store, but believe me, should a bomb drop tomorrow and break every heart on the face of the earth, I'll still be here. I'll still be here. Broken hearts are nothing.'

Outside again, Kozicki nailed the August sheaf of a calendar to the inside of the lid on the big wooden tool box in the back of his truck. 'Gather round!' he called. The crew drifted in from their various

114

jobs—clean up mostly (clean-up for the next goddamn week, Kozicki thought).

'What'd he say?' Trischuk asked.

'What we figured he'd say,' Kozicki said. 'No extensions.' With a grease pencil he crossed off the first row and a half of the calendar's numbers. 'Twenty-one days to go, ladies and gentlemen,' he said. 'Twenty-one days and counting.' He drew a bullseye on the blank square at the bottom of the page and tapped it a couple of times. 'And then we hit the jackpot.'

When he dropped the lid it sounded so much like a gun going off that Lannie jumped behind a tree.

PART THREE

BIG SAM CAPELLE OF BIG SAM'S SPORTS BLESSED THE DAY THE CITY council had approved Thursday late-night shopping. What with all the malls sponging up the suburban trade, a downtown merchant needed a twenty-six-hour day just to keep his chin above water. That and an inventory that looked like a Sears warehouse. You had to carry it all these days—racquet sports, jogging shoes, baseball, football, swimsuits, shoulder pads, fishing tackle—even clothes, for God's sake. Unless you specialized, a route Big Sam was seriously considering. There was a time—donkey's years ago, as Big Sam told his older customers who weren't so senile they couldn't remember the old days—there was a time when Big Sam could count on a steady seasonal demand for his goods; winters, every kid in the city used to pass through his shop, buy a hockey stick and try to steal a roll of tape; summers they used to pass through again, buy a bat or ball-glove and try to steal a baseball. Life was simpler then. Now you had to sell exercise tights and ankle weights, croquet mallets and head-bands. Mind you, lately people were shopping downtown again. Their spending had something to do with summer, he reflected: the nearness of Riverside Park, the heat, the Exhibition coming next week. Even the cave-in at Payless Foods a couple of blocks over attracted the curious. Now that the evenings had warmed up again, people wore bright summer clothes, bought ice cream cones, sauntered. Stores and cafés set up shop on the sidewalk, buskers twanged and yodelled on street corners or in the archway of the old Capitol Theatre. And down there—Big Sam lounged in his store's doorway and peered along the street to the corner of 20th and Central—the patrons at the Queen Anne pub strolled in for a cold one and waited for the sun to go down and the hookers to come out. It was almost like the old days; Thursday night shopping nudged Big Sam towards nostalgia and, he hoped, prosperity.

He stepped back inside the store, stroking his moustache. The moustache was his trademark; a thick, handlebarred triumph that obscured his mouth, lips and a good part of his chin. His wife said it looked like two squirrels mating, so to give it room Big Sam shaved the rest of his face and his head too. His wife said then that his moustache looked like two squirrels mating on a rock. Big Sam guessed she was jealous. What did she know about squirrels?

He eyed his customers. The kid and his father were still muttering over the bicycles. Big Sam would let the kid talk the old man into a ten-speed. The two old geezers were still fingering the fishing tackle as if the number three Len Thompson's were the crown jewels; if they didn't make up their minds soon Big Sam would go over and offer them the Fisherman's Friend gag—a stick of fake dynamite and a basket. The red-headed guy who slouched like an orangutan had homed in on the shotgun rack, though in Big Sam's opinion the guy would've looked more natural wearing leopard skin and carrying a club.

'What do you figger, pardner?' Big Sam talked loud. Guns were a noisy, western thing to Big Sam; he'd even shot one a couple of times when he was a kid. 'What can I do you for? See anything that suits your fancy?'

'I'm not sure.' The redhead's eyes were the size of garden peas. 'It's early in the year yet. I'm just looking.'

'We're into August already,' Big Sam pointed out. 'Fall'll be here sooner than you can turn around. That's why I marked these babies down twenty per cent. I like to see the early bird get the worm.' He followed the redhead's gaze. 'Take a look at this one.' Big Sam fished out his key and unlocked the chain that was threaded through the trigger guards. 'Double-barreled's a good idea, and this Remington has a pump action so you can get your shots off quick. Mind you—' He handed the redhead the gun. '—you might not get the range with this one that you'd pull in with that twenty-gauge there. The twenty-gauge you want for geese. Shove in a number two or a number four shot and you can bring down a high-flying honker. You hunting honkers?'

'Ducks,' the readhead said. He snuggled the shotgun to his shoulder and sighted, both eyes open. The guy had downy hair all over his arms and neck, Big Sam noticed. No nippy October mornings out in a duckblind for this fella. He had his own fur coat.

'Put a number five or number six shot in that twelve-gauge and you got a sweet little gun for ducks, pardner. It'll give you a good spray. Recoils like a rocking chair if you hold 'er snug. Prime 'er with number seven shot and the prairie chickens'll fall right into your frying pan.'

The readhead swung the gun after some invisible pheasants and smiled over the gunstock. 'Think I could bring down two at once?'

'More than that, pardner.' Big Sam confessed. 'With a number seven shot you'd get a pattern that could air-condition a barn.'

The redhead hugged the gunstock into his shoulder. 'It feels good,' he said. 'I'll take it.'

'And shells?' Big Sam slid smoothly behind the counter. His wife said he moved graceful, for a big guy.

'Give me a box of number six and number seven,' the redhead said. 'I'll want a broad pattern, as you say.'

Big Sam punched the numbers into the cash register and filled out the necessary papers. 'Anything else, pardner?' he asked, before he rang the total. 'I got coveralls, caps, duckcalls, decoys, hand warmers, thermos flasks—the whole ball o' wax.'

'No thanks. I've got everything I need.' The readhead glanced at the plastic mallards and smiled. 'I don't like to use decoys,' he said. 'I like to give sitting ducks a sporting chance.'

'That's a pretty fair attitude, pardner,' Big Sam boomed. He never went hunting himself—too much blood. 'But if you find there's something you forgot, come on back. We can outfit you top to bottom.'

The readhead thanked him and left the store. From experience, Big Sam knew that one good sale could trigger others. He stroked his moustache. The two old geezers had a mittful of Len Thompson's already and were nosing around the wet flies. And the kid had dragged his father away from the regular racers to an eighteen-speed Peugot. No doubt about it, Thursday night shopping was looking better all the time.

'Howdy pardners. What can I do you for?'

'You know what I wisht we had?' Corny Fergus asked Ironeagle on the fourth day of clean-up after the storm. 'One of them big friggin guns. You know, like the kind they got out in the mountains that they fire at friggin snow packs to make them avalanches come down? Them guns got a shell in 'em as big as a sewer pipe. We could just stand down here and aim that big gun up at them broken branches and split tree trunks and *blam*! Shoot the friggin things off, clean as a whistle.'

'You'd end up with toothpicks,' Ironeagle said.

'I'd rather pick up toothpicks than carry this friggin chainsaw up that ladder again.'

'You don't got to carry that chainsaw. I told you, I'll do this one.'

'You done the last two.'

'That's cause I don't want to see you cut the rest of your nose off.' Ironeagle pointed to the bandage Corny wore over the tip of his nose. 'How'd you get that cut, anyways?'

'Accident. You wouldn't friggin believe me if I friggin told ya.' Corny laid his hand on the tree's rough trunk and gazed upwards. It was some friggin tree, all right. Eighty feet if it was an inch. The undersides of its leaves glinted like dimes in a sack. A silver maple, Kozicki had called it. 'Now who in his right mind,' Kozicki had asked earlier, 'would plant a silver maple that close to a house?' Corny couldn't imagine who would do such a thing. He *could* imagine, however, somebody being killed by a silver maple planted that close to a house. Thirty feet above his head the storm had splintered one of the tree's main limbs and torn it down to the balcony, so that now the branch lay draped over the stone balustrade Dominico was examining. Like a giant dislocated arm hanging out of a car window, the limb's thick end was still jaggedly attached to the trunk, its slender branches brushing the stone slabs of the balcony floor. That branch weighed close to three hundred friggin pounds in Corny's estimation, and to bring it down was going to be a friggin tricky piece of business. Why, just standing underneath it he could come up with half a dozen ways that friggin branch would kill him. If he balanced on the ladder to undercut the branch, the limb would droop, vice-grip his chainsaw bar so it got stuck; he'd pull on the friggin saw, pop it loose, and hack his right leg off just above the knee. If he climbed the tree above the branch, he'd fall and break his friggin neck, or overbalance in the tree's crutch, pitch forward and tear both hips out of their sockets and hang there like a busted puppet. Or he could stand in the tree and cut the branch, watch it barber-chair and drive a friggin wood splinter the size of a crowbar into the soft part under his friggin chin. His oldest daughter Marilyn had once wrote a school report on one of them castles where they axed off a guy's head and spiked it on a pole. That's what Corny'd look like once that branch got through with him—a friggin onion on a ice pick. If he let Ironeagle prune the branch, he'd be down below hauling on the control rope just long enough to pull half the tree and Ironeagle too down on top of himself. They'd all end up like friggin bugs on a windshield. Even if he sat in a bucket on a friggin gooseneck crane—which a friggin skinflint like this Rawlings wouldn't hire anyways—Corny'd probably brush a power line, sizzle and drop to the friggin ground like burnt bacon. Anyway you cut it—ha, big joke—Corny didn't like the look of this friggin tree at all.

'How'd you cut your nose?' Ironeagle asked again.

'Forget the friggin nose.'

'If you tell me how you cut your nose, eh, could be I'll cut this tree.'

'If I tell you how I cut my nose, will you come and see my daughter again?'

'What for? It didn't do no good the first time.'

'How would you know? You left before dessert.'

'I remembered. I had to see some people.'

'Sure.'

'They came in on the bus.'

'There wasn't no buses runnin that night. That was the night of the Big Piss.'

'Could be it was the train station.'

'Yeah, sure. Okay. Well, you sure left in a friggin hurry. My wife figured you hated her rhubarb pie, the kids figured you hated them, and little Rosalee didn't know whether to cry or steal third. Did you see the way she was lookin at you?'

'Could be that kid makes me nervous.'

'Could be you make *her* nervous.'

'So it was a good thing I left, eh?'

'Aw jeez, Eagle.' Corny looked up. On the balcony, the broken branch partially obscured Dominico and Paterson as they chiselled gently at something at the far end of the balustrade. From Corny's perspective, the little stone mason was a pair of baggy trousers and a torso of shiny leaves. Paterson was a pair of boots.

'How'd you cut that nose?' Ironeagle asked again.

Corny lowered his voice and jerked his thumb at the men above them. 'Don't tell nobody.'

'Why would I wanna tell them guys?'

'I mean *nobody*.'

'Who else am I gonna tell?'

'I don't know. People who come in on the friggin bus.'

'Moony-ass,' Ironeagle snorted. 'How'm I gonna do that? There was no buses runnin that night.'

Corny pushed back his hard hat and studied Ironeagle appreciatively. He grinned. 'You're such a friggin jerk, you know that?'

'It's a gift, eh. What about the nose?'

Corny pulled Ironeagle confidentially under the eaves. 'The night you left, Rosalee was feelin down, well all the kids didn't feel too friggin happy. They don't get visitors often because I mean the place is such a friggin madhouse who's gonna come? Anyways they had all kinds of things they wanted to show off to you, like little Kennie can burp "O Canada" and Susie and Marilyn can play the piano both at the same time. So anyhow they're all feelin like cats in a friggin bathtub because it's pissin rain and their guest of honour has frigged off so I done the straw trick for them. I stick this milkshake straw in my mouth and I tell this story about a crocodile and how he eats this snake one bit at a time only it's not a snake it's his own *self* he's eatin, see. So each time he bites I take the nail scissors and snip a bit off the straw only this time I don't got the nail scissors I got my pruning shears and I nip the end of my nose off. And you can stop friggin laughin, you're as bad as them friggin kids.' Corny pointed to his bandaged nose. 'If you'd stayed for the friggin rhubarb pie this never woulda happened. Hey, look out!'

A shoebox-sized block of stone clattered down the wall and thudded at their feet. The stone was smooth, as creamy white as mozzarella cheese.

Corny plastered himself against the wall. 'I'm gonna break you friggin neck, Dominico!'

Dominico's voice came to them thin and wavery. 'Corny Ferg, you hokay?'

'I'm gonna grab you by the friggin nuts and see if you can fly.'

'It was an accident,' Paterson called.

'I'm gonna take that chisel and carve a keyhole in your friggin forehead,' Corny promised, although he still hadn't moved. Backed tightly against the rough stone wall, tensely staring upwards at the protective eaves, breathless, he waited and listened for the sounds he could not describe but had heard in his dreams all his working life: the telltale groan of weakened wood; the tearing creak of a parting branch, like a spike being pried from a board; the plaintive moan; the cracking, sinuous splinter of collapsing lumber; the innocent swish of leaves, the silence, the numbing thump. That's how Corny would meet his doom, he knew. The friggin sky would smash his head.

Ironeagle stepped out and climbed the ladder. Corny could hear them muttering up there.

After a while Paterson called: 'Corny, are you going to hide under there all day?'

'Tie the friggin branch off!' Corny shouted.

More muttering; someone scuffled in the tree.

'Okay, it's tied off.'

'Tie the friggin ladder off!'

'Corny Ferg, already we do that. Whaddayou think?'

'What else you got up there? A bomb? A friggin knife?'

'I got the tools, moony-ass,' Ironeagle said. 'I got the Swedesaw and the chainsaw. We can take this branch down in sections, eh.'

But Corny waited.

Dominico said, 'Corny Ferg, Corny Ferg, Dio canne. Whaddayou think? I drop the astone, that's it. I makea the sbaglio—whaddayou say—the mistake. That's it. I apologize. You come up now, Corny Ferg. I got no more astone.'

Corny sidestepped out from under the eaves and tentatively approached the ladder, whose top rung had been anchored to a chimney above the balcony, while its feet had been dug into the ground. Like a broken arm in a sling, the splintered tree limb had been jury-rigged in a complex looping of yellow polypropylene rope. Ironeagle, Paterson and Dominico gazed down at him benevolently, like saints—or idiots.

'Where's that chainsaw?' Corny asked them. 'You got it near the edge? You gonna crank it up and kick it in my friggin face once I'm halfway up?'

'The saw's behind me,' Paterson said.

'You climb up anow, Corny Ferg. You gonna be hokay anow. I tell you true. You don' gotta cuta the tree, you don' gotta toucha the tool.' Corny mounted the ladder. 'You gonna be a supervise, Corny Ferg, a bigashot. You gonna be the Pope, Corny Ferg.'

Corny eased himself onto the balcony and spent a few seconds rubbing his knees. 'Jeez, look at me. I'm shakin like a friggin dog shittin razor blades.'

'You gonna be safe anow, Corny Ferg.'

He was, too. After several minutes he could see that. He checked himself over: faller's gloves, steel-toed boots, rip-stop pants, long-sleeved shirt, safety glasses and earplugs in his pocket, hard hat. Bandage still on nose. Tensor bandage snug on elbow. The ladder was solid, the branch wasn't going anywhere. The sky was clear, the balcony flagstones lay securely under his feet. He felt, if anybody wanted to know, like a friggin king. From the balcony he could see the breadth of Rawlings's estate clear out to the road. Down there Kozicki and Lannie were replanting junipers; Trischuk and Anna dredged the moat for fallen branches; a white van swept through the open wrought-iron gates and wheeled smoothly along the curved pebbled drive. Corny closed his eyes and sucked in a lungful of refueling air. Life was good. If he *was* a king, he'd stand up on this friggin balcony and tell his subjects that yessir, he could see they got this friggin job done on time. Majestically, he leaned against the stone balustrade; it disintegrated. Against his weight, it crumpled like breakfast cereal. He pitched headlong into the air, swore once, windmilled a little, then watched as the newly laid sod twenty feet below suddenly rushed up and smacked him in the face. And then—oh, he should've known, he should've guessed—every friggin thing went friggin black.

Kozicki knew his way around hospitals. Exits and entrances were his compass. He understood the desperate protocol of emergency rooms, knew when to stand back as attendants whipped the stretcher out of the ambulance and scooted a gurney down the tiled corridors. He recognized terminologies and procedures; BP's, sutures, contusions, vital signs and IV's held for him no surprises. He expected curtains around the beds, was accustomed to the whimpering complaints of the patients in the waiting area—the arms in slings, the bloodied heads, the fretful red-faced children. When harassed duty nurses and baggy-eyed interns asked him questions, he appreciated what his calm terse answers meant to them. In a hospital he embraced his humanity, assumed sadness, compassion and a yearning for life. He hated every minute he was there.

The duty nurse called him to the nurses' station. 'Cornelius Fergus,' she said. 'Who would be his next of kin?'

'Marion Fergus. Look, is Corny okay?'

'Has she been contacted?'

'A couple of guys I work with went to pick her up. Is Corny conscious?'

The nurse, a West Indian girl no older than his daughter, smiled. 'I'm sorry, sir, it's too early to comment on that.'

'I mean he's breathing okay, isn't he? We had to dig under his face to get air to him. His schnoz was stuck in the grass. Is he conscious?'

She shook her head. 'I can tell you that his vital signs are stable.'

Down the hall a man's voice shouted, 'Forty-five minutes, I been here forty-five minutes! Why don't you just give *me* the needle and thread and I'll do it *myself*!'

Kozicki leaned over the counter. 'Look,' he said. 'What is it? What's the matter with him? Come on, I'm the guy's foreman. He got hurt working for me. What is it, a concussion?'

'Sir, it would be premature for me to speculate on a diagnosis. The doctors are just seeing him now.'

'It would be premature for me to jump over this desk and wrestle you for your clipboard,' Kozicki said. 'Please, you were in there. What is it?'

The nurse relented. 'A mild concussion, yes. The doctor also suspects some spinal trauma, but more tests will have to be administered before he can be certain.'

'Spinal trauma. You mean Corny's paralyzed?'

'Sir,' the nurse said firmly, 'we'll have to wait and see. Your friend is being transferred to the second-floor ward for spinal injuries. I suggest you wait up there.' She glanced at Kozicki enquiringly. 'Sir, are you in pain?'

Kozicki pulled his right hand from under his belt. 'No.'

'Did you injure yourself in the mishap?'

'No, no.' Kozicki pointed to his groin. 'Old war wound.'

'Because if you are in pain—'

'No. Thanks.' He waved to the nurse and escaped to the elevators, which were occupied. He took the stairs, and climbed through a burgeoning odour of soap powders and cleaning fluids.

Other people frequently maligned a hospital's antiseptic scents, but Kozicki prized the smell of cleanliness. After his father died, he'd ridden boxcars out to British Columbia in search of work, and what with the dust and the cinders from the railway engine, and the unabashed filth of hobo jungles, railroad bunkhouses and logging camps, he knew the difference between clean and grubby when he smelled it. 'You put me any place without soap, water, and a bathtub,' he'd once told his wife, whose illness at this very hospital marked the last time he'd wanted to come in here, 'and within six months I'll find a place to wash.' 'Why so long?' she'd asked dreamily from her hospital bed. 'Emily, I'd need some time to get *dirty*.' He was pleased when she rewarded him with indulgent chuckling, then worried that his jokes would tear the stitches in her chest. Sick or well, he'd loved the smell of her. And she was kept clean until the end, he reflected. You couldn't fault the hospital on that score.

Up in the second-floor waiting room Dominico and Ironeagle slouched gloomily in a couple of chrome chairs while Corny's wife, Marion Fergus, stalked around the room tapping the walls and the furniture. Short, squat and freckled, Marion Fergus reminded Kozicki of a cop on a vice squad who approached his clients with an extended cup of coffee in one hand and a fistful of knuckles in the other. Ten children and marriage to Corny had taught her a thing or two about reality. If life had any surprises left, Marion had yet to hear about them.

'Mike,' she said when she saw him. She stopped tapping the coffee table and approached. 'What have you heard? I can't squeeze anything out of the nurses and these two boneheads aren't any help. He fell, that's all anyone will tell me. Is Cornelius injured or blemished?'

'It's an injury this time, Marion.' He hugged her. Her pug nose poked the middle of his chest. 'Who's staying with the kids?'

'Marilyn.' In fulfillment of an alliterative dream, Marion had christened all her daughters with names that began with M: Marilyn, Marlene, Muriel, and Marie. By the time her last daughter came along, she was fed up with the pattern but too steeped in precedent to reverse it: she dubbed the baby Marliss. The boy's names—her attitude was what did boys need, anyway—were scattered all over the alphabet. Her newest girl had arrived with her own name— Rosalee Good Sky—and how could an M-name improve on that?

'Tell me, Mike. Is it worse than the hip?' Once Corny had slipped off a truck box into a front-end loader bucket and fractured something called his ischial tuberosity. Kozicki wasn't sure what an ischial tuberosity was, but apparently a fractured one kept a fella off his feet and in a cast for three months and, according to Corny, twanged like a jew's-harp every time the weather turned cold.

'Worse, Marion. This one's right up there with the kidney.' He told her what the nurse in Emergency had said about concussions and spinal trauma.

Marion Fergus withdrew her thick arms from around his waist and looked up into his face. For an instant her frank grey eyes watered at the edges; then they hardened. 'I'm going to demand compensation, Mike. If my Cornelius is paralyzed, we're going to need compensation.'

'We don't know anything for sure yet, Marion. Look, why don't we hunt up a doctor right now and find out?'

She shook her head. 'I can wait. I'm used to waiting. You start looking for doctors and you'll only interfere with them doing their job. I'd rather they worked on Cornelius than deal with me. They'll get to see me, don't you worry. In the meantime I want you to be clear on this.' She raised her voice to include Dominico and Iron-eagle, who moped in their chairs and eyed her apprehensively. 'If my Cornelius is paralyzed, we'll demand compensation. If he dies—' her voice caught, and Kozicki moved toward her, but she waved him away. 'If he dies, Mike, you and your crew and this Mr. Rawlings will feed and clothe Cornelius's children forever.'

'He's not going to die, Marion.'

She drew herself upright. 'You'd be surprised what Cornelius can do once he gets an idea into his head.'

'We don't know if he's got *that* idea, Marion.'

'From what you've told me , we don't know if he's got anything in his head *at all.*' She cried silently. Marion Fergus favoured print dresses that she wore like tents. Kozicki watched helplessly as a whole wall of primroses shuddered and shook. He laid his hand on her shoulder and fumbled in his back pocket for a handkerchief. She looked at the cloth and pushed it away.

'Mike, don't you ever do your laundry?'

'Come on, Marion.'

She accepted the soiled handkerchief and dabbed at her eyes.

'Look, Marion, we'll wait here with you.'

'No, you won't.' She smoothed her dress. 'I'll wait here alone. I'm used to this. Just remember what I've told you.' Kozicki,

Dominico and Ironeagle had huddled around her. The woman had forearms like a blacksmith. In her own way she was familiar with iron; Kozicki imagined her lashing out a well-timed wallop on one of her kid's ears. The little bugger's head would ring like a fire alarm. 'Get those looks off your faces,' she told them. Her eyes were tearless and wet at the same time. 'My Cornelius isn't gone yet. He's had more injuries and blemishes than you've had cups of coffee. He's always pulled through, and he will this time too. And even if he doesn't, when the job is finished Cornelius will get his fair share.'

Dominico's voice came out lightly strangled. 'Mrs. Corny Ferg, I'ma gonna give Corny Ferg halfa my pay for thisa job. I'ma gonna give for him fifty percent. That's it. He'sa good friend for me, that Corny Ferg.'

'Fifty percent?' Marion Fergus teased him. 'What is he, *half* a friend?'

'One hunnert percent.' Dominico gulped, tugging his trousers up to his armpits. Kozicki thought the little stone mason looked sick.

Marion Fergus patted Dominico's hand. 'I don't care what you give him,' she said, 'as long as he gets his fair share.' She turned to Ironeagle. 'As for you—don't think this accident of Cornelius's lets you off the hook. You still have to come to my house and eat a piece of my rhubarb pie.' She waved her hands at them. 'Now go away, all of you. Please. Go back to work.'

'We'll check in later tonight,' Kozicki promised.

In the elevator Ironeagle observed that Marion Fergus was a strong woman. Kozicki agreed. Silently, he wondered if all women weren't strong. Certainly his wife had been. During her last days she pursued determined, halting, post-operational walks around the neighbourhood, during which she provided a running commentary on her progress. 'Now Emily's coming up fast on the outside,' she'd say, 'and as they round the turn Emily's right foot is stretching out in front of her left.' Or she'd remark on other people's gardens, as if they were part of a grand and stimulating tour. 'Oh,' she'd say, 'look at Mr. Halpern's ivy. Do you think he'd mind if we dug it all up and replanted it on our trellis?' Anguished, Kozicki and his daughter cast each other self-pitying glances and took the dinky little steps that most grown-ups would use to walk a toddler. If Emily noticed their condescension, she never let on. Frequently she kicked them out of the house, and later out of her hospital room. 'Go out for a while you two,' she'd say. 'Wear some of that flab off.' Though in the end she resembled a bag of pretzels and was as easy to lift as balsa wood, Emily had the strength of reinforced concrete. She wrote her will, said her goodbyes, and cried only because she couldn't stay longer to help them deal with her going. At the time Kozicki had wished he could've traded places with her. She was so much better at the death business than he was.

On the hospital's front steps he sent Dominico and Ironeagle off to the Rawlings estate and, as soon as Dominico's huge car disappeared into the traffic, he sneaked back to the second floor and instructed the ward nurse to keep an eye on Marion Fergus. 'Just tell her the truth,' he told the nurse behind the desk. 'And check on her now and then, okay? She's a nice lady but she likes to bump the furniture.'

He took the stairs down to a side exit, where he stepped into the bright sunlit parking lot, recalling those times he'd led his daughter by the hand through a maze of planter dividers and cedar-chipped shrub beds to the safety of his truck. Gillian had followed him readily enough, and sometimes had strutted along the concrete curbs like a tightrope walker, guiltily aware, it seemed to Kozicki, that her mother was simultaneously walking a rope of her own. In those days, Kozicki had deliberately parked his vehicle in the furthest corner of the lot, behind a white spruce's protective bulk, or a rock pine's spiky resilience. The long walk, he figured, would make their departure less abrupt; they wouldn't breezily drive off, but stop once in awhile to wave at the windows—although they weren't always sure which one was Emily's.

The habit of distant parking remained with Kozicki, even now when he should've been behind the wheel and tearing off to Rawlings's place, since the job, by his morose, slow-fused calculation, had squirted so far ahead of his crew that they'd have to run themselves to death just to catch up. A little over two weeks to go. Kozicki could feel the deadline hanging over his head like a boulder suspended from a shoelace.

Poor Corny, he thought, and was so engrossed in his own feet that he didn't see Cargill until the picket captain popped up in Kozicki's truck cab and said, 'Hey, brother. You got troubles?'

During his four years in the air force, Kozicki had heard his share of patriotic flapdoodle and optimistic rumour—stories that involved mythical flyers who, downed in obscure and dangerous circumstances, used courage and luck to escape certain annihilation. If they crash-landed in the Mediterranean, they managed to swim to Bournemouth; if they fell from the sky over the Alps, they landed in a beautiful countess's Swiss haystack; if their kite was a colander and their fuel tanks empty, they skimmed the Channel like a flat rock and rested on the beach at Dover. It was all *Per Ardua ad Astra* for those flyers: through adversity to the stars. Now, sitting in his truck next to Cargill, Kozicki would've been happy just to get off the ground. He climbed in behind the wheel and sat next to Cargill.

'How are the knackers, brother?' Cargill asked pleasantly. 'Last time I saw you, you had a hand dipped in the old jewel box. Got 'em fixed, have ya?'

'Not yet. Due for a check-up, though.'

'Ah, those check-ups.' Buddy-style, Cargill slapped his big red hand on Kozicki's knee, and gave it a squeeze. 'I go for check-ups on a regular basis. Pulse, blood pressure, cholesterol, that kind of thing. The doc wants me to avoid the triple bypass.' He removed his hand from Kozicki's knee and tapped his own chest. 'You know, the ticker. I told one of your guys about it. Brother—?'

'Paterson.'

'Yeah. Brother Paterson. Haven't seen much of Brother Paterson lately.' Cargill's already sanguine face coloured slightly, as if he'd spent all day in the sun and the burn had just now kicked in. 'Fact is I haven't seen much of Brother Paterson or Brother Ironeagle or Brother Trischuk or Brother Anybody for a while now. Seems every time I drive by they're on a break somewhere.'

'We got a friend in the hospital.'

Cargill inhaled deeply and stuck out his chest. 'Really?' He exhaled as he spoke, and Kozicki watched the chest drop to the belly. 'Brother Kozicki, why are you fucking the union?'

'Am I fucking the union?'

'That's what *I* asked *you*.'

'In what way would I be fucking the union?'

Cargill threw back his head and laughed humourlessly. Veins surged up and down his neck like boa constrictors. If he busts one of them, Kozicki thought, we'll be up to our hips in blood.

'In *what way?*' Cargill suddenly exploded. '*In what way*! Brother, do you think I'm naive? Do you think I'm stupid? Don't you think I know what you and your guys are up to, who you're visiting in the hospital? Don't you think I've seen you at Clarence D. Rawlings's place? Playing footsie with Dreedle at the greenhouse? Brother, don't you think—' Cargill sputtered. White spittle flecked his lips. Through a veiny alchemy that Kozicki guessed had something to do with tickers and cholesterol, Cargill's face shot through several shades of deep red and headed for purple. His outburst dwindled to a gasp, a choke, a fine screeching wheeze that soon had Kozicki worried. If the tubby guy flopped over the front seat, would Kozicki have room to jolt him with CPR, manoeuvrability to lay on some mouth-to-mouth resuscitation? 'Take it easy,' he told Cargill. What if the poor guy slumped over onto the driver's side, pinned Kozicki between the steering wheel and the back of the seat? Kozicki would be stuck there, honking SOS on his horn while Cargill had a heart attack on his lap. 'Breathe slowly,' Kozicki instructed. 'Breathe.' He hooked his right arm around Cargill's thick shoulders and with his left hand undid the man's belt, trousers button and fly. The action caused Cargill's already protruding eyes to widen, as if for one wild moment he thought Kozicki was going to make kinky forays into *his* underpants. 'Take it easy,' Kozicki assured him. 'Just relax and try to breathe.' Under Kozicki's grip Cargill went limp and sucked in great shivering draughts of air. They sat together for several minutes, as if they were on a date. 'That's it,' Kozicki said, 'that's better. Take it easy.'

Gradually Cargill's colour subsided to a bright pink and his breathing slowed.

'You okay?'

Cargill nodded.

'Any pain in your chest? Numbness in the left arm?'

'No.'

'I'm going to drive you over to the hopsital.'

'Not yet.'

'You don't look so good.'

'I haven't finished.'

Kozicki braced himself against Cargill's bulk. 'You feel more coming on?'

'I mean about the union. I haven't finished about the union. Say, you got a drink somewhere?'

133

Kozicki pulled a plastic water jug from behind the seat.

Cargill sipped experimentally. 'Nice and cold.'

'I freeze it the night before. What about the union?'

Cargill took several deep breaths. 'I've got to blow the whistle on you, brother.'

Kozicki withdrew his arm from the man's shoulders. 'What for?'

'You're breaking the terms of your collective agreement. What would be the point of a strike if all the brothers and sisters were pulling in big bucks from other jobs?'

'We do our picket duty.'

'Not always.'

'Most of the time.'

'Fuck that,' Cargill said. The water seemed to give him strength. 'It's all or nothing, brother. Can't you see that? Can't you see how your actions jeopardize your union? Goddammit, the bargaining team fights tooth and nail for salary and working conditions. How can they do that in all conscience when some of the brothers and sisters can moonlight lucrative private contracts? It's a bullshit deal, brother. What if management finds out? What's our bargaining team supposed to say when management finds out that the brothers and sisters really don't need the benefits the rest of the union went out on strike for? That kind of thing punches a hole in the whole goddamn balloon, brother. It fucks the union.'

Kozicki laid his hands on the steering wheel and considered. Maybe he should listen to Cargill. Maybe he shouldn't. Maybe he should grab the fat little walrus by the neck and give him a *real* heart attack. Who would be the wiser? They were sitting in an isolated corner of the parking lot, almost obscured under a weeping birch. 'Your fly's undone,' he told the picket captain.

'Oh yeah. Thanks.' Cargill stretched his legs to adjust his clothing. Kozicki watched the man's pudgy fingers fumble with the belt buckle.

'Listen,' Kozicki said, 'we only got a couple of weeks left. I did you a favour here, can't you do me one? Keep the union off my back. For a couple of weeks, that's all.'

Cargill tucked his shirt in. 'I don't know.'

'Look, what if I took part of what I make on the Rawlings job and donated it to say, the union strike fund. Or the pension fund, or union dues, something like that?'

Cargill looked at him shrewdly. 'And the others?'

'Let the others keep their earnings.'

'I can't do that, brother.'

'Why not?'

'They're scabs, brother. Scabs. And by rights the union should not only have their earnings, but their balls as well.'

'They're not all men.'

'You know what I mean.'

Kozicki rubbed his nose. 'How much of our earnings would you want?'

'Not *me*, brother. The union. I've got to check this out with the executive. I've got to stand between you and your irate brothers and sisters, brother. The brothers and sisters don't take kindly to scabbing.'

'You don't have to tell them everything. Say the donation's anonymous.'

'Are you *trying* to make me laugh, brother?' Kozicki sighed. 'How much?'

'Fifty percent.'

'Get stuffed. Ten percent.'

'Forty.'

'Twenty.'

'Twenty-five, brother. And no guarantees. I go to the executive with twenty-five percent of the crew's earnings and the executive might find it in their hearts to let bygones be bygones.'

'Okay. Twenty-five percent of our earnings.'

Cargill laughed. 'That would be a good deal, brother, except for one thing. You forgot to mention the deadline.'

Kozicki kept his face composed. 'What deadline?'

Cargill laughed again. 'The Rawlings deadline. Come on, brother. I asked you before: Do you think I'm naive? Do you think I'm stupid?'

Kozicki drummed his fingers on the steering wheel. The sun had risen higher in the sky; the ragged shadow of the weeping birch had shrunk away from his truck and left the dull metal baking in the bright sun.

'Brother,' Cargill asked gently. 'How much are you going to make on the Rawlings job?'

'Each of us?'

'Each—if you finish on time. How much?'

'Forty-eight hundred dollars.'

Cargill sipped the water. 'And how much will you make each, if you blow the deadline?'

'At worst?—Nothing.'

Cargill handed Kozicki the water. 'All right, here's the deal. I'll give you your couple of weeks. I'll go to bat for you with the executive. If you finish on time, the union gets twenty-five percent of the crew's earnings. How many workers you got—eight? At twelve hundred bucks apiece, that's—what?' Cargill rolled his eyes to the ceiling, figuring. 'That's ninety-six hundred bucks. Let's make it an even ten thousand.'

'Let's make it ninety-six.'

'Surely the foreman can kick in some extra.'

Kozicki sat for a while. 'How do you define extortion?' he asked.

'Dictionary stuff doesn't interest me, brother.'

'What if we turn down your offer? What if I was to tell you to go have a heart attack? What if I was to *help* you have a heart attack?'

'You wouldn't do that, brother, and you know it. And if you refuse, I won't go to bat for you with the executive. Then you and your crew can turn in your cards and look for work in the want ads.'

Kozicki stared at him. 'You'd do that?'

'It's solidarity forever, brother. You know that.'

Kozicki pondered. 'That's some deal.'

'That's the package.'

'You should be on the bargaining team.'

'They don't need me.' Cargill stretched. 'As a matter of fact, the bargaining team has negotiated a package all their own with management. They're ready to bring it to the membership for ratification.' He smiled into Kozicki's startled face. 'If you'd attend a few union meetings, brother, or take your regular turn on the picket line, you'd know that already. We vote on it a week from next Tuesday, but that's just to rubber-stamp it. It's a done deal. Think of it: two weeks from Wednesday all the brothers and sisters will be back at work. So you've still got what?—thirteen, fourteen more days?'

Kozicki hugged his steering wheel and watched the Rawlings job drift away. One minute it was anchored to his front bumper, the next it was floating among mare's tails somewhere above the trees. 'Why didn't you show your face a little sooner?' he asked Cargill. He wished Cargill would turn purple again so he could tighten the fat bugger's belt and zip his fly up to his Adam's apple. 'Why did you wait so long?'

'I had to be sure,' Cargill said. 'I had to give you a chance.'

'What for?'

'Hey,' Cargill said. 'Do you think I call you brother for nothing?'

Re-raking the water-clotted soil in front of Rawlings's house, Anna blamed the three-day rainstorm. That was it. The rain, the weather. Kozicki called it the Big Piss and it certainly had been. Piss, piss.

Since the storm the image of Trischuk's daughter followed her. Anna even knew the girl's name: Alice. Clumsy Alice. Hopeful Alice. Alice who wanted to be a figure skater but whose feet were size nines although she was only thirteen. Trischuk called her Snowshoes. He didn't see, *couldn't* see, what Anna had seen that day in the mall.

Alice was Auntie May. Trischuk and his wife had produced an Auntie May!

If there is no justice out here, Anna thought, how will I find it in law school?

She wished the job would end. She was tired. Tired of getting up at four o'clock every morning, tired of thinking cars were following her, tired of expecting Alex to knock on her door at any moment. Kozicki had said Alex had gone to the greenhouse—so where was he? She was tired, tired. Tired perhaps even of Trischuk, now that she knew his Alices were Auntie Mays. She needed time to think.

There were moments when she wanted to open Kozicki's tool-box lid and cross all the days off the calendar, she was that tired. Everybody seemed tired—as if Corny's fall had pulled them all down.

Someone ran up to her carrying a shovel. It was Lannie. He smiled and nodded, and then without warning dropped his shovel and waltzed her around in a circle.

'What is it?' she laughed. 'What's the matter?'

But he spun her a few more times, then picked up his shovel and was gone.

'Woof,' he called over his shoulder. 'Woof, woof.'

Lately Lannie noticed that his sense of smell was getting keener. If smells were food he had landed face first in a smorgasbord. Every-where odours assaulted him; scents that had hitherto sidled shyly up

137

to his olfactories and tapped on the window now stormed up the sidewalk and kicked down the door. Aromas charged his nostrils like spear-waving Zulus. A simple fragrance, like a shovelful of loam, slashed at his senses like fresh-cut onions. The plants Mr. Bistritz delivered in his van reeked of rainforest and marshland, a rich funk that catapulted Lannie right back to the muskeg where Kozicki's dog Churchill had yipped after invisible whirring grouse. On that occasion Kozicki had flipped through his dictionary to find—what was the word?—*fecund*. '*Fecund*,' Kozicki read. '*Fertile*.' Lannie wasn't sure *he* was fecund, but his nose sure was; it gave birth to a new smell every time he turned around. Spilled coffee, rain, dog poop, cheese on a bun, vinegar, living leaves, dead leaves, beer—there was no end to the smells. But that wasn't all. He could smell *everything*. Fear, love, hate, greed, truth—*everything*. Oh, at times the aromas jumbled together, like a train hitting a perfumery, but if one strong odour was there, he'd sniff it out.

One strong odour was guilt. Phew-wee! A clammy, acrid stench, like old gym socks on a radiator, limburger cheese in a can. That smell really went after people. It clung to Dominico, tried to flatten his straw hat and pull his arse closer to the ground. It tugged Ironeagle's sagging face—already gravity's triumph—closer to the centre of the earth, and spiked his sweat with beer foam and cheap whiskey. Guilt formed a cloud around Anna and Trischuk; where Lannie used to smell on them the sweet musk of joyful humping, now he caught whiffs of regret and horny despair. Guilt slowed Paterson's pen to a walk; his daily entries included the date and snatches of verse that began "Do not go gentle . . ." and "Death be not proud . . ." Guilt—and something else—wiped the smile from Kozicki's face and hauled his jokes off to the gallows.

'Did you get in to see Corny?' Paterson asked Kozicki one morning.

'I poked my head in the door,' Kozicki said. 'The nurse said only relatives, but Marion let me in.'

'How is he?'

'Conscious. Asked me where his friggin TV was.'

'How's he look?

'Like a goddamn mummy. They got him plaster-casted from his neck to his ankles. He can move his arms okay, but he's still hasn't got much feeling in his legs. His feet look like a couple of pork chops. I bet they've never been that clean since he was in the cradle. His wife sits by his bed, reading legal books. She says it's nothing personal, but she's going to sue the pants off everybody.'

'Can she *do* that?'

'She can do it, but I don't know how serious she is. I told her, "Marion, you sue the pants off us and that's what you'll get — pants. None of us has got any money." She says, "Rawlings has got money."'

'What does Corny say?'

'Corny says the accident was his own friggin fault. He says he'll take it to the Workers' Compensation Board.'

'Would he have a chance for a settlement?'

Kozicki shook his head. 'Does a snowball freeze in hell?'

'That Corny Ferg,' Dominico put in. 'Mike, you asay Corny he want a TV. I'm gonna get for him a biga TV.'

'He's already got one,' Kozicki said. 'I rented him one last night. Otherwise he would've got up and kicked me.'

'Whena they gonna let us asee that Corny Ferg?'

'In a day or two, I guess.' Kozicki was kneading his groin, and Lannie could smell something new in the air. He lifted his head and sniffed: fear. Fear slumped in the air over Kozicki's head like doo-doo weighting a baby's diaper. Lannie recognized that aroma; simultaneously sharp and stagnant, chemical and rotted, it was the same smell that permeated the Eastview Centre for the Emotionally Disturbed. Liquid cleansers and dust, medication and mildew. People like Tall Bennie lost themselves in such redolence and wound up in Ward Six, as vacant as yoghurt, nodding at the cinder blocks. Just thinking of the centre gave Lannie the shivers, and he recalled with explosive clarity the Man With the Great Big Gun. Who else but the Man With the Great Big Gun had shoved Corny Fergus into a swan-dive with the ground? And who else but the Man With the Great Big Gun would have alerted Cargill to what the crew was up to, and exacted a promise for twenty-five per cent of their earnings and the possibility of being thrown out of the union, if not some spittle-lipped psycho who got his jollies at gun point? When Kozicki told the crew about his run-in with the picket captain, Lannie's nose floundered under waves of anger and frustration. Blood was up. Violence was in the air.

'Goddamn Cargill,' Trischuk said. 'How do we know we can trust him?'

Kozicki shook his head. 'We don't. But we're in it now. There's no going back.'

'Back to where?' Trischuk snarled. 'We got nothing to go back to.'

'That's what I'm saying.'

'So what the hell are we suppposed to do?'

'Work.'

For a while Lannie feared the crew would rip the throat out of Cargill, Kozicki, or anybody they could sink their teeth into.

But they stopped themselves. Because behind everything, like a skunk under the porch, Time waited. Each day Rawlings's deadline loomed closer—seven days, six, five, four . . . a countdown, a tick-ticking.

Once on a school visit to a museum when he was twelve, Lannie had wandered away from his class into a workroom where, amid piled crates and iron shelving, he discovered an elaborate eighteenth century gizmo whose system of springs, cogs and wheels inexorably propelled a clutch of lead balls up ladders, along trestles and down chutes. Since no one was around, Lannie poked a curious finger into the mechanical workings. Levers shot across the floor, lead balls clogged flywheels and coiled springs fired delicate brasswork all over the floor. 'Hey!' a man yelled behind him as he took off. 'What the hell have you done to that *clock*?' Lannie had sprinted, convinced that his pursuit, like the clock, like his father's criticism, would be perpetual. Even on the bus home he'd watched for a crazed Father Time who would scythe him off at the knees. Pile fear on guilt and screw the concoction down with time and Lannie figured the safest place for him right now might be back in his old ward, where he could flatten himself against a wall and live out his life as a starfish.

But in the midst of his agitation, Kozicki was saying, '. . . can do it, if we bust our humps. We might have to work around the clock, that's all.'

'In the *dark*?' Trischuk asked.

'I was thinking of lights.'

'What about the sod?' Trischuk pressed. 'We'll need delivery for that. We've got nearly an acre to turf—what if we run out in the middle of the night?'

'We'll get the sod dumped in one load.'

Dominico tugged at his pants as if the prospect of laying sixteen tons of lawn turf for several nights running had opened up new vistas of adventure. 'Sure, you takea the sod from the truck and you put awater on it, keep it afresh, keep it anice. The sod, she don' gonna die for you.'

'You still gotta fix them stones Corny broke,' Ironeagle reminded him. 'The speed you work, that job'll keep you busy, eh. Could be you'll help us haul that wet sod sometime, eh. About Thanksgiving, I guess.'

'Sure, yah, big ajoke, Thanksagive. Whaddayou think? That job with astone takea maybe one, one and a half days, that's it. Finito. After a that, I'm alay the sod, alay the sod, you don' gonna see my hands amove, I'm ajust alike a machine.' Robotlike, Dominico carried and flung invisible strips of sod in front of him. 'A binga, bing! That's it. Finito.'

'Speaking of finito,' Anna said—and to Lannie Anna looked *finito* herself, paler than usual, as though she'd been dipped in bleach, 'when is it they vote for the union package, Mike?'

'Tuesday,' Kozicki said.

'That's September first.' She looked around, as if remembering herself, then smiled sheepishly. 'Of course, we all knew that already, didn't we?'

Kozicki rumpled her hair. 'Yeah, we did.'

Paterson cleared his throat.

I was ever a fighter, so—one fight more,
    The best and the last!
I would hate that death bandaged my eyes, and forebore,
    And bade me creep past.

'What the hell's that?' Trischuk asked.

'Robert Browning.'

'I mean what the hell does it *mean?*'

'It means—Get Pumped, I suppose.'

'But he's talking about *death*,' Anna said.

'Morte.' Dominico crossed himself. 'No morte, holy cow.'

Paterson blushed. 'Maybe he meant it as a metaphor.'

'What's a metaphor for, anyways?' Ironeagle wondered.

'You guys—' Kozicki said.

Lannie listened to them argue. An enormous balloon inflated his chest. He might've been mistaken, but he believed the balloon was filling with all the scents he'd ever taken in through his nostrils; his chest was loaded with trees and flowers and the crew and the Eastview Centre; it swelled with deadlines and clocks and Rawlings's cameras mounted on poles; it expanded with the dogs at the Burdock Experimental Station and Corny Fergus in his hospital bed; it stretched around Paterson's Browning's poetry; it strained at the seams at the thought of the Man With the Great Big Gun. His chest was the size of a ship's spinnaker, as lung-ed as a breaching whale. If he didn't let some air out soon he would burst; he had, he realized, deadlines of his own.

'RALPH!' he barked, and plunged his shovel into the soil.

The crew shut up.

'That's what I been saying,' Kozicki agreed. 'Let's get back to work.'

At his library console, Clarence Rawlings idly switched from one camera monitor to another and wondered if his program of so-called relaxation wasn't in fact boring him to death. Business had taken him out of the country in recent weeks, and before his return he'd gotten Andrews to have the tedium of the crew's activities edited into a more streamlined package. At one of his television stations Sanders, the manager, claimed to have hired a girl-wonder in the editing department, a skilled technician who, Sanders said, could make drying paint sensational news. Rawlings didn't know if the girl-wonder had a hand in editing the tape he was watching; but if she had, she'd failed.

Hours and hours of drudgery. He thanked God for the turns his own life had taken.

Which reminded him: he'd told Claymore in publishing to put out feelers for ghost-writers. Someone professional, someone who could deliver on time—someone like the guy who did Coletti's bio, or the Kaufmans'. On the plane back from Japan, Rawlings had doodled with titles: *Dame Fortune and Me; Accruing Interest*. Well. A writer would be able to come up with something snappier.

Whatever its title, his life story would sell. Not because he was immoral, eccentric or artistic, but because he was rich. He was successful. People liked to read about a successful person, especially when they weren't successsful themselves. They wanted to know his secret. They wanted him to distill his life into a single aphorism that they could use to inspire their own ambition and success. What would that aphorism be? Clarence Rawlings glanced at the bank of monitors. Some showed live action, others played recorded scenes. On one screen the big-nosed worker in the hard hat lay at the bottom of a ladder. Look at *the time* the crew wasted after he'd fallen! Two people

142

helping the man, and the other five *standing around!* Looking worried. Looking concerned. He could appreciate their feelings, but if there was one thing he understood that they didn't, if there was a maxim that had garnered him millions and held money forever out of their reach, it was this: in matters of business, nothing is personal. Don't take business personally. Just *get on with it.*

But they hadn't got on with it. Not them. They'd waited for the ambulance, a sentimental tableau that reminded Rawlings of the day his ex-wife, surrounded by their grown-up children, announced that she was leaving. Thirty years congenial, on the day of youngest son Peter's birthday Lillian proclaimed her unhappiness, her sugary manifesto on the sanctity of family and hearth, and ran away with a dentist. Once in an interview, a journalist had hit upon this sore point, and asked Clarence Rawlings if the divorce had affected his relationship with his children. 'I'm their father,' Rawlings said. 'They can come to me for anything except money. I believe my children should earn their own way, like everybody else.' His children did not visit him at all now, so apparently they were doing well. They were getting on with it. Fantastic.

Casually, Rawlings switched on camera five. The foreman Korchinsky and the silent, curly-haired boy were unloading flats of white flowers from the back of a white van whose driver wore tight white pants and a bouffant hairstyle reminiscent of certain Vegas showgirls who had been offered to Rawlings from time to time—and declined. The three seemed to be talking, and not for the first time did Rawlings find his mind wandering. In a way he envied the gardeners. At least with this job they had a deadline to meet, and could actively pursue it. For his own part, the deadline was a dormant issue, an investment waiting for a date of maturity; a bond.

The foreman was leaning close to the curly-haired boy—having to repeat already oversimplied instructions, no doubt.

The telephone rang. He'd told Andrews to let the private calls through. There was no advantage to isolation.

It was Bob Harkness, one of the in-house lawyers.

'Two items, Clarence. One, an update on Payless Foods.'

'Yes?'

'Inquiry completed. Roof collapse liability of architect and engineer. They're represented by Berger and Reece, so all queries and correspondence goes to them. We're out from under Payless Foods. That's a pun.'

'And number two?'

'Second item, Mrs. Marion Fergus.'

'Don't know her.'

'Wife of the gardener who took a header off your balcony.'

'Yes.'

'She's filing a lawsuit.'

'Against my balcony?'

'Against the property owner. If you recall, I was going to direct her to the foreman, but he's only the subcontractor.'

'Korchinski?'

'Kozicki.'

'Pardon?'

'The foreman's name is Kozicki, Clarence.'

'Are you sure?'

'I've got the woman's letter in front of me now. Kozicki.' Harkness waited. 'Clarence?'

'Oh. Yes.'

'We could drag in the foreman, and possibly even Dreedle, and stall until the Workers' Compensation Board kicks it around. There's the union, too.'

'But?'

'Too messy.'

'What do you suggest?'

'We settle out of court.'

'Who's her representative?'

'Legal Aid.'

'Fantastic.'

'I've contacted them. Lawyer's a kid fresh out of the blocks. She's eager, but her caseload's left her a little breathless. I think we can settle. Got a figure in mind?'

'Whatever's the going rate,' Rawlings said. 'Are you *sure* it's Kozicki, Bob?'

'I'm sure, but I can double-check.'

'Do that. And Bob?'

'Yes.'

'Find out if he has a daughter.'

'Right.'

For the life of him, Kozicki couldn't understand why he hadn't hit on the idea of night lights long before this. What had he been thinking of? Where was he living—on the moon? Technology goes to the trouble of developing this stuff, it surrounds you like a baby's blanket, and you don't *use* it? What was this, for crying out loud—the old days?

Kozicki had fairly vivid memories of the old days—clearer, in fact, than those of his more recent experiences. Ask him how many times his remorseless bladder propelled him to the john last night or how many cups of tea he'd drunk at breakfast, and he'd be hard-pressed to tell you; but query him on the time of his wife's death or the face of his father sightlessly gazing at the city morgue's ceiling, and he could deal out a whole deck of verbal snapshots that caught the curve of Emily's brow, the prominence of his father's deathly beak, the grey light seeping through the windows. Lately Kozicki had become long on reminiscence and short on memory. Even now, driving through cleanly scrubbed suburbs, he had to ask Paterson, "What the hell did Bistritz say that address was again?'

'Thirty-seven Dominion Crescent.'

'Dominion Drive?'

'*Crescent.*'

'Jeez.'

He hated the suburbs. He hated wasting time like this. He hated the deadline, Cargill, Rawlings, Corny Fergus's cast, his own bladder. He hated Dominico's long face, Ironeagle's long face, Anna's long face, Trischuk's long face. He couldn't keep up with them. One day they were up, the next down; you'd think somebody beat them every night, tickled them every morning and stretched their goddamn jawbones in between. Of course, was he any better himself? Yo-yoing through his list of burdens, like a bigshot running his finger down a restaurant menu. Let's see, what'll I have? A little deadline? A little gland trouble? A bowl of union executive? Million-aire on toast? Daughter-in-a-glass? Self-pity on a goddamn shingle?

'Thirty-five?'

'Thirty-seven.'

'Okay, this is it.'

They parked the truck in the driveway. Sylvia was a narrow woman in a man's shirt and blue jeans who strode hiplessly out of the house, lifted the overhead garage door, and peppered them with questions. 'You're Mike? And Paterson? I'm Sylvia? Well you should be careful with these, not that they're fragile but they're halogen? Nigel built these crates for them so they could be transported? And these are the poles, they fit the stands like this? And the power bar? And Bisty didn't say, but I assume you'll want the generator? In case you're a long way from a power source? We didn't use it with the *Pirandello*, but it worked okay with the *Pinter in the Park*? We do the P plays in the Park, you know? *Poe in the Park*? *Pushkin in the Park*? Maybe you've seen them? Anyway, you can bring back the lights on the fourth, Nigel has a children's folkie thing the week after—a birthday party?'

'Do you want me to pay you now?'

'If you don't mind?'

'Sure.'

Kozicki wrote her a cheque. Back in the truck, Paterson asked him if this Rawlings job was the best one he'd ever had.

'Are you kidding?'

'Okay," Paterson said, 'maybe not the best, but the most lucrative.'

'That depends.'

'On what?'

'On what you mean by lucrative.'

Paterson laughed. 'You know what lucrative means.'

'Not in this day and age I don't.'

'In what day and age did you know it?'

'I don't know.' Kozicki speculated as he drove. 'Maybe never. Maybe when I was young.'

'What was your first *lucrative* job?' Paterson persisted.

Kozicki frowned. 'Why do you want to know that?'

'Because this is mine.' Paterson studied his hands. He wasn't writing anything down, Kozicki noticed. 'Come on, Mike. What was it?'

Kozicki pondered. Written, his work history would read like a petty thief's convictions, a record as long as an arm. A catalogue of day-labour vocations, part-time, full-time, inside the weekly forty-hour ballpark or outside the fence where bosses threw safety and minimum wages into the weeds. Kozicki hadn't worked at everything, but had managed the patchwork earnings of a born scrambler. He'd sandblasted bridges and planted barley, pulled cows' teats and driven nails, delivered lambs, pizzas and once, false teeth. Gandy-danced on the C.P.R. and fried fish in a roadside eatery. Cut trees, pigs' nuts and longstemmed roses, established a name as a solid if unskilled worker who ate big and shovelled hard, another fella who'd jacked all trades and mastered none.

'My first real job was at a lumber camp in B.C. in 1935.'

He was fourteen then, and if he did not tell Paterson all the facts, he at least let the young fella catch his drift. Kozicki's daddy lay as dead as cold cuts on the mortician's slab, a death no one was fingered for, no one charged or convicted because Kozicki the tailor had passed on during an unlawful gathering, booted into eternity by a Mountie's horse. You couldn't say it was the Mountie's fault, but what galled Kozicki was his daddy's death didn't even make the papers. In fact, twelve stiffs lay in the funeral parlour after the Market Square riot, but the newspapers reported only one, a city detective the Mounties accidently plugged during the excitement. Not even an obituary to mark Kozicki the tailor's passing. Kozicki had taken one look at his daddy's nose, fleshless in death, meatless as an axeblade, borrowed the dead man's shoes and walked out of there. He headed straight for the railyard. But it turned out he had to wait a couple of days during which he tried to comfort his mother who sold the sewing machine to pay for the funeral and who asked, with Welsh curiosity, what would happen to them now? She packed him bread and cold potatoes and filled a mason jar with water, and with that he rode a boxcar from Saskatchewan clear out to the Pacific Ocean, once catching a face full of cinders in a tunnel through the Rogers Pass. In Vancouver he bunked in a railroad shed, then shipped north with men who called themselves loggers, holey-shoed prairie dogs like himself, eager to cut the big trees and eat three meals a day.

'The first year I skidded out logs with a team of horses and the snow was up to my armpits which didn't please me at all. Towards the end a horse squashed my knee against a tree and I was lucky to walk out of there. The second year I worked as a flunkey for the cook, washing dishes and setting tables. We ate like kings: barrels of soft-boiled eggs and sausages stacked like cordwood; pancakes the size of manhole covers. Enough syrup to float the *Queen Mary*. But no toast. We didn't make toast—no time to watch it. I got the same pay as the outside workers, but nobody wanted my job. They were smart, those outside guys. They quit work when it got dark while I did the dishes and set tables until ten-thirty or even midnight. Then I got smart, too. I swiped sausages, biscuits, Spanish onions and went around to the card games after hours. "You want a wiener?—Two bits." I made all the spending money I needed. Sent the paycheque home to my mother.'

Kozicki grinned as he drove, retrospection the universal relaxant. 'I thought I'd forgotten all this stuff,' he said.

'What else?'

'One night I got scared and told the cook what I was doing. He said to hell with it—the company paid for it all anyway. He whipped up a batch of molasses, yeast and brown sugar, boiled it for two weeks and when it was clear we siphoned it off and called it Brown Alcohol. "Want some Brown Alcohol?—Fifty cents." The loggers had their own bottles. Potent stuff—put hair on your *teeth*.'

'So you were at it even then.'

Kozicki started. 'At what?'

'Well, you know. Unofficial overtime work.'

'Yeah. Yeah, I guess I was. Above and beyond the call of duty.' Though in truth he'd never thought of it that way before. Whizzing through traffic and short-cutting back to Rawlings's place along the circle road, he took a few quick bearings and figured that he might be right back where he started. His work life—all the jobs, the overtime, back pay, holiday pay, deductions, bonuses, lay-offs, re-hirings—all of it, was funnelled into this moment when he and a kid zipped along an intracity truck route carrying halogen bulbs as big as tubas so they could cheat daylight, beat back darkness, grab just a little more. A little more, a little more—jeez, they might as well be peddlers of Brown Alcohol, hustling that extra buck while normal people—now, late in the afternoon—headed home for the newspaper and slippers, the kids and the dog tearing each other apart in the back yard. As he turned off into the leafy avenues of Riversdale, he saw a young couple walking arm and arm under the trees, like lovesick doves on a movie marquee, and he suddenly remembered his daughter with her Peter Plants, the two of them probably headed west right now. And what about Charlene? And the Incas? Possibilities beckoned him like a woman in a window. Fatigue crept up his arms and bunched his shoulders. A guy needed a break. Would he be ready? Would the job be finished, the strike over? Maybe he'd clean the sand out of his fishing reel. He saw himself landing lake trout the size of Volkswagens.

'Hey,' Paterson pointed. 'Isn't that Cargill?'

The picket captain's truck was parked to one side of Rawlings's wrought iron gates. Porcine and doughty, Cargill stood next to his vehicle, a referee waiting for the game to start. To Kozicki, the man appeared to have more colours in his face than a paint store, more cords on his neck than Houdini.

Paterson turned to his foreman. 'What do you suppose he wants?'

'*Pinder in the Park*,' Kozicki said.

'Pinter.'

'Who?'

'Pinter.'

'Yeah.'

Cargill carried a manilla envelope that he held out like a subpoena. 'I have a letter for you from the executive, brother.'

Kozicki kept his hands in his pockets. 'I'm not too good with letters.'

'The executive wants you to read it.'

'Haven't you read it already?'

'Yes.'

'So tell me what's in it.'

'I'm not supposed to tell you what's in it. You're supposed to read it, see what's in it, and then tell me if you understand what's in it.'

'Did they write it in *English*?'

Cargill's face throbbed as he thrust the envelope into Kozicki's chest. 'Read the damn letter.'

Kozicki read the letter. Twice.

'Do you understand it?' Cargill asked. 'Do you have any questions?'

'I wonder,' Kozicki ventured. 'Do they want my balls in a pickle jar, or will they take them as is?'

'That's not funny, brother.'

'You're not kidding.'

'They could've come down harder.'

'How?' Kozicki said. 'Firing squad?'

'You're not taking this well.'

'I'm not taking it *at all*. Jeez, Cargill, you said you'd go to bat for us. What happened?'

'They started throwing fastballs.'

'Didn't you ever hear of *bunting*?' Kozicki paced up and down.

He hooked his hand into his pants, like someone who's eaten too many green apples. From inside the truck Paterson watched apprehensively. Kozicki went on: 'We got less than forty-eight hours to finish this job. A sixteen-ton flatbed of lawn sod is coming in any minute.'

Cargill coughed. 'It already came in.'

'What?'

'The truckload of sod. It's in.'

'Wonderful. Great. It's in. And I've got floodlights ready to go and you come at me with this shit.' He waved the letter at Cargill.

'What is it?' Paterson got out of the truck. 'What's it say?'

'It says shit.' Kozicki handed him the letter. 'See? Read it. "Dear Shit: Eat shit, breathe shit, be shit. Shitfully yours, Shit."'

'So I can assume you understand the letter?' Cargill remained stoutly on his big legs, but had backed off a little, as if now that he'd heard the dog bark, the next thing to do was wait for the bite.

'I understand the letter, sure I understand the letter,' Kozicki fumed. 'What I can't understand is you. I don't understand the union. I been in unions most of my life, and I thought I understood them, but I don't.'

'They're ordering us to quit right now,' Paterson said. 'Today. Immediately.'

Cargill pushed his back against his truck. 'That's right, today. Why not today?' He opened the palms of his hands to them, like a fugitive showing the cops he has no gun. 'You don't get it, brothers, do you? You honestly don't get it. Oh—' He shrugged and rolled his eyes. '—you'll take the wage hikes that the union wins for you, you'll grab the benefit packages when the shooting's over, you'll pat each other on the back when somebody else gets you a forty-hour week, but when your union needs you, brothers, *you won't go to the fucking wall.* Do you think strikes and negotiations are penny-ante stuff? Do you think the union's some kind of handball club, some kind of steambath you can drop in on any time you feel like working up a little sweat? Brothers, do you think the union's *a fucking country club?* Well I've got a news flash for you, a weather report. *The union is your life, brothers. It's your sunshine, it's your rain.* Without the union, you've got nothing. If you're not for the union, you're against it. *That's* what this letter is saying: make a choice—the union, or nothing. You're lost sheep, brothers. Come back to the fold. Come back to the fold, or *get fucked.*'

Cargill was panting. From a vial in his shirt pocket he withdrew a capsule and placed it under his tongue.

'You okay?' Kozicki asked.

'I'm perfect,' Cargill gasped. 'I'm great.' He closed his eyes for a minute, like a Tibetan monk grabbing some meditative shut-eye. Calmer—calmed—he opened his eyes. 'You've got to choose, brothers. Either you're in or you're out.'

'The job's not finished.' Kozicki said. 'We got two days left.'

'Tough shit.'

'I helped you,' Kozicki pointed out. 'That day at the hospital.'

Cargill patted his shirt pocket. 'I got pills now.'

'You're telling my guys they've worked eight weeks here for nothing.'

'I'm not telling them that.' Cargill climbed back into his truck. 'You are. You're telling them. If they finish this job, they're finished. It's up to them. You can also tell them that I'll be waiting right out here for their answers.'

The Big Picture, Kozicki thought as he and Paterson drove up Rawlings's curving drive, you got to look at the Big Picture. But the trouble with the Big Picture was, well, it was *big*, and you never really got to see all of it. At times he thought he'd witnessed some large-canvassed events—the Market Square riot, World War II, and thanks to his father, Emily, his friends in the air force, his mother, Churchill and strangers on TV the biggest Big Picture of them all—Death. But what had he actually seen of such things? A corner here, a smear of colour there—what did a guy actually see of life besides a pile of smudged snapshots taken from a moving train? Out of focus, most of them, like the ones Gillian used to send of herself in her school uniform, her face as goofy as Silly Putty, her teeth like a rabbit's, her legs sticking out of her kilt like a lawn flamingo's. What had his job been but to straighten those teeth, pack meat on those legs? Let Churchill hear a gun go off; sit in a chair and look up a big word in a dictionary. These were the things Kozicki had pursued—little details. Cargill was right: he'd never paid attention to the union, never taken it seriously. It was just another big machine that hummed along out there, as dependable as a refrigerator, about as far away as the government. Unions, bosses, if it wasn't one of them ready to jump you through a hoop, it was the other. Kozicki thought of his father, the private enterprise socialist, playing both ends against the middle. Look what happened to him.

He stopped the truck on the driveway near the front of the house. Paterson climbed out, and the rest of the crew silently gathered around. Along the drive the flatbed delivery truck had left a dozen or so wooden pallets, on which lawn turf was stacked four feet high and four feet square—enough sod to build a pioneer village or a good-sized fairway. Already awash at the transom, Kozicki's heart started to ship water along the gunwales.

'Did anybody sign for this load of sod?'

'Rawlings did,' Trischuk said.

'Is he here?'

'He's here, but so what? What've you got for us? Cargill's been parked out at the gates for over an hour. What'd he tell you?'

'Bad news.'

'Hey,' Trischuk said. 'I'm so surprised.'

Kozicki read the letter to them. It was written in the formal style he'd always thought he'd fancied for himself—full of ten-dollar words that made his mouth water just to pronounce them. If language was food, then the union's letter was a seven-course meal, dessert included. He smacked his lips over 'dereliction of union responsibilities and disregard for union principles'; tucked into 'violated the precepts of strike action and collective bargaining'; filled up on 'unethically undermined the solidarity of your union in the eyes of the employer and the membership at large'; and nearly bloated himself with, 'You are hereby instructed to cease and desist non-union employment at this point in time, subject to Section 14, Subsection D of the Constitution of the University Public Employees' Union Local 97, from which organization you and your crew's membership (see attached list) is immediately suspended pending an investigation by the ad hoc Strike Disciplinary Committee, George Cargill, Chairperson.' There was more, but Kozicki handed the letter to Anna, and loosened his belt. You had to hand it to the union executive. When it came to language, their dictionary was right up there with the best of them.

'Heya, Mike,' Dominico scowled. 'Whatsa gonna happen, Dio canne.'

'Yeah.' Ironeagle said. 'What's that mean, anyways?'

Anna held the letter in front of them. 'It means it's over. It means we have to quit working here, right now. If we don't, we risk being kicked out of the union. As it is we're suspended. We won't be able to vote on Tuesday night, and we won't go back to work Wednesday when the contract's ratified—in fact, we might never work at our jobs again. And in the meantime, we go on trial before the union. They don't call it a trial, but that's what it is.' She turned to Kozicki. 'Is that how you read it?'

'You're saying it better than I can.'

'Thatsa bullshit!' Dominico exclaimed. 'We still gotta two adays for dead-aline.' He appealed to the others. 'Two adays, Dio canne! Mike, didn't you told him we got two adays?'

'I told him,' Kozicki said, 'but he's not interested in that.'

'What about the twenty-five per cent we offered them?' Trischuk said.

Kozicki consulted the letter. 'They don't want it.'

'Do they say that?'

'I think they consider it a bribe.'

'They say *that*? A bribe?'

Anna traced the line with her finger. 'They call it "unsolicited remuneration." They seem to think,' she skimmed the letter again, 'that by taking on this job we—how do they put it—"threaten solidarity" and "jeopardize the integrity of the union."'

Trischuk held out his hand. 'Lemme see that.' He perused the letter while Anna read it over his shoulder. 'They got us screwed six ways,' Trischuk decided.

'Well, I haven't counted them all up,' Kozicki said.

'But what's this other stuff in here about the new contract?' Trischuk lifted his head. 'You never said anything about this stuff.'

'It's not a new contract yet.'

'But it probably will be.'

'Whadda new contrack?' Dominico asked.

'Probably,' Kozicki said.

'Heya, Mike,' Dominico repeated, 'whadda new contrack?'

The crew waited.

'The one they'll ratify tomorrow night. Look, there's a good chance that once the new contract kicks in there'll be some full-time jobs opening up for seasonals. Dominico, you and me and Corny are in line to work the rinks in the winter. And the word is the union's landed more jobs for snow removal.'

'Is that supposed to cheer us up?' Anna said.

'It cheers *me* up.' Trischuk said. 'I've got kids to raise.'

Ironeagle agreed. 'I guess that wouldn't be so bad, eh—workin full time. A fella wouldn't hafta work so hard lookin for another job.'

The crew held their breaths. 'The question is,' Kozicki said, because he knew they expected to hear it, 'do we want to give up our regular jobs to finish this one?'

Dominico took off his hat and shook his head. 'Porco Madonne, that'sa pretty biga question, Mike.'

'There aren't too many bigger.'

'I don' like thisa biga question.'

'It's the only one we've got.'

'Maybe it isn't.' Trischuk said slowly.

'How do you mean?'

'Today's Monday. Tomorrow's the first. If we go by the union, we can't work from Monday to Friday, is that right?'

'That's right.'

'But we *can* work weekends.' Trischuk looked around at the crew. 'Well, can't we?'

Kozicki nodded. 'The union can't tell you how to spend your weekends.'

'So,' Trischuk said. 'We'll finish it on the weekend.'

'But,' Anna reminded him, 'we'll be over the deadline.'

'I know that. Say we finish next Sunday night. From Tuesday midnight to Sunday midnight: how many days over the deadline is that?'

Dominico counted on his fingers. 'Five adays.'

'Five days,' Trischuk said. 'Then we'd lose five weeks' pay.'

Paterson scribbled some figures in his notebook. 'We'd lose three thousand dollars each.'

'Dio canne!' Dominico said. 'How mucha money we gonna make, Patersoni?'

'Eighteen hundred each.'

'Eighteen hundred dollars,' Trischuk said, nodding to Kozicki. 'Maybe *that's* the question. Do we want to've worked sixteen hours a day for sixty days for eighteen hundred dollars?'

Ironeagle dug his toe into the ground. 'Eighteen hundred dollars is a lot more than nothin.'

'On the other hand,' Anna pointed out, 'what if we do finish the job on Sunday, and find out we're out of the union anyway? I for one need this job for next year, but I'm not sure I want to give up three thousand dollars, either.'

They were worried and who could blame them? In hard times a worker should no more throw away a job than an Eskimo a parka. It was a cold world out there. In the past Kozicki had walked down to the day labour exchange every morning—*walked*, to save the dime on the bus fare—on the off-chance he'd get an afternoon unloading pig iron from a boxcar. Security?—He couldn't have spelled the word. All he'd thought of in those days was new shoes for his kid and enough money so Emily could buy a can of Spam that she could drench in melted brown sugar. Jeez, what was the matter with his head? He'd racked up nineteen solid years with the union, rode it smooth and rode it bony, his longest stint of employment in a lifetime of work and, though there'd been lean times, there'd been fat ones, too. He could remember raises of seventeen per cent; five-day work weeks and guaranteed coffee breaks. For nineteen years he woke up every morning knowing exactly where he had to be and how much he'd get paid for being there. He'd picked up his paycheque on the middle and last day of every month. When Emily was sick the union helped him get compassionate leave, and when the job was unsafe his shop steward handed him a hard hat and gloves. The union was like a hammock from the first day on the job to the gold watch at the retirement dinner. It was the safety net he would've given his right leg for during the war when he'd flown terrified over Berlin with the knowledge that when the bottom dropped out of *that* job there was no where to go but down. The union was a quilt, roast chicken, new shingles on the roof. So why was he gawking at piles of lawn turf on their pallets, why was he surveying the acre or so of naked topsoil that fell away from Rawlings's house, waiting to be fertilized and sodded so that it wouldn't look like the Sahara? Why—during the twenty minutes his crew procrastinated and argued and finally agreed that they would swallow the three thousand dollar loss and finish the job on the weekend—did it seem like a crime to see a job go unfinished? Why, after they left, did he stand there like a wino outside a liquor store trying to figure another angle? What was wrong with him anyhow?

'Maybe you're ambitious,' Clarence D. Rawlings suggested. 'And I don't mean that in a pejorative sense.'

'In a what sense?'

'As an insult.'

'Jeez, that's the way I took it.'

'Perhaps *ambitious* is too strong. *Conscientious* might be better.'

'I got a dictionary in my back pocket,' Kozicki said. 'In case you run out.'

Over his glass Rawlings squinted at Kozicki. Kozicki, Kozicki: that was the name, all right. And if Bob Harkness was correct, Clarence Rawlings was sitting opposite the father of the girl who'd stolen Peter's heart. *Stolen* was right. In matters of sentiment, his youngest son was a full wallet in a den of thieves. The boy was like his mother, a soft-headed, weepy sort of woman whom Rawlings had divorced as soon as the children were grown. His son Peter reminded Clarence Rawlings of the septuagenerian American tourist he'd once observed in—where was it—New Delhi? A sweet, homemade-cookie-faced old duck who arrived at the hotel via a taxi from the airport. In paying the turbaned cabbie and the scimitared doorman, the old woman pulled out a wad of Indian banknotes and asked querulously, 'Twenty rupees, how much is that? Are they the orange ones?' The two men plucked several bills from her hand like a magician's audience choosing cards. The old lady had been ripped off and, if Clarence Rawlings was any judge, his son would be too. But just as Rawlings hadn't intervened with the old lady, he would keep his nose out of Peter's romances. Let the boy learn.

Let this Kozicki learn as well. Look at the man—played it dumb. Insisted on removing his boots at the door. Padded into the library in his sock feet as if the place were a cathedral or a museum. Refused twelve-year-old Scotch and settled for a beer Andrews had to retrieve from the kitchen. Splayed himself out in the wing chair as if he were exhausted. Any minute now he would begin his excuses, possibly plead for mercy, an extension to the deadline, payment for work done—something. All the while keeping his trump card up his sleeve, waiting for the right moment when he could lean forward with his common-man elbows on his common-man knees and say, like an old neighbour who'd just dropped in for a chat, *Oh by the way, I hear our two kids are in love or something, isn't that a kicker? Yeah, you could've knocked me over with a feather. I hear they're both coming out here to pay you a visit, Clarence—you don't mind if I call you Clarence?—so I guess we'll have to have a little get-together, huh? And say—it's kind of embarrassing not to've finished on time, so what do you say—*

And here it came:

'You gotta understand,' Kozicki was saying. 'Most of them have got families, and if they don't, they got big plans. The woman, for instance, needs a summer job for the next four years—she's putting herself through law school. There's a young fella wants to be a writer—wants to go off to someplace cheap. Dominico's got a house and a car to pay for. There's a boxer who hasn't seen a regular pay-cheque since he quit the ring. What I mean is we all need the money, so it's only natural we'd go along with the union. It's safer in the long run.' Kozicki sipped his beer.

Rawlings smiled. If a biographer ever asked him what was the easiest part of transacting business, he'd have one answer: human predictability. He watched Kozicki unblinkingly. 'She won't make any difference, you know.'

The man did a good job of appearing startled. 'Who?'

'Your daughter.'

'Gillian?' Kozicki put down his beer.

'Your daughter and my son.'

'Your *son?*'

'Peter, my son. He attends the University of Toronto.'

'Peter Plants is *your son?*'

'His name is Peter Rawlings, and he's not in line for any inheritance or age-of-majority payoff or anything like that. My children earn their own way.'

But Kozicki was laughing, head flung back, strong teeth bared. 'Your son,' he spluttered, 'is *Peter Plants?*' He guffawed, wheezed, slapped his knees and broke into a paroxysm of coughing. At length he sagged back in his chair and wiped his eyes. 'Peter Plants! I'm sorry, but you got to admit it's funny.'

'Yes.' Rawlings remained calm. 'You must've split your sides the first time you heard it.'

'I *did*,' Kozicki chuckled. 'This *is* the first time I've heard it.'

'I'm sure.'

'It *is*.' Kozicki's face sobered: really, Rawlings thought, the man was fantastic, the way he could switch from one transparent pretence to another. Now the gardener was doing *realization dawning*, an expression Rawlings had learned to appreciate in certain business associates who weren't too proud to flatter. Kozicki had the look almost down pat: if the gardener's head had been a building, Rawlings could have sworn he saw a caretaker running upstairs to turn the lights on.

'Hey,' Kozicki pointed. 'Hey, you thought I already knew about Gillian and your son, didn't you?'

'Did I say that?'

'For crying out loud.' Kozicki shook his head. He paused. 'You're a real curveball, you know that?' He spoke quietly. 'I can't catch you coming or going. You've got more tunes than a goddamn jukebox.'

'I believe I commented on your swearing in my house before, Mike.'

'I believe you did. And I can't tell you how goddamn sorry I am.' Kozicki stood. From where he sat, Rawlings saw plainly the other man's knuckled fingers, the narrow, thick shoulders. Kozicki leaned forward. 'What did you think I was going to do, use my daughter to ask you for an extension? Use her to lever some money out of you?'

'You're the one who came in here with excuses, Mike. You're the one whose crew ran away from the job.'

Kozicki stood in front of Rawlings's desk, his face twisted. Rawlings himself settled back in his chair, stretched his legs and crossed his ankles—his favourite stance in such situations. Give the opponent room to breathe, a chance to collect his wits and review common sense, and he would accept his loss and head for the nearest exit.

Kozicki smiled faintly. 'Okay. All right. You gotta hit me over the head a few times, but I get the idea. I only got one question.'

'What's that?'

'Have you got some place out there where I can plug in an extension cord? I got some lights I want to set up.'

Revenge—number six shot, binoculars, the Remington twelve-gauge—lay under the seat of Berenson's rented Chrysler, which he'd parked in a leafy cul-de-sac not far from the rich man's iron gates through which his wife passed every morning on her bicycle, and through which she reappeared every night. And Mister Muscles. They didn't fool him, even if they rode their bikes yards apart, even if they waved goodbye and cycled in opposite directions. They didn't fool him.

He'd have to get them together. They had to be together. So they'd know, so they'd realize.

Tonight might've been it. But they cycled out of the gates early, stopped at the pick-up truck where a porker eating a bag of doughnuts spoke to them briefly. Then they left. Berenson followed discreetly. When they separated, he followed Mister Muscles, who pulled into a public swimming pool where he met a blonde woman and a couple of kids. So much blondness. Like Swedes.

He circled back to the wrought-iron gates. Beyond the brick wall he could see flickering lights, so perhaps she'd go back to work. But dusk fell, and he saw no sign of her. No sign of anybody. Even Doughnuts was gone.

Anna decided that whatever tied her to Trischuk, it wasn't just her bum. Not just her bum, not just his muscles, and once you took away bums and muscles, what did you have left?—Love, or something like it. She loved him, and he probably loved her, and for that reason the idea of their having a future together was absurd. Because love did not conquer all: love *complicated* all. This revelation struck her now—almost physically, like the bare foot of her karate instructor booting her in the chops. Revelation, enlightenment, self-awareness, love: the ads on TV were right. You could get just about anything from a trip to the mall.

Not that she'd been shopping for those things. Her seeing Trischuk and his family was unintentional—an accident, like stepping off a curb and being mowed down by a firetruck. Little alarms went off inside her, sirens, people screamed from fourth-storey windows. Self-preservation told her to run, but masochistic curiosity kept her there. She'd looked at his wife, but now she realized she'd glimpsed another country whose passport she would never carry. Barren, she was Berlin-Walled off from motherhood, Iron-Curtained from family. She watched Trischuk's arm around his wife's shoulders, his wife's around his. Like buddies on a fishing trip. They weren't merely lovers, he and his wife. They were friends. Trischuk and his wife had done not only what Anna and Trischuk had done, but more. Out of the moans and chuckles, saliva and jism, they'd made two daughters who could Auntie May them together with something as simple as a laugh.

Having a revelation could be lonely sometimes. Once, she'd joined a feminist transcendental meditation group and quit when she wondered why she had to be in a room with only *women* in order to *think*. Now, away from the shopping mall, she could think. *He loves his wife. And his daughters. They love him.* And then: *Daughters! He has daughters!* Women and girls. She imagined him divorced, sending child care payments to his wife—or not sending them, weasling out of the rent money, ducking the purchase of new shoes, figure skating fees. *She was going to law school to protect women against men like him, and*—why stop at one revelation?—*against women like herself!* Because if he had betrayed his wife and daughters—women, Anna's sisters—then she, their sister, had betrayed them too.

'Strong Enough to Stand the Strain,' she told him when his bicycle rolled alongside hers. 'Woman Enough to Bear the Pain.'

'Knock it off.' He pedalled with his head down. 'What's your problem?'

'I've transcended the physical.'

'Whoopee. Where's that leave me?'

'Where you should be.'

'On the ground.'

'I'm sorry.' And, perhaps to her surprise, she really was. 'I'm sorry, Rob. But it's got to stop. It's got to finish.'

'Hey,' he said drily, 'that was my guess, too. I figured it out from the brooding and the silences. Oh—and the no-sex. That's how *I* figured it out. What tipped you off?'

'Don't be angry. The job's over too.'

'We'll be back at work on Wednesday.'

'Not me. I'll be going back to classes.' They pedalled slowly, under listening trees. She thought she heard a car behind them but when she looked she saw only a yellow Chrysler parked on the edge of the street. 'I want to say goodbye, Rob.'

'Sure. So long.'

'Properly.'

'Oh. Goodbye.'

'Please. Meet me at the union meeting.'

'Where?'

'At the Memorial Gym. Then you won't have to tell any lies about where you're going.'

'What's with lies all of a sudden?'

'Meet me.'

'We're suspended. We can't vote.'

'We can listen to the speeches. Or pretend to. Then we can slip out the back, by the greenhouse road. It'll be quiet there.'

They'd reached the corner where he had to turn. He hesitated, wobbled on his bicycle.

'Meet me,' she insisted.

He rode in a circle once, twice. Finally he asked, 'Should I wear clothes?'

She smiled. 'Coveralls,' she said.

Ironeagle couldn't understand why Dominico wanted to take *him*. If the stonemason was going over there, why didn't he take Paterson? After all, Paterson had been up on the balcony, too.

'No job, a no job,' Dominico mourned as he drove. 'Whadda you think, I'm gonna take a skinny bambino likea Patersoni to say to her we gotta no job? Whadda good for is Patersoni? Whad he gonna do, usea hisa notebook for protection me? The wife of a Corny Ferg, she'sa gonna *kill* Patersoni. She'sa gonna kill Patersoni and then, *she's gonna kill me!* But she don' gonna kill a boxer. How's she gonna kill a boxer? A boxer, he'sa gonna move, makea the body likea this, makea the body likea that.' Dominico started to bob and weave behind the wheel; his car bobbed and wove down the street.

'Looks to me like *you're* gonna kill a boxer.' Ironeagle gripped the armrest.

Dominico steadied the wheel. He would have to calm down. He asked himself what Leonardo da Vinci would have done. Well, the Maestro he wouldn't be driving a car, they had no cars in the Maestro's time. And the Maestro wouldn't have had to steal a tiny block of Carrara marble, the Maestro would've had a hundred workmen deliver a block of it to his studio. Maybe the Maestro would've stayed home to sketch. Or, like Patersoni, stayed home to write. Dio canne! The more Dominico thought about the Maestro, the more he saw how different he was from the great man. Would the Maestro have caused a friend to flop like a bird of death on the ground—and on the nose, too? Porco madonne, whad kind of Maestro gonna do a thing likea that?

'What's wrong with you anyways?' Ironeagle had been watching him.

'I think abouta Corny Ferg. Whad he gonna do when hisa legs don' work?'

'Somethin else, I guess.'

'Dio canne.'

They drove for awhile in silence. Then Dominico said: 'My gran'father—you know, gran'father—Babbaluche, he worka the astone. He'sa a bigashot, Babbaluche. When the people wanna know something, they aska Babbaluche. So—sometime when I'ma kid, I do a bad thing. I steal a lamb, justa one. I hide him, makea the food, the water, I make it anice for him. Then onea day, when the lamb he'sa big, I takea the sharp stick and makea the little cut on the neck, justa likea this—' Dominico jabbed his forefinger at his own neck. 'The lamb he'sa get tired, he'sa go to sleep. Finito. He'sa died. I makea the lamb into meat. I don' feel nice, but I makea the meat. Then I puta the meat ina sack and I takea the sack home and I say to momma, "I finda the lamb!" Babbaluche hears this. He sees momma cry and say *grazie* to the Madonne, and Babbaluche say to me, "Dominico, you makea the astone crook.' I say, "Gran'father, I don' makea the astone, I makea the meat." Babbaluche say, "Is no youra meat, Dominico. You makea the astone crook. Always, you gotta makea the astone straight. You givea the meat to the one who has the lamb before. Then you don' makea the astone crook, you makea the astone straight." So thisa time, I makea the astone straight. I makea the astone straight for Corny Ferg.'

Dominico stopped his car in front of a once-painted frame house whose finish now resembled a skin disease, and whose veranda roof had been so buffeted and blistered that its eaves had the undulated appearance of cardboard left too long out in the rain. Like a garage sale gone bust, the front lawn was littered with kids' toys, wheeled, round, stuffed, lurking in the tall grass, jungle traps for the unwary. Down in front of the latticework, the native Indian girl Rosalee crouched with two others and a grubby little boy in a swimsuit and T-shirt. All stuck their rumps in the air and shrieked in high falsettos, 'Major! Major! Major! Come here, Major!' like demented dwarves. The front screen door slapped open and a pimply boy no wider than string chased two squealing girls down the front steps, threatening to set fire to their eyebrows.

Dominico sighed. 'Ah, Corny Ferg, Corny Ferg.'

Ironeagle sat in the car without moving. 'One time I asked Corny how long he'd been married, eh.'

'Whad he say?'

'A hunnert and seventy-three years.'

When they stepped out of the car they were mobbed. Kids grabbed their hands, their shirtsleeves, their trouser legs; kids rushed them up the steps and through the front door like rugger players would a ball in a scrum.

'Dominico and the Eagle-man are here!'

Marion Fergus stood in the kichen, up to her elbows in flour. 'Well, look what the cat dragged in.' She dusted her hands on her apron.

'The cat's under the house,' one of the girls said.

'It's just an expression, Muriel.' She spoke to Ironeagle. 'You're too late. I'm all out of rhubarb pie.' She sat at the kitchen table and invited the two men to do likewise. 'Marilyn, get us some coffee please. Now—' She spread her stubby, floury hands on the table '—what can I do for you?'

Dominico held his hat in his hands. He cleared his throat as prelude to the garbled speech he'd bounced around in his mind during most of the drive over. A speech was like a block of stone, he decided: it needed to be cleaned, chiselled, polished, washed. It needed grace. But here in Corny's wife's kitchen, Dominico held no mallet, no chisel, no brush. What grace was there in a hat? What could he say to this woman and her children—all these bambinos!—who crowded into the kitchen, on the counters, on the chairs, in the doorways—Dio canne, a lota kids! What could he say? That he was sorry? That in removing one little stone from the balcony he had made crook God's holy line, he had made crook his friend Corny Ferg? How could he tell them that he had grabbed the Carrara marble, that in his rush to find God's stone on which to carve his *firma*, his *segno*, all the things Babbaluche had taught him had flown right out of his head? He glanced into his hat; mio Dio, even if he put it on it would still be empty!

'Mrs. Corny Ferg, I come to aska you how isa Corny Ferg.'

'Cornelius? Cornelius is fine, thank you. Cornelius is, in fact, dandy. Two days ago he moved his big toes. Both of them.' She raised her voice to her children. 'What did he call that—Marlene?'

'"A friggin miracle,"' Marlene said.

'That's right.' Marion Fergus nodded. She raised her voice

again. 'And how did he feel about that?—Rosalee?'
'"Friggin grateful,"' Rosalee said.
'That's right. And what else did he say?—Leonard?'
'"Where are all my friggin friends?"'
'Wonderful.' Marion Fergus paused as Marilyn set three cups of coffee on the table. ' "Where are all my friggin friends?"—Well?'

Dominico squeezed his hat. The straw crackled. He wished he could squeeze his own head. He wished he could pull his heart from his chest, dance on it, kick it in the corner. What else could a man do with such miseria? He spoke: 'Mrs. Corny Ferg. I work alla night, I work alla day, all the time I work. I wanna see Corny Ferg, but I don' gotta time justa now. But somea time *now*, I gotta time for justa now, but before now, I don' gotta time for justa now. Mrs. Corny Ferg—' He tapped his chest '—I gotta the sorrow, Mrs. Corny Ferg. The miseria.'

She leaned forward and patted his hand with flour. 'I can see that, Dominico,' she said gently. 'I can also see that I don't know what the frig you're talking about.' She looked to Ironeagle. 'Eagle, do you know?'

'I guess he's tryna tell you some bad news. That Rawlings job—we just got kicked off of it, eh. The union won't let us work there. We might do it on the weekend, but it looks like we're not goin to get much pay for workin at that place.'

'Mrs. Corny Ferg,' Dominico blurted, '*I* breaka the astone.' His voice cracked. 'I, Dominico.' He punched his chest. 'I break the astone. Corny Ferg, he fall because I break the astone. Dio canne, I don' feel agood, I don' feel anice. He'sa my friend, that Corny Ferg. All the time I wanna go see Corny Ferg, but I ascare. I wanna give Corny Ferg fifty per cent my pay, fifty per cent—but now *I don' know if I gotta my pay!* Mrs. Corny Ferg, whad I am gonna do?'

Marion Fergus spoke slowly. 'You didn't push Cornelius off the balcony.'

'No, Mrs. Corny Ferg! I don' *pusha* Corny Ferg—Dio canne, he'sa my *friend. I break the astone!* The Carrara astone. I take away the Carrara astone, I put in different astone, but the mud, the *mortaio* isa too soft. The rain makea him too soft. The new astone fall, and Corny Ferg, he fall also.'

'But it *was* an accident?'

'Si, si, *accidente*, Mrs. Corny Ferg. Whaddayou think, I'ma *kill* Corny Ferg?'

Marion Fergus held his hand. 'What do you want, Dominico?'

'I want to say to Corny Ferg, I'ma sorry.'

'So? Say it.'

'I want to say to Corny Ferg, I'ma sorry, here'sa fifty per cent, that's it. But Mrs. Corny Ferg, didn't I already told you I don' know if I gotta my pay? Maybe I gotta nothing—whad I gonna do, give Corny Ferg fifty per cent ofa nothing?'

'Corny's getting money,' Marion Fergus said.

'Corny Ferg gotta money?'

'From Rawlings.'

'Corny Ferg gotta money from Rawlings? But Corny Ferg, he don' work for Rawlings.'

'Cornelius *fell*,' Marion Fergus reminded him.

Dominico scratched his head. 'Thisa Rawlings. He *pay* Corny Ferg to fall?'

'He's *going* to pay him for falling.'

Dominico slapped his forehead. 'Porco Madonne! He wantsa Corny Ferg to fall another time? Corny Ferg, he'sa gonna die!'

Marion Fergus laughed. 'No, no—Rawlings is paying compensation—for the accident.'

'Ah, *compenso*.' Domico knew the word. 'Compensation.' He rubbed his chin thoughtfully. 'For compensation, that Corny Ferg, he'sa maestro. For compensation,' he said, suddenly illuminated, 'that Corny Ferg, he'sa da Vinci.'

Da Vinci. If there was one thing Ironeagle was sure he was not, it was a da Vinci. And didn't want to be, either. In England, his trainer Morrie Green had considered himself something of the sort—a tin lid moony-ass genius of the London streets, a Whitechapel Einstein. 'Stick wiv me, mate. I'm yer bread, I'm yer butter, I'm the polish on yer daisy roots. Yer can't go wrong wiv Morrie, Eagle. Ask anyone. Brains—not 'alf. I come from a long line o' brains on me muvver's side. 'Course, on me dad's they was all barmy.' Morrie was a scrapper, a humorist, a wiry little Cockney whose face revealed that though he'd been knocked to canvas, he'd never been counted out. He'd lived in the slums all his life, as a youngster had fought featherweight in the little clubs when to be a Jew in the ring was to suffer catcalls, shied boots, and rancid bacon wrapped in newspaper. Morrie was the first white man Ironeagle had ever met who'd had to hoe a row as tough as an Indian's. When Morrie died, Ironeagle sat *shivah* with the family for two days until an ancient man in a black yarmulke looked up haggardly and said, 'Who's det?' 'That's the boxer, zeyde.' 'Det's the Red Indian?' 'He was Morrie's friend, zeyde.' The old man gently slapped his own cheek. 'A Red Indian. Oy.' Then he rose majestically, shuffled over to Ironeagle and said, 'Tenk you, tenk you, Red Indian, but vat? You don't got no buffaloes you can wisit?' And despite the family's protests, Ironeagle had gone away. Tribeless again.

Well, there were no buffalo here, either. Just a kitchen full of big-beaked Ferguses attacking the banana muffins their mother pulled from the oven, the little kids clammering for more as the older ones handled the bread knives and the butter. Ironeagle accepted the food and the coffee and ate slowly as the massacre went on around him. Next to his chair stood Rosalee, and he couldn't help but notice he and she formed an Indian island in this lake of moony-asses. What did they want from him—from *them*—these white people? A Morrie Green to train their kid to be a perfect little bow-and-arrow?

Dominico was talking about da Vinci again, how he was a great maestro.

Da Vinci, da Vinci. Once, when he was first in London, Ironeagle had followed Morrie on a quick cultural sprint of the city— Trafalgar Square, Big Ben, Westminster Abbey. In a rainstorm they ducked into an art gallery—the Tate, he learned later—and there Ironeagle saw the *Mona Lisa*. A faded serene woman—'wiv a smarmy smirk on 'er clock,' as Morrie said. 'But look at 'er eyes, mate. It's true wot they say about them eyes. They follow a bloke about the room. That's what yer've got ter be like in the ring, Eagle. Like the bleedin *Mona Lisa*, always on the lookout.' If Ironeagle was to teach Rosalee anything, it would be only that: always be on the lookout.

Rosalee was shyly tugging at his arm. 'Mr. Eagle? Mr. Eagle, I got something for you. My mum helped me make them. Come on, I'll show you.'

Ironeagle looked enquiringly at Marion Fergus, who waved through the muffin uproar. 'It won't take long—go ahead.'

Led by the hand, he trailed the child out of the kitchen, down a hall and out onto the back porch. Daylight was gone. The back yard, cut off from the front streetlights, lay in shadow. Somewhere a frog croaked.

'You got a pond here?' he asked.

'That's Terry's toad. He's got it in a box and he says we're not s'posed to let it go.'

'So that's what you got for me, eh. A toad.'

'No.' She sounded annoyed. Even in the poor light from the windows he could see she was a funny looking kid—big hands, big feet, big head. Had she been a different age, she might've been his own kid. He had one or two out there somewhere.

'Wait here,' she said.

He found a lawnchair and sat down. No point in wandering around, he thought. All those toys, a fella could cripple himself. Corny was lucky to go off the balcony, eh; at least in the hopsital he was safe.

'Here.' She was back, handing him a paper bag.

'What is it?'

'Oh. I'll turn on the light.' She reached inside the door; a bulb flared.

In the bag he found three cylinders of cloth, each not much larger than a cigarette. One was white, one black, one blue. He lifted them to the light, sniffed them.

'Mr. Eagle, do you know what they are?'

'Tobacco ties. Where'd you get them?'

'I told you. My mum and I made them.'

'Mrs. Fergus?'

'She's my mum.'

He held the tobacco ties in his palm. 'What are they for?'

'For the Uwpi ceremony. You know, the healing ceremony. They got other colours, but I want you to have these ones. I gave my dad a white one. White's for healing the mind and the body and the spirit.'

'What about the black one?'

'That's for protection. I think I should give my dad one of them, too.'

'And blue?'

'That's for wisdom and name-giving. My mum says—' she stopped. In the kitchen someone was singing, then broke off to laugh.

'Your mum says what?'

'My mum says maybe sometime I could have an Indian name—and maybe sometime you could give me one.'

Ironeagle rolled the tobacco ties in his fist. 'For a little kid, you sure know a lot about this Indian stuff. Where'd you learn about it, anyways?'

'From a book. Marilyn got it for my birthday.'

Ironeagle opened his palm and studied the tobacco ties. 'Well, you better hang onto that book, eh. Could be a fella might want to borrow it sometime.'

Paterson loved books. Every time he read one he wanted to write one, but every time he tried to write one he went back to reading another. Reading was easy. Writing was hard. It had something to do with the Muse. And time. And money.

Money! Now that the Rawlings job had fallen through, he would have to kiss Spain goodbye—unless the union reinstated him. *Then* maybe he could afford a ticket to Madrid. In Spain he could Hemingway for months. Lately he'd been reading Hemingway. Hemingway was good. Spain was good. Having no job was bad.

He told all this to Lannie Dougal, to whom he gave a ride home from the Rawlings place. They drove in Paterson's Volkswagen, whose muffler baffles clattered, so Paterson thought, like castanets, or Republicans' rifles. The baffles were good.

'Do you ever find that when you listen to someone for a long time, you start to imitate that person's voice?'

Lannie shook his head.

'Sometimes when I'm at home in bed I hear people talk,' Paterson confided. 'You know, people I work with. Dominico, Kozicki—all the others.' He paused. 'Not you, though.'

Lannie smiled.

Paterson drove. Darkness fell, streetlights blinked on. He fancied he was adrift, a sailor recently dumped by the seat of his pants over a frigate's railing. The Rawlings job had been scuttled, its crew shanghaied, its paycheque run aground. What next, sharks?

Lannied pointed at a road.

Paterson whipped the car left, shot along the edge of the university campus, then turned again to rattle down a narrow pot-holed road that sliced through the agricultural college's experimental fields of asparagus. 'Asper-grass,' undergrad agros routinely called the crop—in the moonlight a sea of eery spears and ghostly nailheads, an

East Indian fakir's nightmare. The car was headed for Sunderville, once a farming community now a suburb, a glowing profusion of clapboard houses, mini-malls and apartment blocks that was dominated by a long-necked, anachronous grain elevator that rose above the other buildings like a giraffe trying to escape a crowd of pygmies.

'Jeez,' Paterson ventured over the noise of the engine. 'We're unemployed.'

They drove glumly. The suburb's light hung in a peculiar dome over the grain elevator which tent-poled the penumbra of an infinite arc. 'All the time you don't talk,' he hollered, 'do you hear voices? Do you see things? Sometimes I catch you looking.'

Lannie shrugged.

'Okay,' Paterson said.

Paterson was disappointed. He saw things all the time—well, often. On good days his brain was a picture show with gum stuck under the seats, popcorn scattered on the floor and fat ladies with wailing kids under their arms trying to push past his knees in the dark. The sound between his ears was a party line for gossip mongers and blatherers, it was a town hall debate, palace mob, seventeen short-wave radio stations pulled in on one band. Literary stuff if he was lucky, junk if he wasn't: metaphors stacked up in his skull like planes over an airport, similes planted as thick as landmines, alliterations working his imagination like pickpockets in Petticoat Lane. He used it all, scribbled it into notebooks that he piled up like bales of shingles, his rainy-day protection for when writer's block roared at him like a storm over the Atlantic. On writer's block days the projector shut down, the crowds went home. All that was left was a hardwood floor and an old man in the corner, leaning on a broom.

'If you could talk,' Paterson said, 'how much would you have to say?'

Lannie thought for a moment, then held up his hands as if he were measuring a long, long fish.

'That much?'

Lannie shook his head, pointed out the window, and with his arm swept up everything out there.

Paterson looked out the side window. Spain or no Spain, Hemingway or not, even here the world was a big place. Beyond the suburb lay the prairie, and beyond the prairie the rim of the earth. *Lannie knows that*, Paterson thought suddenly. *Even if he can't talk. He knows that. How many others know that? Even if they can't talk? Even if they* can *talk but don't say it? If Lannie knows then maybe we all do—Dominico, Corny, Trischuk, Anna, Ironeagle. And Kozicki.*

'Kozicki knows,' he said.

Lannie looked at him, puzzled.

Paterson parked outside the stuccoed bungalow whose basement suite Lannie rented.

He got home after midnight, after driving around and around the city. On his desk lay a book he'd been reading—an Irish poet who claimed to dig with his pen. 'Between my finger and my thumb/ The squat pen rests.' the poet wrote. 'I'll dig with it.'

Make my pen a shovel then, Paterson wrote.

And wrote the line again, and again, one hundred and forty-seven times, while in a corner of his brain an old man leaned patiently on a broom.

That's okay, Paterson told himself as he rolled into bed. *That's all right. There'll be time.*

Kozicki was late, he knew that. And getting later every minute. His dad used to say that time waited for no man, and whoever said that first sure knew his ass from his elbow. Certainly time hadn't waited for Kozicki's father. Dead at—what was he, thirty-nine, forty? And shoeless, too. Kozicki hoped his dad wasn't laying sod up in the big beyond. Tough job, barefoot.

Tough job anyway, rolling the grass strips into forty-pound jellyrolls, muscling a wheelbarrow load of them over planks because the ground was still too soft to keep the wheel from sinking up to its axle. I must be nuts, he thought. Hook me up to one of those brain scanner whaddaycallits Lannie said they use in the bughouse, and I bet you'd get more idiot squiggles on my readout than dance night at a worm farm.

Kozicki had never considered brains his strong suit. As a kid in school he'd always thought of himself as a grinning lump, not bad at arithmetic, so-so in reading, numbskull in everything else. And later, how had he qualified for rear gunner in the air force—through his genius? Not likely. A genius didn't fly over the target range and hit every bullseye he saw; a genius didn't gaze at the medical officer's eyechart and say, 'Doc, I could read those letters from the other end of a hockey rink.' A genius didn't pass his navigation tests in the top five per cent of his class and then jump eagerly behind two Browning machine guns *just so that other geniuses could shoot him down!* A genius was somebody who knew when to keep his mouth shut and his head under a table.

The night the crew left he'd taken nearly an hour and a half to connect the lights. At first Rawlings didn't have enough extension cords to reach the outdoor outlet. Andrews, the butler, rooted around in garages and storage buildings until he found half a dozen. Kozicki joined the cords to each light, plugged them all in and blew a fuse.

'I'll have to use the power bar and the generator,' Kozicki told Andrews, a portly, smooth-skinned man who tilted oddly backwards, as if balancing a ping-pong ball in his navel.

'Would a generator be noisy?' Andrews enquired.

'It would.'

'Then it would have to go off at eleven o'clock.'

'Gee, I don't think so.'

'Mr. R retires at eleven o'clock.'

'Oh yeah?' Kozicki said. 'I'm retiring at sixty.'

Andrews favoured him with a thin smile. 'I shall relay that information.'

'And I shall crank up the generator.'

Crank up was the word. Gas-engined, the generator flooded twice before it fired and caught, chugging uncertainly like a morning cough and spewing smoke like a four-alarm fire. Kozicki tinkered with the needle valve and the air filter and finally got the machine running, just as two of the lights, their cowlings outfitted with clamps, apathetically slid down the poles like melted ice cream. Finding the clamp bolts stripped and the wingnuts shot, in the absence of replacement parts Kozicki duct-taped the lights to the top of their poles, where they shone over what appeared to be, at such a late hour, a quarter section of unturfed soil. The lights attracted clouds of moths and mosquitoes bent on suicide and, listening to the insects sizzle and pop, Kozicki guessed they had more common sense than he did.

He carried sod all that night and most of the next day, catnapping for a couple of hours in the truck cab. He drank cold coffee from his thermos and ate day-old cheese sandwiches. In the delerium of fatigue, he imagined demanding the crew's payment in small bills, a briefcase full of it like a mobster's pay-off, which he would unzip on a table in the middle of them. He'd divide the stacks of bills evenly, like Jesus with the fishes and loaves. 'Go ahead, dig in. You earned it,

171

for crying out loud.' He used to be one for gestures, lugging home extravagant bouquets from the greenhouse for Emily, later Gillian, still later Charlene—sometimes admitting that the flowers had no market, were to be tossed in the compost anyway. It was the thought that counted.

What counted now?—Time. Hours, minutes, seconds. After Andrews had come out of the house at eleven o'clock and informed him that on careful consideration Mr. R had decided to allow the generator to chuff along indefinitely, Kozicki rarely glanced at his watch. The music of the job took over, led him through a lugubrious dance he knew by heart. He rolled the sod, loaded the sod, wheeled the sod, laid the sod. Raked; spread the pellet fertilizer by hand (Dominico's words in his head, 'Feeda the chicks, feeda the chicks')—and then rolled the sod, loaded the sod, and so on, moving to the mood and rhythm of the job, the job, the job.

And wound up exhausted. By the time the sun rose on August 31 he was a stumbling hunchback and, when he turned off the generator, the explosive silence nearly clubbed him to his knees. At seven o'clock he stood dazed and stiff, with roughly thirty-seven sleepless hours of work under his belt, in addition to the familiar pressure in his bowels that made him want to lie in a hammock on a beach somewhere in Costa Rica. He was beat. He had barber's itch of the eyeballs, hands like a crab's pincers, and sweat so soured on sweat that his shirt wished his skin would move out of town.

Andrews appeared with a tray of tea and toast. 'Compliments of the house.'

'Thanks.'

Standing, Kozicki ate delicately, lured to tender etiquette by the feeling that if he sat down he would never rise again. When he'd finished, he wiped his hands on his pants and announced he was going home for a while.

'I believe,' Andrews said, 'that midnight is the witching hour?'

'That's still about sixteen hours away.'

'Might I wish you luck?'

'You might.'

He drove home in a stupor, clumped up the back steps and stripped as he stumbled towards the bathroom. He peed, peed, and peed. Under the shower he considered the sweetness of death; out, refreshed, he padded in a towel to the front door to retrieve his mail. A roofing company flyer, ignorant of his bladder, promised him a leakless next fifty years. The secret was plastic. A postcard from Gillian ('Hello from Thunder Bay!—Peter and I arriving Sept 3'). And a slim brown package. The book he'd ordered.

Machu Picchu: Echoes of the Sun.

He sat down on the hall carpet in his towel and looked at the photographs. They were in black and white. Dark cutstone towers trailing rags of mist rose above bulbous wooded mountains. Grassy terraces climbed up rock bluffs like flights of stairs. Stone houses lay roofless and deserted on the mountaintop, their foundations a marvel of geometry. The place was asleep. Nothing but stones, grass and air. Quiet. Peaceful. With a hammock and a rain tarp, a guy could sleep there for two hundred years.

He had to look up the phone number. When she answered, his tongue turned into leather.

'Is there something wrong?' she said. 'Are you all right? Your voice sounds odd.'

'I got a proposition.'

'Should I listen to it?'

'Proposition, that's a noun. Hang on. It means—' he reached for his back pocket and knocked his towel off. 'Oh jeez, I'm naked.'

She laughed. 'Is that the proposition?'

'No, no.' He fumbled for the towel, gave up. Air shivered his nethers. 'First I gotta know: have you moved in with the priest?'

'Who told you he was a priest? Mike, why are you naked?'

'My towel fell off. Roger said he was Maurice the priest. Have you moved in with him yet?'

'You've phoned me at Roger's, Mike. I'm here, at Roger's.'

'So you're not moving in with the priest.'

'I didn't say that.'

'Well don't, okay? I mean not until—not until September the fourth, say.'

'A few weeks ago you said something about September first.'

'Well yeah, but that's another thing. That's the job. September fourth. Labour Day. Yeah, don't move in until Labour Day, okay?' Next to the phone hung an ivy. Kozicki picked off two of its leaves.

'What's the proposition, Mike?'

'I got a book for you.'

'That's the proposition. A book? What book?'

'A special book. And I got a daughter.'

'I know you've got a daughter.'

'I mean she's coming here. Gillian's coming here, with a man. So I thought maybe you could come over. On Labour Day. We could barbecue or something.'

Charlene was silent. Kozicki could hear her breathing. 'Why?' she asked.

He pulled a few more leaves off the plant. Goosebumps were forming on his buttocks. 'Why?'

'*Why*,' Charlene said. 'I think it's an interrogative pronoun.'

'I want you to meet her. You always said you wanted to meet her. And I want you to take a look at her man for me. And I want to give you your book, Charlene.' He waited.

'I can't promise you anything, Mike.'

'Will you come over?'

'All right.' She paused. 'Get some clothes on.'

He set the alarm clock for 11:00 A.M., crawled into bed and fell asleep.

In his dream he and Emily were building the patio. On their knees, they set flagstones into fine sand, tapping the corners with great wooden mallets. 'I don't know,' Kozicki said. 'Do you think these stones are intransigent? Some stones are like that. Intransigent written all over them.' Emily kissed his cheek. 'You're so mendacious,' she said. 'Sleep now.' He said, 'What an intransigent thing to say.' She kissed him again. 'Sleep now.'

He slept flat on his back, arms outflung like a drunk on a pool table, his snores the first three notes of a badly-timed Massey Harris tractor, the kind with a crank at the front. He woke with a mouth full of rabbit fur and a jangling in his ear that had his feet running down the hall before he knew they had hit the floor. It was Marion Fergus on the phone. Some of the crew were going to visit Corny after the union meeting. Would he like to come along?

'I might show up a little later, Marion.'

'Are you saying you're too busy? With what?'

'I'm saying I'll try to make it.'

He hung up. Standing naked in his kitchen he raked his fingers over his scalp, tousled what hair he had, yawned and slapped his belly. Outside the window, something was wrong. Where Churchill was buried beneath the roses, the grass was bathed in orange light. Long shadows lay on the lawn.

He spun to look at the kitchen clock. It was after six in the evening. He'd been asleep for over nine hours.

At first Lannie had planned to carry everything in the gunny sack. He had too much equipment to do otherwise. The bolt cutters were longer and heavier than he expected; if he smuggled them under his jacket, he'd look excessively perverted; if he slid them down one pantleg, he'd look excessively disabled. Since he was travelling to the campus by bus, he didn't want to alarm his fellow passengers. People who alarmed other people got remembered. As a choirboy Tall Bennie had once slipped into his church-minister father's surplice and rushed down the centre aisle during a wedding to announce that he was the ghost of Anne of Green Gables. People remembered *him*.

The clothes were a problem. On a warm summer's night, not many people wore a black wool turtleneck and a watch cap. He *could* give people to understand that he was a sailor on shoreleave, but with the nearest ocean fifteen hundred miles away, wouldn't they simply peg him for a weirdo? Also, he'd have to find a place for the milk-bones and the gloves. The gunny sack seemed to solve his difficulties but, when he slung it fully packed over his shoulder and looked at himself in the bathroom mirror, he saw a dishevelled vagrant bent on either picking up beer bottles or blowing up the post office. He wished he could look, well, normal—like Paterson, say, in his jeans and running shoes and plaid shirts, hiding his subversion under the guise of Regular Guy.

Lannie dug through his closet. Jeans, running shoes, shirt. The rest of the stuff in a sports bag. He checked the mirror again, shaved, combed his hair, composed his face. A healthy looking young fellow, probably on his way to the gym. He only hoped that when the time came the dogs would be ready, and that when darkness fell he would be Regular Guy enough not to run screaming into the night.

He looked at his watch. Almost seven-thirty. The union meeting would have already started. It would be over by nine or nine-thirty, and then he would lose himself in the crowds as they swarmed out of the F.R. Haverston Memorial Gym. Just another hound in the Everlasting Night. Who was going to notice *him*?

Seven-thirty, getting on for eight o'clock. Lannie gulped. Not long now.

Ya-rooooww.

Seated next to Trischuk on a plastic chair in the hot, overcrowded gymnasium, her neatly rounded head aimed in a semblance of rapture towards the speaker's platform from which ruddy-faced Cargill and other union executives delivered speeches about contracts, labour strife and solidarity, Anna rehearsed a little speech of her own. It was one that talked about love and finding oneself and broken hearts and two ships passing in the night; it was full of tears-but-no-regrets, happy-memories-but-sad-goodbyes. It was, so Anna realized, a masterful blend of clichéd sentimentality and platitudinous poop more suited to a sixteen-year-old's dumping a boyfriend than to a thirty-eight-year-old's farewell to her lover. She supposed she would have to give up on the speech and tell him the truth instead. The truth was she loved him. The truth was he loved his wife and children. The truth was she loved him *because* he loved his wife and children.

The truth was making her perspire.

Still, she sat through the union meeting composed, as did Trischuk, as did the other members of the crew—except Lannie, who never attended meetings, and Kozicki, whom nobody had seen since they'd abandoned the Rawlings job. Before the meeting was called to order, Cargill had approached them and asked, 'Where's that foreman of yours?'

The crew stared into space. Paterson had said, 'Kozicki's dog died.'

'I wouldn't sweat a dead dog if I was him.' Cargill had looked around the crowded floor as if to confirm that no dead dogs had sneaked in. 'I'm putting forward a special motion to allow you brothers and sisters to listen to the proceedings, even though you won't be voting.' Expanding, he added, 'Your presence here won't go unappreciated when the committee meets to discuss lifting suspensions.'

'We wan' you to liff the suspend fora Corny Ferg,' Dominico said.

Cargill nodded. 'He's on the list, brother. You'll all get your chance when you come before the committee. I'll let you know when that will be. You'll hear from me on Friday.'

Anna had listened numbly and, later, during the discussion, the debate, the interminable wrangling, her bum fell asleep. When the time came to vote, she stumbled with Trischuk out a side entrance, like a dowager too long on an ocean cruise. After the gymnasium, the darkness was a relief; the air smelled cool and fresh.

176

'Have you heard the story of F.R. Haverston?' she asked as they walked.

'Who?'

'Haverston. Where we just were—the F.R. Haverston Memorial Gym.'

'No.'

'He was a physical education instructor—in the 1920s, I think. One day in a fitness class he was beaned by an Indian club one of his students was using for calisthenics. Died instantly.'

'The student?'

'Haverston. He did such a good job of dying they named a gym after him.'

'Is there a point to this?'

'Yes.' She took his hand. 'At least we're not F.R. Haverston.'

They strolled across the darkened campus towards the greenhouse, across the parking lot in front of the gates where they'd leapt at each other that first time. In the shadows, she could see the warehouse where Kozicki had discovered them.

'Remember?' she asked.

'It wasn't that long ago,' he said. 'Where are we headed here—memory lane?'

'I'm afraid so.'

'And that's it.'

'That's it.'

'No hands, no lips, no shoot the moon?'

She shook her head. 'None of those things.'

'What makes you think I'll go for this?'

'Because you're strong enough to stand the strain,' she said.

They continued to walk past the greenhouse compound, beyond the animal experimental station whose dogs began to yip and natter to each other in the dark. On a knoll overlooking the river he held her—just held her—and said, 'Now, I suppose you're going to tell me something.'

In the dark, Lannie waited under the willows, flattened against the fallen leaves, unable to move. The sports bag lay next to him. Any minute now he would pull on the leather gloves, black turtleneck and watch cap, slide the bolt cutters from the bag, stuff the milkbones in his right pocket, then roll up the bag and tuck it under his sweater. Any minute now. Any second. All he had to do was heave the Everlasting Night off his back. Once that Night was off there, he'd spring into action like a greyhound out of the blocks. He'd slash through the fence links like a butcher cutting cheese, peel back the wire like an orange, whistle heigh-ho to the dogs and they'd all gallop to the river. In his mind he saw himself leap light-footed, every dog's pied piper, freedom singing in his ears like the hit parade. Once at the river he'd ditch the bolt cutters and gloves and there he'd be, a frolicsome master with fourteen dogs jogging through a riverside park. Any minute now it would all happen. Any minute. In the meantime he would gather the courage to lift his head.

In the distance an engine idled softly and died. Lannie shuddered. He had already seen the campus security police once this evening. Those security guards with their big shoulders and enormous flashlights. Some day he would laugh at them. Ha.

He had to pee. And he was itchy. As soon as he pulled it on, the turtleneck sweater prickled his back like a nest of fleas. The dogs, for a long time fretful, had settled. From where he lay he could just make out Bluey's pale shape at the end of her kennel. She seemed to be scenting the breeze. He couldn't be sure, but her ears seemed to be twitching back and forth like metronomes.

Something stirred in the leaves, like an out-of-his-burrow gopher. Above him voices murmured.

He stiffened, his heart knocking holes in his ribs, his tongue crawling down his throat. He hoisted himself on all fours and crept forward, carrying the sports bag in his teeth. The hanging branches of the willows brushed against his face. When he reached the end of the line of kennels, he remained on his knees, panting. Where the wild bunch grass opened onto the bare hills that overlooked the river and the city beyond, two people stood in one another's arms. Silhouetted against the distant city lights, they resembled a two-headed gargoyle sharing the same body. He watched them fearfully.

Distance softened their voices. One of them laughed. It was Anna. And the other one, looking like a shirt full of walnuts, was Trischuk. Lannie relaxed. He watched them for awhile, and when his teeth started to ache he remembered the sports bag and put it down. He massaged his jaw. Still they talked. He yawned, scratched his ear. Maybe if he barked he would scare them away. He yawned again, and at first he thought his jaw had clicked, or that Bluey or one of the other dogs had raked a claw over a kennel's cement floor. But the dogs, wary now, snuffled and growled. Lannie leaned into the night. He would've growled himself if he could've pried his tongue off the roof of his mouth. Trembling, he raised himself on one knee. He'd never been that close to the Man With the Great Big Gun before.

Stuck in the hospital for a solid friggin week and the only friggin visitors you get is your friggin wife and those friggin fightin kids and the first night your friends drop by, what do they do but show up late when visiting hours are nearly friggin over, and then they give you a gift that weighs a friggin ton. Other patients get flowers and chocolates and one guy even got a pizza and a porno book, but what do you get? Heavy little box the size of a football. Must be a lead-lined casket for a squirrel. Must be a friggin *rock*.

'What's in this thing anyways?'

'Just open it, Cornelius.' Marion, chipper as always. A regular Mary friggin Sunshine ever since he moved his toes.

In some ways Corny felt cheated. One look at the body cast and he'd figured for a life in a wheelchair. At least a fella didn't have to be on his feet all day. And steering one of those gizmos down the street would sure as hell make everybody move out of the friggin way. But no; the doctors came in and looked at his charts and shone lights in his eyes and pinched his toes and poked him places where only his wife had poked before, and they all seemed pretty proud of themselves. He was one of the lucky few, they said, he'd be walking in six weeks, they said, maybe he'd even be back to work within three friggin months. Already he'd been wheeled along to the physiotherapy room for a looksee. They had a nurse down there looked like a friggin Olympic athaleete who made those other poor wasted buggers do chin-ups, parallel bar stunts and he couldn't remember what else. All of them sweatin like friggin firemen. They probably wisht they'd of been hurt a lot worse so's they could lie around and have a friggin holiday for a change.

He sighed and struggled with the box's ribbon. Dominico stood at the foot of the bed, hat off like he was at a friggin funeral. Maybe that's what the little guy's give me. A friggin tombstone, a friggin headrest. And over on the other side of the room Ironeagle waitin like an undertaker. Marion said him and Rosalee hit it off, so why's he lookin like he just left his saddle out in the rain? And Paterson, kinda jumpy and nervous, but who could figure young fellas nowadays? Half the time they walked around like they'd got butterflies up their ass.

It *was* a rock. Pretty friggin nice one too.

'Marble,' Dominico said, in a voice like you'd use in a cathedral or someplace. 'Carrara astone.'

Corny lifted the stone from its tissue paper wrapping. It glowed under the lights like white honey.

'I makea the astone smooth, nice. Patersoni, Eagle, they help me makea the astone.'

Corny held the stone up to the light. 'Hey, what's this stuff on here?' In one corner of the creamy marble, Corny's hospital-clean fingers traced a deeply etched Gothic D.

'My *firma*,' Domico said. He puffed his chest, 'My *segno*. D isa for Dominico.' He leaned his face so close Corny could see the friggin hairs on the little guy's nose. 'I tell you true, Corny Ferg,' Dominico explained. 'Someatime when I work for Rawlings I tella myself, "Dominico, when you finish the astone you gonna cement one Carrara astone someaplace—one nicea stone—and that astone she gonna say: 'Dominico Babbaluche, He Work Here.' So I finda the astone, but also I finda you ba-boomba on the aground. So I tella myself, "Dominico, someatime you usea that Carrara astone for Corny Ferg, and that astone gonna say: 'Corny Ferg, He Work Here.'" But Corny Ferg, I tell you true: This astone isa for ayou, but this astone is no for ayou.'

'It's for me,' Corny repeated slowly, 'but it's not for me?'

'Si.'

'Have you any friggin idea how much sense that don't make?'

'Look at the astone.'

Corny studied the stone's side. Besides the Gothic D an eagle soared in full flight towards the rock's upper edge.

'I don' gotta told you what is thisa bird: Eagle. Patersoni, he draw thisa bird. I makea the bird in the astone.'

Corny fingered the characters; they had been flawlessly chiseled into the stone. Big friggin deal. What good were they? Pretty fancy friggin doorstop.

'Now, Corny Ferg,' Dominico said gently. 'You turn this astone to 'nother side.'

When Corny turned the stone over, he saw:

II   II

ROSALEE

Ironeagle took the stone from him and touched the vertical lines with a blunt index finger, first one pair, then the other. He handed the stone back. 'You tell that Rosalee kid of yours that those are her Sun Dance scars. She don't have to do everything the old way, eh.'

Corny laid his hand on the stone and stroked it. 'You could tell her yourself.'

Ironeagle lowered his eyes. 'I been thinkin maybe I'll go back home for a while. I haven't been on that reserve for a long time. Could be I got a kid of my own up there, eh.'

Corny frowned. Life was a friggin horse race. You never knew where you were. Think you're in front and look up just in time to catch a faceful of tailshit as all them other nags blow right by you. Jeez, everywhere you looked was an accident waitin to happen. You couldn't count on nothin. Even lyin in a hospital, even a friggin *spinal injury* couldn't protect you from the world's changingness. Corny raised his eyebrows over this last thought. He'd never had one like that before. Most times his brain didn't work like that. How could a spinal injury protect you—a thing like that was friggin bad for you, wasn't it? But look at that stone—there was somethin good. Bad and good at the same time—that was one of them whaddyacallits, them things Kozicki looked up in his book one time—a pair of docks— wasn't it?

'Hey,' he remembered suddenly. 'Where's Kozicki? Wasn't he gonna come with you guys?'

The others' faces went blank, like they hadn't given a friggin thought to Kozicki, like he was a wallet they'd dropped someplace and didn't know it until they reached for a pocket that was flat. 'Where's Kozicki?' they asked each other, like they were pattin their friggin clothes. 'And where's Anna, and Trischuk? Where's Lannie?'

'Anna and Trischuk were at the union meeting,' Paterson said. 'They left together.'

'I guess Lannie left the meeting early.'

'No he don'. He don' leavea the meeting. He don' *go to* the meeting.'

'That don't answer my friggin question. Where's Kozicki?' Ideas started to blossom in Corny's head, jeez, they were poppin up like friggin weeds. 'Think about it for a minute. He told Marion over

181

the phone that he'd be here, right Marion? That he'd come to visit.'

'He said he might be late, Cornelius. He sounded busy.'

'Busy? Sure. Busy doin what? Curlin his hair? Watchin the friggin stars? I worked twelve years with that guy. I never seen him late, and I never seen him quit in the middle of a job.' Corny grew agitated. Under his cast, his shin started to itch. 'Marion, slide that knitting needle up in there again, wouldja?—Ah, that's better. Now, where was I?'

'Kozicki doesn't quit in the middle of a job.'

'He don't stop. He don't come to visit me, and he don't go to the union meeting. He don't drink much no more, and I heard his girlfriend cut herself loose weeks ago. So where's that leave 'em?'

'At the Rawlings place,' Paterson said.

'At the Rawlings place,' Corny nodded. 'Makin the money we're s'posed to help him make.'

'Whaddayou think, Corny Ferg? Mike, he gonna do that?'

'You friggin right he's gonna do that. I betcha he's workin right now.' Corny scratched his nose, which had been broken the instant he'd hit the ground. The flesh under his eyes had swelled and coloured a peculiar shade of mauve that upon healing faded to a mottled yellow, so that every time he looked into the mirror to shave he saw a raccoon with jaundice. There was nothing wrong with his sight now, though. Even with his eyes closed he could've seen Kozicki clearly, carrying rolls of sod to the unturfed lawn, sweatin like a friggin boiler.

'It ain't right, though,' he told the others in the room. 'It ain't right that he should do all the friggin work himself.'

'What about the union?' Paterson asked.

'Listen,' Corny said, 'let me tell you somethin. Lyin here for a week I figgered somethin out. What's the worst friggin thing that can happen to a person?—Bein dead, right? Bein dead is the worst friggin accident there is. Now, you gotta ask yourself: if you help Kozicki finish the job—'

'Assuming he's finishing the job.'

'—if you help Kozicki finish the job, what's the union gonna do to you? Bust your head? Put ya in a wheelchair? Kill ya?'

'They don' gonna kill us, Corny Ferg.'

'That's what I'm sayin.'

Corny waited. What did a guy have to do, lead them by the friggin nose?

Paterson glanced at his watch. 'It's after nine. We've got less than three hours.'

'Hey moony-ass,' Ironeagle asked Dominico as they went out the door, 'does this mean you're gonna hafta drive real fast?'

In the dark, unbidden words filled Lannie's mouth until he couldn't breathe. 'WATCH OUT!' he shouted, leaping from the bushes. 'WATCH OUT!'

His first swing with the bolt cutters clipped the Man's shoulder and so jolted the Great Big Gun that it exploded into the darkness. Lannie heard the pellets snick through the grass. The Man staggered backwards into the hillside's shadow. Lannie swung the loaded sports bag again, a low, looping sweep that caught the Man just above the knees. The Man stumbled forward, and clamped Lannie's neck in the crook of one hairy arm while with the other hand he tried to push the gun barrel into Lannie's ear.

'Fucker,' the Man hissed.

Lannie's voice squeaked. 'Woof yourself.'

The two wrestled and fell to the ground. Lannie heard the gun drop into the grass; he kicked and squirmed, grabbed for balls and twisted. The Man screamed, gouged Lannie's mouth with his thumb. Struggling free, Lannie tumbled down the hill, the bolt cutters in their bag clutched to his chest. The gun roared again. A shower of lead slashed the ground just beyond his feet.

'WATCH OUT! WATCH OUT!'

'Who's there?' Trischuk called. 'Lannie?'

'THE MAN! THE EVERLASTING NIGHT!'

'Lannie? Jesus, have you got a gun?'

But all hell had broken loose. In their kennels the dogs flung themselves against the chain link fence and barked and howled like wolves. Somewhere in the dark the Man fumbled with the gun. Trischuk hollered, 'Anna? Anna?' and Lannie, scuttling crabwise through the grass yelled, 'Watch out, you bastard, watch out! I'm coming, so watch out!'

He could make out the Man With the Great Big Gun crouched below the hill's crest; above, and to the Man's right, Anna's slender figure appeared against the night sky. Suddenly the Man With the Great Big Gun straightened; for an instant he faced Anna. Lannie shouted, 'ANNA WATCH—' as she pirouetted daintily and kicked the Man three times in the face.

The Man With the Great Big Gun dropped without a sound.

Part way up the hill Lannie stood quivering.

The dogs had stopped barking; they were waiting.

'Lannie? Is that you?'

'I've got to go, Anna. The security guards will be here.'

'You can *talk*, Lannie.'

'Yeah, I know.'

Trischuk's massive shape appeared beside her. 'Are you okay, Lannie?'

'I'm all right.' Already he was moving down the hill away from them, pulling the bolt cutters from the bag. 'But I've got to go. You'd better go too,' he called. 'The security guards—'

'Lannie—'

But by then he'd reached the kennels.

The engine on the portable generator was an eight horsepower Briggs and Stratton capable of producing 3600 watts of electricity, but Kozicki could tell it was having breathing problems. For the past hour it'd been sputtering a series of herniated hiccups so that the halogen bulbs flared and faded like glow-worms who couldn't decide whether to stay at the party or go home to bed. Kozicki felt sorry for the machine: had it been human, it would've crawled into the nearest bar and ordered a brandy. The engine was—what was that word the school nurse had used that year Gillian needed iron pills—amoebic? Anaerobic? Whatever the word, the engine was getting more amoebical as the night wore on. He wouldn't have been surprised if it suddenly rolled over on its back and anaerobicked right where it lay. Well, he was too busy hauling sod to tinker with it now.

And there was a lot of sod. Kozicki figured if he loaded up the grass he still had left and moved it west, he could sod Alberta. What would the deadline be on that sucker, three thousand years?

Kozicki lifted his head. He thought he heard a pop. Then another one. Like fireworks, from a long way down the river.

Somebody else was having engine trouble.

Anna was so filled with her own strength that she didn't need to speak of love. When the gun had gone off she'd flung Trischuk to the ground, *she'd* flung *him*, and raced towards Lannie's voice through the smell of the sweet grass. Now Alex lay unconscious at her feet.

'We'll have to get him to the hospital,' she told Trischuk.

They bent together and somehow (Where did the light come from that allowed her to see it?) she saw Trischuk's hand gently cup the back of Alex's head. And she remembered now, that day in the shopping mall. Trischuk had leaned over and briefly—so briefly!—cupped the back of his wife's head in his hand.

Trischuk carried Alex in his arms like a child. Across the campus, under the trees and streetlamps, past the deserted greystone buildings. A student, hurrying to the library, asked if she could help.

'The hospital knows we're coming,' Anna said.

They left Alex at the emergency entrance and hurried away from the glass doors into the darkness. At the corner a security car shot past them, siren wailing, lights flashing. Another vehicle squealed out of the parking lot, pinned them in its headlights and screeched to a stop.

'Dio canne! You buncha guys. Don' justa stand there! Whadda I'm gonna do, waita for you alla night? Come on, come on, holy cow!'

As Lannie ran, the secret he'd just discovered threatened to burst his lungs. He knew he should be quiet, but after he pitched the bag, cutters and gun into the river he threw back his head and bayed like a bloodhound. The remnants of fear still soured his mouth, so he scooped a handful of water, rinsed and spat. The river tasted of mud, but he didn't care. 'Yarrrrooow!' he howled. 'We did it!'

The dogs milled around him. In the light reflected from the buildings across the river Lannie counted fourteen of them. Already most of them were crashing through the underbrush, up the bank and away. He couldn't stop them. Only Bluey pressed herself against his leg; her frantic tail flailed him like a rope. He bent to take her muzzle in his hands. 'We did it, Bluey.' She licked his face and knocked him backwards on the path. He tousled her ears and thumped her sides. How could she know or understand? She was just a dog.

But then what could he tell her? How could he explain the fear that propelled the sports bag through the dark? Without thinking!

Without cringing! Swinging pure and angry because *I knew, I knew!*—that for the Man With the Great Big Gun, *I* was part of the darkness. *I* was the Everlasting Night. That for the Man With the Great Big Gun, *I was the Man With the Great Big Gun*!

Lannie jogged along the river path. Somewhere on the campus a siren yowped, but the siren wasn't here. Darkness was. He would be safe.

What had Kozicki told Paterson that time? Paterson had written it down in his little notebook and read it out to them. 'Every job has its music,' Kozicki had said, 'and we dance to its tune.'

As he ran with Bluey at his heels, Lannie felt as if he were dancing.

Peering out beyond the lights, Kozicki watched Dominico's monstrous Buick and Paterson's VW bug motor jauntily towards him (he supposed Andrews the butler had let them in), a two-car cavalcade. Dominico's car was outfitted with a horn that was the mating call of a Guernsey cow. 'Moo!' the horn cried. 'Moo! Moo!'

'You're early,' Kozicki greeted them. 'This isn't the weekend.'

Dominico pointed to his wristwatch and held up his hand, pinching an invisible grass seed. 'Early, whaddayou mean! It'sa ninea forty-five!'

Kozicki massaged his groin. 'Cargill and the union won't be happy about this.'

'Paisano, paisano.' Dominico shook his head with infinite patience, and spread his arms to show the obvious. 'That'sa why we don' brought them!'

The crew set to work quickly. Trischuk adjusted the generator, reseated its idle and feed screws, tapped the carburetor like a heart-and-lung man thumping an asthmatic's chest. Dominico, Ironeagle and Anna rushed between the sod piles and the lawn. Paterson squared the sod's edges and at a jog peat-mossed what had already been laid. In the rhythm of work they accommodated each other like frantic dancers. In five minutes they were sweating, moving swiftly around each other; no stumbles, no bumps. In half an hour they were a machine—to Kozicki a thing of beauty. They all fit together, like gloves, like socks. They avoided speech.

'How's Corny?' he asked once.

Corny was fine.

'Where's Lannie?'

They didn't know. But at 10:30 Kozicki raised his head and watched Lannie struggle up from the riverbank in a sweat-bagged turtleneck and a pair of jeans that were ripped from ankle to crotch so that they flapped in front of the kid's skinny legs like a cowboy's chaps. Burrs and thistles snarled Lannie's hair; from the neck up he looked electrocuted, and wore a grin like the split in a Chiclet box. If the crew paused at all, it was to gape when Lannie said, 'I was running. I saw the lights.'

Kozicki wiped his muddy hands on his pants. 'Who's your friend?'

The dog at Lannie's heels had a fine firm muzzle and solid haunches and a bristle-haired backbone the colour of iron filings. When Lannie moved, the dog moved. When Lannie stopped, the dog stopped.

'Her name's Bluey.'

The crew whooped.

'Hiya, Bluey!'

'You got a nice voice, kid.'

'Where are the other dogs, Lannie? We heard others.'

'How come you never talked before?'

'What're you gonna do, stand there talkin all night? Grab some sod, eh.'

'Dio canne.'

They worked on. As they carried the rolls of sod across the turfed portion of the lawn, Kozicki watched the crew as he watched himself. He didn't think in words. He matched his steps to theirs, carried his burden the same way, grunted when he had to, blew his nose with his fingers, wiped the sweat away when it ran into his eyes. Something odd was happening. He could see it in each of them. He could see it in himself. The job was his taskmaster. Not Rawlings, not Cargill, not Corny Fergus, or the crew; not even the money. The job had become the taskmaster. They were working to finish the job.

Time wound down. Ten forty-five; eleven o'clock; eleven-thirty. At five minutes to twelve Rawlings stepped out of the French doors from the library and watched them silently. He went back in, then came out again carrying a case of beer. At midnight he called out: 'It was a good try, fellas.'

Kozicki waved, but didn't stop. Nor did the crew. The beer sat

on the patio table. 'It's here when you want it,' Rawlings said, and stepped back inside. The light in the library went out, but Kozicki imagined the man sitting there in the dark, facing the window.

The others' voices came to him through a haze:

'Whaddayou think, thisa rich guy, he wanna work too?'

'He can't work, eh.'

'What'sa matter him?'

'His butler's asleep.'

Laughter.

And:

'What do you think security will do?'

'Charge him.

'Charge Alex? What with?'

'Dog theft. Over two hundred dollars.'

Laughter.

And:

'. . . time is it?'

'. . . time is it?'

'. . . time . . . ?'

They worked on, through the night, when the moon slunk behind the trees and Emily's face drifted away from his hand like a fallen leaf, and at 2:00 A.M. he turned on the hose and lined them up for a drink. They worked through the graveyard hour, when the tailor lay in the morgue, his sharp nose aimed at the ceiling, and the darkness was as lightless as dirt. They worked through the pearly dawn when the birds woke singing like girls in a boarding school let out for the summer. At five o'clock Ironeagle, Trischuk and Kozicki sliced open bags of peat moss and Dominico raked it over the turf.

At six the last of the sod had been laid. Anna and Paterson banked the edges with soil while the others piled the tools in the truck.

Kozicki took down the floodlights. Up on the ladder he nearly dropped a bracket. Lannie climbed up to help him.

By seven they were finished. Too tired to cheer. Kozicki led them to the patio where they stood foolishly, slumped and gritty in the morning light. Kozicki crossed the flagstones to the French doors, rapped sharply several times. Rawlings emerged, dishevelled, in clothes from the night before. Kozicki handed him an open beer.

'To—' he began.

'—a shot in the dark—'

'—Leonardo da Vinci—'
'—Corny Fergus—'
'—Charles Dickens—'
'—money in the bank—'
'—us.'
After which Rawlings wrote out a cheque for each of them and sent them home.

The day his daughter arrived, Kozicki was transplanting flowers in Mrs. Burkmar's begonia patch. Rising on stiffened knees, he hobbled toward Gillian like an aged cowpoke who spent most of his time whittling, spitting, and sweeping out the sheriff's office.

'Hi Daddy.'

'Hello, Gillie.'

Any time Kozicki hugged his daughter he fell into the snug and conflicting embrace of overwhelming good fortune and awful possibility. He used to think that such a feeling would hit people caught in dicier situations: stuck in a hotel in Reno, Nevada, say, where under glitzy chandeliers and in full view of a neckless goon in a shoulder holster you shoved a quarter into a slot machine, pulled a lever, and found yourself hip deep in silver dollars that some mobster wanted *back*. Kozicki had never been to Reno, suspected mobsters were overrated, but he did understand the question a guy might ask himself under such circumstances: What'd I do to deserve this?

But holding his daughter as he did Kozicki marvelled at his luck. When he finally pressed Gillian to arms' length he saw more spark in her eyes than a welder's torch. She was tough, Gillian. In some mysterious way she'd become her mother's daughter. Even if she'd inherited some of his stupidity, Kozicki guessed she had brains enough to hide it.

'Daddy, you're so thin.'

'Not thin. I'm just—whaddayoucallit.'

'Skinny.'

'Naw—give me some more.'

She laughed. 'Angular? Bony?'

'Maybe. Keep trying.'

'Lean? Scrawny? Willowy?' She laughed again, played harp on his ribs. 'Meagre? Twiggy? Svelte? Spare?'

'Yeah, that's it.'

'Spare?'

'No, svelte. Yeah. I been svelting up like crazy.'

She herself possessed a whiplike slenderness, although thicker in the shoulders and heavier in the bust than Emily had been. If he held her long enough, would she live forever?

He looked over her shoulder and faced the young man who waited patiently on the sidewalk.

'Peter Plants?'

'Peter Rawlings.' The young man approached, hand extended. He was a head taller than his father, heavier, looser-jointed, more shambly. He had fair hair and an easy grin, a firm handshake and a shy, diffident manner that Kozicki would've trusted immediately if the guy hadn't been interested in his daughter.

'Pleased to meet you, Peter.'

'I'm glad I'm finally meeting you, Mr. Kozicki.'

'Call me Mike. What do you mean, finally?'

'I know a lot about you. Your daughter's a big fan.'

'I hope she lied.'

They'd driven three thousand miles in a Japanese tea tin on wheels, so what could Kozicki do but invite them in and smile and agree with everything they said? The young people sat together on his couch hand-in-hand, drank his tea, ate his graham crackers, apples and cheese, and gazed at each other with unabashed pleasure. They described the winds east of Winnipeg and joked about the hailstorm that pounded them on the Trans-Canada just outside Regina. Without the precise words, they told him by look and gesture that they were in love, that they were immortal, that in spite of their education they were just as dumb as he was.

'We'll be staying here tonight,' Gillian said. 'But this afternoon we thought we'd visit Peter's father. Peter and his dad don't—' Kozicki watched her squeeze the guy's hand. 'They don't see each other very often.'

'Dad and I argue,' Peter Rawlings admitted. The roots of his hair flushed pink, and Kozicki found himself wondering at the young fella's childhood. What had Rawlings done, given the boy a deadline on puberty? ('Kid, I want you to have hair on your knackers by Easter or you're out of here'?) But then—the idea slapped Kozicki like the flat of a shovel—as a father, had *he* been much better?

Kozicki heard his own voice saying, 'I'll go with you.'

He might've been on his way home, so familiar was the drive to the Rawlings estate; he knew the road as well as the alleys of his boyhood—the broad tree-lined boulevards, the stately, aloof houses, the high squeak of the wrought-iron gates as they opened, the low rasp as they closed. Along the pebbled drive, Gillian exclaimed over the shasta daisies and the hump-backed bridge that spanned the cobbled moat.

'The place sure has changed,' Peter Rawlings said. 'Look at those *potentilla davurica*! They're so *lush*! See, Gill?' He pointed. 'The ones with the white flowers? And back there—above that rock garden. Those junipers and what's that?—*Arctostaphylos*? It must be *alpina*.' He turned to Kozicki. 'Black bearberry,' he explained.

'Yeah.' Kozicki liked the way the young fella talked. 'Nice shrubs.'

'The whole place is magnificent,' Gillian said. She pivoted in the front seat. 'Imagine the challenge of being a gardener here, Daddy.'

Because of course he didn't tell her. Nor did Clarence Rawlings when he met them outside the library doors, the perfect if distant host, awkward with his son's height and choice of companions. The strain shrivelled the millionaire a little. In a way he didn't quite understand, Kozicki saw that Clarence Rawlings's discomfort greatly comforted *Kozicki*. He wanted to see the rich guy squirm, but why? Not for revenge, that was for sure. The man hadn't shafted them. He'd paid up when the bill came due. Why then did he want to see Rawlings humbled in some way?—not humiliated, but at least brought down a peg—though Kozicki couldn't say what the peg was or what hung from it.

Maybe it was a game, the same game that others had been playing from the time Kozicki was a kid. Like those policemen with their baseball bats in Market Square. And even himself, sending his own kid thousands of miles away. Who did they think they were? Who did he think *he* was?

In the course of the afternoon, he found himself alone with the millionaire. Gillian and Peter had wandered away together, like lovers in a park. Kozicki and Rawlings stood outside the camouflaged bunker.

Rawlings remained silent, then without turning asked, 'So, what now?'

'You mean about *them*?'

Rawlings gazed after the two young people. 'They can take care of themselves. No, I mean about you. I understand the union has reinstated the rest of your crew. But you've lost your job. And part of a pension.'

Kozicki whistled. 'Boy, you're pretty good. Do you happen to know what colour underwear I got on?' He pushed his hands in his pockets. 'Well, you're right about the job. Wrong about the pension, though. I'll get my twenty years.'

'How's that?'

'I belong—I *used* to belong to a strong union.'

Rawlings frowned. 'I don't get you.'

'It's in the contract. Sick leave. I got over a year of sick leave coming. I can put that towards my pension. Might have to go to court to do it, but I'm not busy these days.'

Rawlings studied him for a moment. 'Let's walk.'

They strolled along the driveway towards the moat. A breeze stirred the branches of a weeping birch. 'You might know I own a few holdings,' Rawlings said. 'Properties that have to be landscaped or need maintenance. My managers subcontract that kind of work. There'd be an opening if I let them know.'

Kozicki was looking at the moat's surface, which rose sluggishly against the stones. 'I don't like the looks of that filter system,' he said. 'I'd get it checked if I was you.' He raised his eyes, shook his head. 'I appreciate the offer, but no thanks. I been working a long time. Maybe I oughta try something else.'

Kozicki was unprepared for the greenery of the place. From the black and white photographs he'd expected the roofless houses and temples to be smudged in dead lichens, the rocks to be as lifeless as bone meal. But the stones seemed to breathe, and brilliant green grass—thin in spots, but green—carpeted the terraces like moss. Dark jungle crowded the edges of the city but here, near the Tower of the Sun, the levels fell away from him unobstructed and lush. To be resurrected, all the place needed was a couple of carpenters and a crew of landscape gardeners.

Oh some people would say he'd made a mistake coming to Machu Picchu this time of year. Not much happening in October, they'd say. June 21 was when you wanted to hang around here. That was when the whaddayoucallems—*touristas* showed up. That's when the light of old Inti Rami peeked over San Gabriel Mountain and shot through the window in the Torreon temple. Kozicki had read up on that part. There were all kinds of equinoxes and lunar movements he'd miss, but he didn't mind. Holy Hannah, that professor at the university had just touched the tip of the iceberg on this Hinca business. Kozicki'd have to get a whole other dictionary to look up that stuff. They had words as big as the ones Doc Brandell had used.— What were they?—hyperplasia, peri-urethral, mictri-whatever-it-was.

Older than Kozicki, Dr. Brandell was a leathery coot with a paunch and sweeping arm movements that made you think he must be good at tennis.

'Michael,' he'd asked. 'Pee-pee trouble?'

'Something like that, Doc.'

'And this appointment was made by Charmaine Wendelhauser?'

'Something like that, Doc.'

Dr. Brandell had swept a backhand shot over the net, slipped on a rubber glove and held up his index finger. 'Let's see if the train's in the tunnel, shall we?'

The train was part way in the tunnel. 'Prostate slightly enlarged, but nothing to brag about,' Dr. Brandell had said. 'The X-rays, blood tests and the whiz in the bottle show no malignancy yet, but we'll want to keep an eye on it.'

'I don't know much about prostates, Doc.'

'I'll teach you, Michael.'

Kozicki didn't know much about the Incas, either. Maybe Charlene would teach him about them.

And she would come. He'd sent her the ticket, she had the book. In a few days he would take the bus back to Lima, squeezed between chickens and people with faces as weathered as his, to meet her plane. She would be there; she would. And when she was, the two of them would make the return journey up through the mountains, along the switchback roads where rivers dropped into the valleys below. And somewhere in this ancient city Charlene would wrap her arms around him and whisper the name of the Inca king whose head had been buried away from his body.

Kozicki planned to whisper the name right back to her, over and over, until he knew it as well as he knew his own.